Maka *but so was he!*

Kenyon Blake was standing in front of her as if it was the most natural thing in the world. The years had been kind to him. He had transformed from an adorable teen into one fine-looking man. Kenyon was extra tall. Extra dark. And extra handsome. The width of his shoulders suggested he was a man of great strength. His straight nose, sensuously wide mouth and smoldering brown eyes fueled his bad-boy look. His skin was a dark shade of brown, clear and nice. A single diamond stud clung to his right ear, and the chain around his neck held a cross at the end.

"You must be Ms. Stevens," Kenyon said. "Sorry I'm late, but Terrance's hockey practice ran long. I'm his—"

"Oh, of course," she replied. "You're here for the interview."

Books by Pamela Yaye

Kimani Romance

Other People's Business
The Trouble with Luv'
Her Kind of Man

PAMELA YAYE

has a bachelor's degree in Christian education and has been writing short stories since elementary school. Her love for African-American fiction and literature prompted her to pursue a career in writing romance. When she's not reading or working on her latest novel, she's watching basketball (go Pistons!), cooking or planning her next vacation. Pamela lives in Calgary, Canada, with her husband and daughter. She loves to hear from readers, so visit her at www.Pamelayaye.com.

her kind of

Man

PAMELA YAYE

KIMANI™
ROMANCE

 KIMANI PRESS™

ISBN-13: 978-0-373-86067-8
ISBN-10:   0-373-86067-6

HER KIND OF MAN

Copyright © 2008 by Pamela Sadadi

www.kimanipress.com

Printed in U.S.A.

Dear Reader,

My dad is a news junkie. So is my husband. I try to keep informed of what's going on in the world, but these days the stories of pain and suffering are just overwhelming. One day last year, my dad called me and I could hear the news blaring in the background (what else is new?). When I asked what he was watching, he told me the story of a seven-year-old girl who was handcuffed and escorted out of her elementary school by police. I was dumbfounded! Once I found my voice, I said, "Could you imagine how much pain that child is in to physically attack someone who only wants what's best for her?" Out of this tragic, real-life story came the idea of a stern but loving teacher, a cute, rebellious student and one hot, sexy uncle!

I wrote *Her Kind of Man* while I was six months pregnant. When my son passed away four days after birth, I was reminded of a Bible verse about destiny. No man is promised tomorrow, so while we're here, we have to make the most of our days. I hope Makayla and Kenyon's story will inspire you to follow your dreams. It doesn't matter how difficult it may seem; with love and faith, anything is possible!

Be blessed and walk in your destiny!

Pamela Yaye

This book is dedicated in loving memory to my son, JUSTICE MOUKALLA YAYE, born on August 14, 2007. Not a day goes by that I don't think about you, miss you and wish that you were here. Your time on earth was brief, just long enough to say hello, but you made a valuable impression on us all and your footprint is still on our hearts. Mommy misses you, Justice. I love you, little one. We all do.

Chapter 1

"**Y**ou're incompetent!"

"Excuse me?" Makayla Stevens gripped the phone so hard, a sharp pain whizzed up her arm. "I've done nothing but help Terrance."

"Has it ever occurred to you that maybe *you're* the problem?"

"No, because Terrance is having issues in his other classes, as well. He—"

"Sure, and I'm supposed to believe you."

"Mrs. Blake, each incident has been clearly documented and—"

Click.

"Hello? Hello?" The dial tone buzzed in her ear. Makayla stared down at the receiver, eyes wide, mouth agape. It wasn't the first time she'd argued with a parent about their child's behavior, but she had never been spoken to in such a scathing manner.

Throughout their conversation, Makayla had heard gleeful

revving noises in the background and knew that Terrance was playing nearby. But that didn't stop Mrs. Blake from punctuating her sentences with lively curse words. It was no wonder the five-year-old was a holy terror.

In the ten years Makayla had been teaching, she had never met a child she didn't like—until now. Only a month into the school year and Terrance Blake had been sent to the principal's office five times. Mr. Gibson gave his support, but Makayla had a feeling he blamed her for Terrance's intolerable behavior. In the last month she'd used all of her "tricks" but there was no change in Terrance. Extra computer time, positive reinforcement and glow-in-the-dark stickers didn't help, either. Terrance was as bad as ever. He swiped things off her desk when he thought no one was looking, bullied his peers and lied openly.

Makayla picked up Terrance's file. It was heavier than the Bible. She had to do something fast. Mrs. Blake had threatened to file a grievance against her with the Philadelphia school board. Still, her co-workers had assured her she had nothing to worry about. One complaint from an angry parent wasn't going to ruin her otherwise stellar performance record.

Unruffled by Mrs. Blake's threats, she picked up the phone and hit redial. On the third ring, the answering machine came on. *How can Mrs. Blake be unavailable when she just hung up on me?*

When the automated voice prompted her to leave her name and number, Makayla said, "Hello, Mrs. Blake. It's Ms. Stevens again. Somehow our call got disconnected. I am calling to remind you that parent-teacher interviews are tomorrow night. Your appointment is at 7:15 p.m. I look forward to seeing you then. Goodbye."

After carefully replacing the receiver, she crossed off the last name on her class list. Now that all of the parents and guardians had been called and reminded about the interviews, she could call it a day.

Pushing herself up from her chair, she rubbed her hands over her chilled shoulders. A draft of cool air rushed into the room through the partially open window. Once the window was closed, Makayla surveyed her first-grade classroom. Vivid paint, colorful posters and children's art decorated the walls. A thick piece of red carpet sat in front of Makayla's desk, a row of computers lined the far side of the room and three lumpy beanbag chairs sat near the overcrowded bookshelf.

The distant sound of car horns suggested rush-hour traffic was in full swing. A quick glance at her watch confirmed that it was indeed five o'clock. If Makayla wanted to be on time for karate class, she had to leave now. Shrugging on her jacket, she swung her tote bag over her shoulder and hurried out of her classroom.

"I hate men," Makayla announced, yanking off her headband and chucking it into her gym bag. "Especially the *fine* ones. They cause the most trouble."

Her best friends groaned simultaneously. The three women were at the King Bonk Institute of Martial Arts in downtown Philadelphia. Their five-thirty class was over and they were in the changing room getting dressed.

"Here we go again," Desiree sang. "What's the problem now?"

Makayla untied her karate belt. "What do you mean, 'here we go again'?"

"Every time you go on a date you whine. You break into this 'I-hate-men' routine at *least* once a month."

"What happened this time?" Brandi asked, freeing her chocolate-brown locks from their elastic band.

"First, he was over twenty minutes late to pick me up. By the time we got downtown, found parking and reached our seats, we missed half the movie. Then, when he dropped me home after dinner, he had the nerve to ask for gas money. Said something about his check being short this month and he'd pay me back soon."

Brandi laughed. "Sorry, girl, but that's a trip."

"What was wrong with Reggie?" Desiree applied blush to her cheeks. "He worked for the city, had his own place and, if I recall, he was kinda cute."

"Loose Lips Reggie? No way. That man was *way* too affectionate for my liking." After a year of man-less days and nights, Makayla thought she was ready to jump back into the dating pool. But like her decision to cut her hair and grow it natural back in university, she'd been wrong.

Brandi frowned. "Too affectionate? Most women beg for romance and all you do is complain."

"Who said anything about romance? Reggie's idea of romance is day-old flowers, a six-pack and Steven Seagal movies." Makayla blew out the air in her cheeks. These days she had a better chance of being struck by lightning than finding a good man. She'd had adolescent dreams of the man she loved sweeping her off her feet. But, at thirty-three, she'd settle for him walking her through the front door. Forget romance, candlelit dinners and wild, passionate sex. All she wanted was a single, gainfully employed man who didn't live at home with his momma. "I'm through with the male species. I'm going to take a much-needed break from the dating scene and just concentrate on me."

Desiree shrugged. "Suit yourself. That leaves more men for me."

Makayla rolled her eyes. Desiree Hill could have any man she wanted—celibate, engaged or married. Men paid special attention whenever she was around. Her short, flirty boy cut drew attention to her oval-shaped eyes, and her pecan complexion had a soft, natural glow. Makayla landed a position at Springs Park Elementary School fresh out of university, and later that year

Desiree joined the staff. Her quirky sense of humor and their mutual love of Jackie Brown movies bonded them instantly.

Makayla eyed Desiree through the mirror. "Like you don't have enough men beating down your condo door."

"A single woman can never have too many options." Wiggling her hands under Makayla's nose, she said, "Do you see any rings on these fingers?"

"But you said you're not ready to get married."

"I'm not, but it would be nice if Elliot proposed."

Desiree had been dating Elliot Parker for three years, and even after all of that time Makayla couldn't figure out what the attraction was. The corporate pilot was ultraconservative, reticent and, quite frankly, boring. Last Saturday, at Desiree's birthday party, he didn't say more than five words the entire night. Makayla didn't care much for the man, but as long as he treated her friend well she had no complaints.

"Twinkie, you're too picky. Stop being so hard on these men." Brandi put a hand on Makayla's shoulder. "You don't want to wake up one morning and realize all you have for company are stray cats, do you?"

"How many times do I have to tell you to quit calling me Twinkie?" Feigning anger, she spread her hands out at her sides. "I lost sixty pounds, remember?"

Brandi stuck out her tongue. "Show-off!"

The two women had been friends since high school, and aside from Makayla's weight loss, little had changed between them. Every time Makayla thought about how they met, she cringed. It was her first day at Lincoln High and she couldn't have asked for a better day. She had a light schedule, made a friend in biology class and her sandals were holding up just fine. Her mom had given her enough money to buy a back-to-school dress, but she'd decided not to press the issue by asking for new shoes, too.

Makayla was shuffling through the cafeteria holding a food tray when she felt her right heel give way. Within seconds, she was sprawled out on the slick tile floor. Cream-of-mushroom soup dribbled down her cheek, gravy-soaked French fries stuck to her sundress and her bare legs were smeared with vanilla pudding.

A riot broke out across the room. Kids chortled until tears coursed down their cheeks. Some pointed, others made faces and a few chucked food. Horrified, Makayla tried to flee but every time she tried to stand up, she slid back down. Sobbing uncontrollably, she prayed one of the kind-hearted cafeteria ladies would come to her aid. But it wasn't Ms. Fletcher or Ms. Petroski who came to her rescue. It was a chubby girl with beaded braids and crooked teeth. The girl pulled her up and practically carried her out of the cafeteria. Her savior introduced herself as Brandi Thomas, wiped her tears and cleaned her up. On the way home, Brandi stopped at the grocery store and bought a tub of Rocky Road ice cream. That had sealed their near twenty-year friendship.

"Where to?" Desiree asked as they exited the locker room and proceeded through the studio. Grunts, wails and groans permeated the air. The 7:30 p.m. self-defense class had started, and eighteen sweaty bodies in a tight space made for one putrid smell.

"Somewhere where I can get drunk," Brandi said with a smirk. "After the week I've had, I need some hard liquor, a foot rub and some jazz."

Brandi was a marketing director at a Fortune 500 company, and had been in a committed relationship with her live-in boyfriend, Jamaal, for years. A free, gregarious spirit, she was open to doing anything as long as it was entertaining.

Makayla laughed. "Well, I don't know about the foot rub, but Bourbon Blue has a live band and cheap cocktails after six."

"Naw, it's always so crowded there. Let's go to Zeke's,"

Desiree suggested, pushing open the front door. Outside, it was a cold but clear September evening. A gentle breeze ruffled the trees. "I could really go for their chicken-and-rib platter."

Brandi nodded. "Sounds good to me!" Since the restaurant was only a few blocks away, the three women piled into her green Chevy Blazer.

Desiree clicked on her seat belt. "Makayla, did you leave work early? I came by your class but you weren't there."

"I was on phone with Mrs. Blake. She was yelling so loud I probably didn't hear you knocking."

"Is that woman still giving you a hard time?" Brandi asked.

Glancing out the window, Makayla said, "Veronika Blake makes the Wicked Witch of the West look like Mami from *The Young and the Restless*."

Laughter erupted from the front seat.

Makayla didn't join in her girlfriends' laughter. Mrs. Blake had Principal Gibson wrapped around her finger and she questioned Makayla's ability to teach every chance she got. Mrs. High-and-Mighty was making her life miserable, and it infuriated Makayla that she wasn't getting more support from administration. "Terrance pulled the fire alarm and she blamed me for not keeping an eye on him! Said if I had been watching him he wouldn't have gotten into trouble."

"Is he really that bad?" Brandi wanted to know.

"Worse. Yesterday he flooded the boys' washroom."

"Well, don't let this Veronika woman bully you," Brandi advised. "Stand up to her or it's going to be a very long year."

"That's easier said than done, Brandi. You've never had the misfortune of meeting the Wicked Witch of the West."

On Thursday, seven-fifteen came and went without any signs of Veronika Blake. Closing her appointment book, Makayla pushed back her chair and stood. *God does answer prayer,* she thought, allowing herself a small smile.

Makayla erased the board, straightened the desks, and put a stray yellow cap in the lost-and-found box. Returning to her desk she contemplated whether or not to notify the school secretary that Mrs. Blake had missed her seven-fifteen appointment. Nixing the idea before it took root, she cleared the clutter off her desk. Wanetta was a sweet woman, but she could out-talk a TV evangelist, and after a long evening of parent-teacher interviews, Makayla was anxious to go home.

Piling notebooks into the homework basket, she checked the time. It was almost eight o'clock. Way past quitting time. Makayla counted the math folders, then slipped them into her bag. She hated taking marking home, but the tests had been sitting on her desk since Monday and she had promised to give them back tomorrow.

Saturday can't come fast enough, Makayla thought, slipping on her jacket. Her gaze fell across the stack of old newspapers piled up in the recycling bin. A smile tugged at her lips. Makayla's very first article was appearing in the weekend edition of *The Philadelphia Blaze* and she couldn't be more excited. A lot was riding on the piece. If readers responded favorably, she'd be one step closer to being a travel writer. One step closer to living her dream.

Swinging her purse over her shoulder, she bent down and picked up her tote bag and basket. She turned off the lights and closed the door behind her. In the empty hallway, the growls of her equally empty stomach echoed. A soggy tuna-fish sandwich and a cup of raspberry yogurt had been her only meal of the day and she was so hungry, she felt light-headed.

Fantasizing about a thick slice of lasagna and some garlic bread, she rounded the corner and slammed head-first into what felt like a brick wall. Loose-leaf papers and notebooks sailed into the air, the contents of her purse spilled onto the floor and her feet slipped out from under her.

"I'm sorry," she heard a voice say. "I didn't see you."

Are you blind?

An arm curled around her waist. Allowing the stranger to help her to her feet, Makayla frantically brushed the dust off her pleated skirt. Straightening her sweater, she wondered why things like this always happened to her. Prone to getting flat tires, spilling food and knocking things over, she kept her cell phone charged, spare clothes in her trunk and an emergency credit card on hand.

"Are you all right?"

Do I look all right? Anger gained control of her mouth, but when she glanced up at the stranger, her lips parted wordlessly. Staring down at her, with a remorseful look on his face, was none other than Kenyon Blake.

"Here, let me help you with your things." He collected the sheets of paper littering the hallway, then proceeded to stack all twenty-two notebooks back into the plastic basket.

Standing rigid with shock, Makayla watched as Kenyon retrieved the contents of her purse. When he picked up her tube of mascara, she scrambled to action. Scampering around like a busy hen, she grabbed the box of gum, her leopard-print change purse and her car keys. Spotting two tampons by the heel of his shoes, Makayla prayed the earth would open up and swallow her whole.

Following her gaze, his full lips curved into a grin.

The heat of her humiliation quickly spread through her cheeks and down her neck. With as much composure as she could muster, she swiped the tampons off the floor and shoved them into her purse.

"Are you sure you're all right?" he asked. "You don't look so good."

Makayla forgot how to speak. The pitter-patter of her heart and her shallow breathing filled the silence. Swallowing, she touched a hand to her chest. *Is this what it feels like to have a heart attack?* she wondered, patting her brow with the back of her hand. "I'm fine" came out of her mouth in a painful squeak.

Kenyon Blake was standing in front of her, as if it was the most natural thing in the world. Makayla knew she was staring, but so was he! The years had been kind to him. He had transformed from an adorable teen to one fine-looking man. Kenyon was extra tall. Extra dark. And extra handsome. The width of his shoulders suggested he was a man of great strength. His straight nose, sensuously wide mouth and smoldering brown eyes fuelled his bad-boy look. His skin was mahogany brown, smooth and clear. A single diamond stud clung to his right ear, and the chain around his neck held a cross at the end.

"You must be Ms. Stevens," Kenyon said. "Sorry I'm late, but Terrance's hockey practice ran long. I'm his—"

"Oh, of course," she replied. "You're here for the interview." Makayla cringed at the sound of her high-pitched voice. *What else would Kenyon be doing here if not for parent-teacher interviews?* Now that he clued her in, she could see the resemblance between father and son. They shared the same dark skin, high forehead and blunt nose.

"I must admit, Ms. Stevens, you're not what I expected."

Same here. "I get that a lot," she confessed. At a paltry five feet, two inches, Makayla was often mistaken for an older sister of one of her students.

Smoothing a hand over her hair, she wondered how her makeup was holding up. Her last three interviews had been back to back, which left little time to catch her breath, let alone freshen up. And the last thing Makayla had expected was to run smack-dab into her old high school crush.

I hope he doesn't recognize me, she prayed. But how could he? In high school, the chips had been stacked against her. Grossly overweight, she had been saddled with thick glasses, colored braces and a severe case of acne. And it didn't matter how many times her grandmother pressed her hair, it still looked like she had stuck both hands in an electrical socket.

Kenyon had been the all-American boy. Teachers loved him, male students emulated him and every girl on campus wanted him. Makayla never had any male friends in high school, let alone a boyfriend, and as her weight climbed, she realized someone as popular and as charismatic as Kenyon Blake would never be interested in a girl like her.

Makayla felt as if she was going to melt. Not only was sweat trickling down her back, wisps of hair were sticking to the sides of her face. Drying her hands on her skirt, she avoided his intense gaze. *Get it together, girl! You're acting like you've never been in the presence of a man!*

"I don't mean to hold you up, but Veronika will kill me if she finds out I missed the interview."

I believe you, Makayla agreed silently. An image of Mrs. Blake flashed before her eyes and she shuddered. "How about we reschedule for one day next week?"

"Sorry, but I'm leaving for Fiji the day after tomorrow. I'm a freelance photographer so I take the jobs whenever they come. "

"I guess I could stick around a little while longer," Makayla said. She cleared her throat to conceal the loud rumbles coming from her stomach.

His cheeks dimpled when he smiled. "Why don't we discuss Terrance's progress over dinner? That is, unless you have someone waiting for you at home."

"That's not necessary. My classroom is just down the hall. Please, follow—"

"I know a nice place up the street. What do you say?"

"I don't know—"

"The service is great, the food is fast and it's quiet."

"I really don't mind staying here."

"I insist."

"Well, I am hungry—" she said out loud.

"Then we can talk over dinner."

Swayed by his smile, she nodded in response. His eyes were every bit as dark and mysterious as they had been in high school. Makayla didn't think she could handle having dinner with Kenyon, but her curiosity got the best of her. She wanted to know if he had lived out his dream of playing in the NFL, if he still jogged five miles a day, but most important, she wanted to know how in the world he had ended up married to a woman like Veronika Blake.

Chapter 2

Kenyon glanced up from his menu, just in time to see Ms. Stevens exit the ladies' room. He couldn't believe this dainty woman with the pretty eyes and sensuous mouth was his nephew's teacher. Her sun-kissed complexion paid tribute to her Caribbean roots, her cute, gumdrop nose gave her a youthful look and her curvaceous figure only added to her appeal. Everything about her from her shy smile to her tiny waist came together perfectly in a petite, compact package.

Hot damn! he thought, as he settled back into his chair. Kenyon must have spoken out loud because the plump-faced waitress strolling by stopped abruptly.

"Welcome to the Barbecue Kitchen. I'm Christine, but my friends call me Sunny." She tapped her pencil on her notepad, her smile growing wider by the second. "Can I interest you in something to drink?"

"I'll have a beer."

"Great. I'll be right back."

Kenyon returned his attention to Ms. Stevens. He had never had a teacher that fine. Despite her low-key appearance and the air of timidity surrounding her, she was stunning. Her hair was pulled back, her makeup simple and her jewelry tasteful. The navy, slim-fitted cardigan, straight black skirt and sensible, round-toe shoes fit the bill for a first-grade teacher, but Kenyon had a feeling beneath all those stuffy clothes was one very sexy woman.

It wasn't just her beauty he was drawn to. There was an innocence about her that appealed to him. "Here, let me." Kenyon stood, pulled out her chair and waited until she was comfortable before returning to his seat.

"Thank you." Makayla picked up the menu.

"See anything you like?"

"The spinach salad looks good."

"Salad? You've got to be hungrier than that." Kenyon helped himself to a roll from the wicker basket. "Don't be shy. Order anything you'd like. It's on me."

Makayla downed her water in two quick gulps. "I'm not that hungry. I, uh, had a big lunch."

An amused expression clouded Kenyon's face. *A big lunch?* It was eight-thirty. Unless she'd eaten a buffet with all the trimmings, she was probably starving. Beckoning the happy-go-lucky waitress back over to their table, he said, "Don't worry. I've got this."

While Kenyon placed their orders, Makayla secretly watched him. This was all too much to take in. She was having dinner with her first crush. The only guy she ever loved. Or, thought she loved. At thirty-three, Kenyon was a husband and a father. How had that happened? Back in high school, Makayla never pictured him the marrying type. Passing him in the congested halls of Lincoln High, surrounded by a bevy of perky cheerleaders, she had been convinced the all-star athlete would end up a life-long bachelor with children sprinkled all across the east coast.

"How is Terrance doing?" Kenyon asked once the waitress departed.

"Mr. Blake—"

"Call me Kenyon. The only person who goes by Mr. Blake is my pops."

"Okay." It took Makayla several seconds to organize her words. Labeling Terrance a nuisance would undoubtedly get their conversation off on the wrong foot and she needed Kenyon's support to turn things around. "Terrance is a strong student. He excels in math and science, he's reading at grade level and he has a vivid imagination. However, his behavior has been—" After searching for the right word and coming up empty, she said, "—less than desirable."

His shoulders rocked with laughter.

"Did I say something funny?"

"Instead of trying to be tactful, why don't you come right out and say he's acting like one of Bebe's kids?" He gave her a re-assuring smile. "I'm not Veronika, Ms. Stevens. You don't have to sugarcoat things for me. Be straight up."

"All right. Terrance is doing well academically but his actions give me cause for concern."

Kenyon suspected he would have any easier time extracting her wallet from her purse than getting a straight answer. "Which means?"

"He's aggressive, defiant, disrespectful and—"

His face showed disapproval, but he didn't interrupt.

"Yesterday I had to sit him out of gym because he kicked one of his female classmates. When I asked him to apologize he said he didn't have to because I wasn't his mother. There have even been a few occasions when he has thrown things in class. Sure, they're small items, like crayons or marbles, but that doesn't excuse his behavior."

The expression on Kenyon's face was serious. "He's been having the same problems at home, but Veronika insists it's normal kid stuff. The last couple years have been tough on all of us, but I think Terrance has been hit the hardest."

"I asked Mrs. Blake if there was anything wrong at home but she said everything was fine."

"Veronika doesn't like to talk about it."

The waitress arrived with their orders and hung around the table until Kenyon told her they didn't need anything else.

Alone with their thoughts, they ate in silence for several minutes.

"Do you want me to order some more?" Kenyon asked, noting the depleted plate of nacho chips and Buffalo wings.

Flushed, Makayla wiped the corners of her mouth with her napkin. "No, thanks. I guess I didn't realize how hungry I was."

"Tell me about yourself, Ms. Stevens."

"But we're here to discuss Terrance."

Kenyon grinned. "When I get home, I'll get a switch from off a tree and give his butt the lashing it deserves. Problem solved."

Makayla laughed, low and soft, her shoulders shaking lightly.

"I'll have a talk with Terrance first thing in the morning. We have a great relationship and more times than not, he'll listen to me rather than his mother. Veronika spoils him and he knows how to win her over."

"Thank you. I think things will get better if we're all on the same page."

Kenyon pulled out his wallet and handed her a business card. "Feel free to call me anytime. I travel a lot but I'm reachable on my cell no matter where I am."

"Hopefully I won't have to call." Makayla took the card and slipped it into her purse.

"I don't even know your name," Kenyon said. His eyes lingered on her lips. Like the rest of her, they were soft, moist and incredibly sensuous.

"My name?"

"You do have a first name, don't you?"

The question triggered the memory of the first time they spoke. More than fifteen years had passed, but their conversation was still fresh in her mind. It was a balmy spring afternoon in senior year. Makayla was lounging under a tree, listening to Salt-N-Pepa, munching on a bag of potato chips. She felt a shadow fall across her face and opened her eyes. Lucas Shaw was towering over her, his thin, chapped lips moving at a rapid pace. Makayla couldn't hear what he was saying, but the sinister expression on his face told her it wasn't good. She slowly pulled off her headset. "Yes?"

Lucas kicked the side of her leg. "Beat it, moo-moo. We need to use this tree for an end zone and your fat ass is in the way."

Hot tears burned her eyes as she gathered her things. Ever since Makayla wiped out in the cafeteria, Lucas had made it his personal mission to make her life a living hell.

Makayla was running across the field when she heard Lucas holler behind her, "Come on, QB, we're ready to play." She looked up just in time to see Kenyon and his girlfriend-of-the-month trot down the steps. After a long, sloppy kiss, the two love birds parted ways.

"What's the hurry?" Kenyon asked. "You're running like Freddy Krueger is chasing you!"

Makayla didn't realize she was holding her breath until he waved a hand in her face. "Hello? Anybody home?"

Suddenly deaf and mute, Makayla blinked rapidly. The sun

was blinding her eyes, so she arched a hand over her head. She had had a crush on him from the first day of high school, much like the rest of the girls in the freshman class. In a navy-blue football jacket, a white T-shirt and blue jeans, Kenyon looked like the poster boy for the U.S. Marines. His low top fade was neatly cut and his eyes, which twinkled whenever he was talking to a member of the opposite sex, were concealed by dark sunglasses. He was carrying his two most beloved items: a football and a camera.

"I'm Kenyon. I sit behind you in Mr. Ivanovich's class. What's your name again?" When she hesitated he said, "You do have a name, don't you?"

"M-M-Makayla Stevens," she said, finding her voice.

"You're the smartest girl in our class and I couldn't pass math if I had a cheat sheet. I bombed the last pop quiz while you got a perfect score." His voice was tinged with sadness. "My pops said if I don't pull up my grades, I'm off the football team. Can you tutor me? I can pay you ten bucks a week. Sound fair?"

Makayla spoke in a whisper. "Y-you don't have to pay me. I'll tutor you for free."

"No, my dad says if you want something done right you have to pay for it."

Lucas yelled across the field, "QB! Why are you talkin' to fat ass? Hurry up, man, we're waitin' on you."

Kenyon smiled down at her. "Can you meet me tomorrow in the library? Say twelve-fifteen?"

Too excited to speak, Makayla simply nodded in response.

Flashing those pearly whites again he said, "Thanks, Makayla." With a smile and a wink, he sprinted across the field toward his friends.

For the rest of the semester, Makayla had been in her glory. Three days a week, she worked with Kenyon to complete his assignments and helped him prepare for the final exam. They chatted over lunch when they finished studying. Rather, Kenyon talked and Makayla listened. He shared his dream of one day playing football and taking care of his mom and stepdad. He never asked Makayla about herself and she didn't volunteer any information. Unfortunately for her, Kenyon aced the next three tests and as quickly as their friendship had begun, it was over.

The sound of Kenyon's voice jarred Makayla out of her daydream.

"I'm still waiting for that name," he teased.

Makayla doubted Kenyon would remember her if she told him her full name, but it was better to be on the safe side. "Everyone calls me Kay," she told him. It was only a fraction of a lie, she reasoned, ignoring the jab from her conscience. It grated on her nerves when people shortened her name but tonight, Kay would suit her just fine.

"How long have you been teaching?"

"Ten years. I graduated from Bryn Mawr College in '96 and I've been at Springs Park Elementary ever since."

"You went to Bryn Mawr?" he asked, his fork suspended in midair. "The all-girls school?"

"Yes."

"For four years?"

"Yes. Why do you look so surprised?"

"Because most of the women I've met from there are—are—" Kenyon's voice trailed off into silence.

"They're all butch, bra-burning feminists, right?"

He shrugged. "Pretty much."

"Bryn Mawr College is an exceptional school with high standards and top academic programs."

"I'm sorry. I didn't mean to offend you."

Her lips were a tight line. "I'm not offended."

"Yes, you are."

"No, I'm not. You're entitled to your opinion."

Kenyon studied her face for a few seconds, then said, "Let me just go on the record as saying you're the finest woman I've ever met from Bryn Mawr College."

Her anger vanished and her lips relaxed into a smile. As far as Makayla was concerned, the compliment was better than the Prize Patrol showing up on her doorstep any day. Makayla felt a twinge of guilt. This was wrong, *very, very* wrong. Flirting with a married man was asking for bad karma. To divert the conversation away from herself, she asked Kenyon about his career. "You mentioned earlier that you're a freelance photographer. How did you get into the business?"

"I've always loved photography, so when I busted my knee and my football scholarship fell through, I decided to get my associate degree. After graduation, I traveled across Europe, Asia and Africa building up my portfolio. When I returned to the States, I settled in New York. I was lucky enough to work with some of the biggest names in the industry."

"It must have been hard being away from your family."

"It was."

"Do you travel a lot?"

"Too much," he admitted, his eyes probing her face. "But I plan to be around a lot more. Terrance needs me now. I set my own schedule, which gives me the freedom to choose which jobs I take. I turn down any gig that's going to keep me away from home longer than a week."

Not much had changed since high school. Makayla still loved hearing Kenyon talk. She had more questions, but the waitress returned to collect their plates. Since neither one of them wanted dessert, Kenyon asked for the check.

"I had a good time," he confessed.

It didn't seem right agreeing with him, so Makayla smiled politely.

"Maybe we can get together once I get back from Fiji. We could catch a movie, or go for drinks. Dave Chappelle is doing a set at the Big Dog Comedy Club the last Saturday of the month. Interested?"

Caught off guard by his question, she took a few seconds to collect her thoughts. *He didn't even ask if I have a boyfriend. Is my single status that obvious?* Makayla tucked a piece of hair behind her ear. Beneath her straitlaced, university-educated facade lurked a very lonely woman. Sure, she had friends and an active social life, but Makayla yearned to find her soul mate. That one special guy who would love her unconditionally. "I don't think that would be appropriate."

"Why not? I won't tell if you don't," he joked. "I can be discreet. Nobody has to know we're kicking it."

Is he suggesting we have an affair? Her feelings bubbled over like a pot of boiling water. Makayla hit him with an icy stare. Kenyon had been making passes at her all night and she was sick of it. *He must think he's something special!* she thought, struggling to maintain her composure. Flirting was one thing but now he was crossing the line. He may be having problems in his relationship but he was still legally married and that meant he was off limits. "How can you be so insensitive? Terrance is broken up over what's going on at home and your wife isn't faring much better. I suggest you spend more time getting your family back together and less time hitting on me."

Kenyon smirked. "My wife?"

"Yes, your wife."

"You don't understand," he said, the humor heavy in his voice.

"No, *you* don't understand." Makayla threw down her napkin. "Your son is acting out because of problems at home and you'd rather play the field than attend to his needs. That's despicable!"

"But Veronika and I—"

"Save it." Makayla pushed back her chair, tossed down enough money to cover her share of the bill and grabbed her coat.

"Wait! It's not what you think."

"Womanizing jerk," she muttered, rolling her eyes.

"Veronika and I aren't married!"

"Whatever." Makayla turned and marched through the restaurant without breaking her stride.

Chapter 3

"Class, don't forget to bring your permission slips on Monday. The field trip to the Philadelphia Zoo is only a few weeks away." Walking the length of the room, Makayla cleaned the chalk residue from her hands. She crouched down and helped Kiska tie her sneakers, then separated two boys who were using the rulers as swords.

After reminding the students to do their homework, she opened the door and took a fleeting look down the hall. Weaving his way through the throng of elementary students was Kenyon Blake.

What did he want now?

The bell rang and students swarmed around Makayla for hugs. Kids waved frantically as they scurried out the door and down the congested hallway. Returning to the safety of her desk, she yanked a random book off the shelf, sat down and started reading.

Terrance's high-pitched laugh rippled outside the classroom door.

"All right, li'l man. I'm going to talk to Ms. Stevens while you play outside. I'll be out in five minutes, so don't drive off without me."

"But I can't drive!"

"Aren't you eighteen?"

Terrance giggled. "No, I'm five!"

Burying her head in the science curriculum guide, she picked up a ballpoint pen and pretended to be making notes in the margins. Makayla could hear Terrance running down the hall and resisted the urge to call him back into the classroom. She had told him countless times that hallways were for walking, not running, but like everything else she said, the message obviously wasn't hitting home.

"By the way you took off, I can only assume you're not happy to see me." Kenyon chuckled lightly. "Now is that any way to treat a concerned parent?"

Makayla kept her eyes on the book. She wanted to ask the two-timing snake what was so funny, but she bit her tongue. His cocksure attitude made her sick to her stomach. "What do you want, Mr. Blake?" Her tone was brisk and professional.

"I came to see you."

"Is there a problem?"

"I'd say so. You think I'm an asshole, don't you?"

"Yes." The word slipped from her mouth with ease. Feeling contrite, she dropped her pen and looked up at him. He was even more attractive today, if that was at all possible. In a black leather jacket, turtleneck sweater and jeans, he reminded her of her favorite detective from the hit series *New York Undercover.* There was a gravity about him, a raw, sexual energy that was so intense, if she wasn't careful she'd lose the good sense God gave her. "I'm sorry. I shouldn't have said that."

"By the way, I like your dress. It hugs your body in all the right places."

Makayla folded her hands. It was a good thing there was a desk between them or he would have her hand impression on his right cheek. If there was one thing she hated, it was conceited men who thought they owned the world. And Kenyon Blake was arrogance personified. "I don't think your *wife* would appreciate you hitting on me."

"I'd better stop teasing you before things get ugly." Kenyon pulled a chair up to her desk and straddled it. "Veronika and I aren't married."

"Common-law unions are now recognized by the courts."

"We don't live together."

She eyed him warily. "Don't insult my intelligence, Mr. Blake."

"I wouldn't dream of it."

"Then what are you saying?"

"Veronika's my sister-in-law, not my wife."

Makayla searched his face for the truth. His smile was sincere and he sounded convincing. "But last night you said you were having problems at home. I took that to mean you were separated."

"My brother was—he was murdered a year and a half ago." His voice filled with emotion. "Felix loved his family. Terrance and Veronika were his whole world. They're still having a really hard time dealing with his death. We all are."

Makayla grappled with what to say. It had been almost fifteen years since she lost her mother to breast cancer, but the pain never went away. Overcome with sympathy, she said the only thing that came to mind, "I lost my mom years ago and I still miss her. I am so sorry for your loss."

Kenyon nodded absently. "I tried to explain, but you blew out of the restaurant so fast, I didn't get a chance."

Makayla wanted to crawl into a hole so deep archaeologists wouldn't be able to find her. "I had no idea."

"I thought you knew. Terrance never mentioned it?"

Makayla didn't want to tell Kenyon that every other word out of his nephew's mouth was a lie, so she said, "Kids talk a lot. Sometimes it's hard to separate fact from fiction."

"You're right. Terrance and his friends come up with the craziest things."

They shared a smile.

"If you don't mind my asking, what happened?"

"Felix was on the Criminal Apprehension Unit. He was shot while trying to arrest a gang member out on parole. It's still hard to believe he's gone."

Kenyon glanced out the window. Seconds passed before he returned his gaze to Makayla's face. His eyes were narrowed slightly, and his face was pinched in determination. "I'm going to help Veronika and Terrance get through this. That's why I want you to call me the next time there's a problem. Veronika has a lot on her plate right now and she doesn't need any more added stress. You understand, don't you?"

"I do. And I'm sorry I blew up at you. I didn't mean what I said."

Kenyon's smile resurfaced. "You called me a womanizing jerk." Clutching a hand to his chest, he used the other to wipe away an imaginary tear. "That hurt. I may be a womanizer, but I'm not a jerk."

Makayla laughed. The delicious warmth of his smile alleviated the tension in the room. "Again, I'm deeply sorry."

"Apology accepted." He leaned forward in his chair, his eyes alight with mischief. "What are you going to do to make it up to me?"

"Excuse me?"

"I think restitution is in order."

"What do you expect me to do? Cook you a five-course meal?"

His face lit up like the Rockefeller Christmas tree. "Sounds great!"

"You can't be serious."

"I am."

"I don't date parents." She was quick to add, "Or relatives."

Kenyon opened his mouth, but when he heard his nephew's voice, he swallowed the flirtatious comeback.

"I'm hungry, Uncle Kenyon." Terrance trudged into the classroom, dragging his backpack behind him. "Can we go home now?"

"Sure, li'l man." Kenyon rested his hands on his nephew's shoulders. To Makayla he said, "We'll continue this discussion another time."

Makayla smiled down at Terrance. Learning about his father's sudden death made her heart soften toward him. She wasn't going to let him continue to undermine her authority, but it wouldn't hurt if she relaxed some of the rules for him. "Bye, Terrance. Have a nice weekend. I will see you bright and early on Monday morning."

He grumbled in response, and Kenyon rumpled his hair. "Playing on the jungle gym must have tuckered the poor kid out."

As she watched them exit the classroom, Makayla wondered just how long she could keep Kenyon at bay. Because one thing she remembered about the former football star was that when it came to the ladies, he didn't take no for an answer.

Makayla poured herself a cup of coffee and took a bite of the lemon-filled doughnut she'd treated herself to. Sitting down at the kitchen table, she opened *The Philadelphia Blaze* to the Real Life section and skimmed the page for her article. Nothing. Brenda had promised her it would be on the front page, though this wasn't the first time an editor had lied to her.

"It has to be here somewhere," she said, ruffling the paper in frustration. But her article wasn't on page two or three, either. Just as disappointment set in, she found what she was looking for. "How to Unleash Your Inner Vixen" was on the bottom right-hand corner of page six. Okay, so it wasn't the front page but at least her article had made it into the third largest newspaper in Philadelphia.

A smile bloomed on her lips. Makayla got goose bumps seeing her name in print. Or rather, seeing her pseudonym in print. After all these years, her hard work was finally starting to pay off.

Makayla knew the article by heart, but that didn't stop her from reading it out loud. Writing had been part of her life ever since college when she became the editor of the school newspaper. After stumbling across an old episode of *Loveline* on cable, the idea for an anonymous sex column was born. Over the next month, Makayla penned articles on everything from self-gratification to sex toys to finding the elusive G-spot. The articles were carried in the Friday edition of the paper, and when sales shot through the roof the first week, "The Lady Sexpot Files" became a daily column. To this day, nobody at the university knew Makayla was behind the racy articles.

She opened her laptop. Depending on the response to "How to Unleash Your Inner Vixen," this could be a one-time piece or a weekly column. Makayla decided not to get her hopes up. But when her inbox came up on the screen, her eyes spread wide.

"Thirty-nine messages!" Makayla scrolled down the page. "This has gotta be a mistake!" She scanned the inbox. All of the e-mails were addressed to Lady Sexpot, her pseudonym.

From the common questions such as "Is whipped cream really an aphrodisiac?" to the crazy ones—"Will you marry me?"— Makayla read them all. She couldn't erase the giddy smile on her face.

The strength of her article was in the frank, straight-talking interviews with self-proclaimed "vixens." Not strippers, dancers or escorts, but housewives, bank tellers and flight attendants. All were intelligent, outspoken women who weren't afraid to break the rules or chart new ground in the bedroom. Makayla had never done any of the things she had written about in the article, but when the right man came along, she would put all of her notes to good use. Three weeks of belly-dancing lessons had helped her feel more in tune with her body and increased her confidence. She couldn't work her hips like Shakira but she could swivel her behind better than the other fourteen women in her class.

Makayla spent the next hour responding to her messages. The tremendous response to her article was bound to bring further success. She was sure of it. Makayla loved teaching, namely building relationships with her students and tracking their progress. Walking into a classroom and seeing children's faces light up was the greatest feeling in the world. But as much as she enjoyed her job, she was ready for a change.

She could see it now. First-class flights. Stays in luxurious hotels. Hours spent at historical monuments. Cozy chats with the locals. It was the kind of life she had always dreamed of, and if everything went as planned, it wouldn't be long before her dream became a reality.

She opened the last message in her inbox and her face radiated with pure joy. The message was from Brenda Van Buren, the senior editor at *The Philadelphia Blaze.*

Your column is a hit! Let's set up a time next week to discuss your future.

She sent Brenda a reply and then logged off the computer. "Time to celebrate!" It had been months since she had had lunch at Alfredo's. The last time she had been at the Italian bistro was with Reggie, and he had spent so much time complaining about the food she hadn't enjoyed her meal. Today there would be no distractions. Makayla licked her lips. She could almost taste the Louisiana-style chicken already. Her eyes strayed to the clock. It was still early. She had enough time to shower, dress and make it downtown for the start of Alfredo's eleven o'clock brunch. Humming softly, she exited the kitchen and headed toward her bedroom.

"Welcome to Alfredo's. How many in your party?"

Makayla smiled at the hostess. "Just one."

"Would you prefer to dine in, or on the patio?"

The weather was unusually warm and the sky was clear. What better way to enjoy the day then spending it out in the sun? "Outside."

"Please follow me." The blonde led her outside to a table shielded by tall willow trees.

Makayla glanced around the patio. It was lined with chatting people, loners reading the newspaper and canine partners with their respective owners. "This will be fine. Thanks."

"Your server will be with you shortly."

From her corner seat, she enjoyed watching the world go by. Three college-aged girls were making eyes at a suit-wearing brother talking on a cell phone, an Asian couple argued in their native tongue and a group of professional women sang "Happy Birthday" to the stick-thin redhead at the head of the table.

Makayla picked up the menu. After a few seconds of perusing the day's specials, she placed it off to the side and pulled out the book poking out of her handbag. If she wanted to have *Sins of a Co-ed* finished by the next book club meeting, she had to get going.

"Hi. I'm Cordell. I'll be your server this afternoon. How are you?"

Makayla looked up at the waiter with a dreamy smile and a friendly face. "Fine, thanks."

"Are you dining alone?"

"Yes, why?"

He winked. "Just checking."

They traded looks. He checked her out; she did the same.

"Do you need a few more minutes with the menu or would you like to order?"

"I'll have the brunch."

"Is there anything else I can get you?"

Makayla smiled. As he eyed her up, something came to mind that one of the women in her book club group said last month. "Men love assertive women," the chef-by-day-dominatrix-by-night had shared. "And the more daring, the better."

"Are you single, Cordell?" Makayla had never been so bold.

"Very. Why don't you give me your number so we can kick it sometime?"

"I don't know—" Suddenly, her decision to swear off men seemed silly. Cordell was cute and he wanted to take her out. Just because she'd had a string of bad dates didn't mean she should take herself off the market. Besides, her column was a hit. What better way to cap off a good day than with a date?

"So, can I get that number?"

"Sure, why not?" She recited her number.

Cordell scribbled it on his notepad and tucked it into his back pocket. "Cool. I'll call you next week."

"I'd like that."

As Makayla watched him go, she wondered why she hadn't been that confident when she talked to Kenyon yesterday. Stop thinking about the man, for God's sake, she ordered herself. But

blocking thoughts of Kenyon was impossible. He was outspoken, had the face of an Adonis, the body of a sculpture and
although she didn't have telepathic powers, she had a feeling he
was a first-rate lover. If he didn't have so much personal baggage,
Makayla might have gone out with him.

Cordell returned to the table with her drink, then escorted her
inside. While she skimmed the salad bar, he told her more about
himself. He worked two full-time jobs, took night classes at the
local community college and hoped to be a concert promoter one
day. Despite his tight schedule, he offered to take her out for
dinner next week. Makayla was weighing the pros and cons of
dating someone eight years her junior when she spied Reggie
standing at the bar. He was talking to a taller, lighter, more
handsome version of himself. Funny, he had never mentioned
having a brother.

If Reggie saw her, he'd stick to her like glue and Makayla
couldn't stomach any more of his worn-out lines. Water had
spewed out of her mouth when Reggie had labeled himself "the
last good man around" and squeezed her thigh. Laughing at the
memory, she said goodbye to Cordell and hurried back out to the
patio. If Reggie Ford was the best the world had to offer, then
Makayla would die a lonely spinster.

Chapter 4

The breeze whipped Makayla's face, sending shivers down her spine. Muffling her neck in the collar of her coat, she rocked aggressively from side to side. Her fingers felt like icicles and her hair thrashed around her face. Rubbing her hands together, she imagined her hands wrapped around a piping-hot mug of herbal tea. Any minute now, the bell would ring, signaling the end of recess, and Makayla would return to the warmth of her classroom.

Makayla glanced around the field at the children. Multicolored leaves whirled around them on the wind, but the kids played on, ignoring the stiff wind.

"Boys and girls, be careful," she warned, watching two girls slip and slide on a pile of wet leaves.

Makayla felt a tug on her coat and looked down.

"Teacher, Terrance took my money."

She stared down at the boy and smiled. He was the cutest little thing, his thin face bitten by the frigid wind.

"Then he told me to—to—" Embarrassed, the boy lowered his eyes. "He said a bad word to me, Teacher."

"Are you sure?"

He nodded furiously.

Makayla's eyes scanned the playground. If she had any doubts about Terrance's innocence, they vanished when he scurried up the slide and dove behind one of the plastic pillars.

She stormed across the field to the troublesome first-grader. "Terrance, come down here now!"

"No! I don't have to listen to you!" Terrance emerged from behind the slide, a defiant expression on his face.

Makayla could not allow the disrespect. She climbed the steps. "You're coming with me to the office."

Terrance stepped back. "No, I'm not!"

"Oh, yes, you are."

"You always pick on me!" he whined, stomping his foot. "I didn't do any—"

Makayla reached out and grabbed his arm. To her shock, Terrance threw himself against her, freed himself and took off running. He leaped off the play structure and landed in the sandbox with a thump. A second later, an earsplitting scream shattered the morning silence.

"Don't tell me I'm overreacting! That bitch hurt my baby and she's going to pay!"

Kenyon tried calming down his sister-in-law, but Veronika only became more irate. Her recent tirade brought a nurse into the room who told them, "Excuse me, but it is far too loud in here." She went over to the wall-mounted TV and turned it down, too.

"Hey! What are you doing? I was watching that!" Terrance snatched the remote off the table and punched up the volume.

Kenyon looked contrite. "I apologize." Ever since they'd taken

Terrance to The Children's Hospital, he'd been apologizing for Veronika's behavior, and his nephew's. "We'll keep it down from now on." He looked at his nephew sternly. "Terrance, apologize. That is no way to talk to the nurse."

His eyes remained fixed on the screen.

"Did you hear me?"

Nothing.

Kenyon put a hand on his shoulder. "Apologize. Now."

"Stop yelling at him!" Sitting on the edge of the bed, Veronika cradled Terrance's head to her chest and rocked him back and forth. "Can't you see that he's been traumatized? His teacher attacked him, for goodness' sake! How do you expect him to behave?"

Unmoved by Veronika's performance, Kenyon took the remote control out of his nephew's grasp and switched off the TV. "Terrance, if you don't apologize to the nurse, I won't take you and your friends to the arcade next weekend."

Terrance fiddled with his ID bracelet. "Okay, I'm sorry."

"That's better."

"Any word on the X-rays?" Veronika asked the nurse, cradling her son in her arms. "I don't need X-rays to know my baby broke his arm, but my lawyer said it wouldn't hurt to have some hard evidence."

"Doctor Harvick should be here any minute with the results."

"Thanks." Kenyon smiled at the nurse as she turned to leave. "And sorry we've been such a pain."

Veronika smoothed a hand over Terrance's cheek. "Mommy doesn't know what she'd do if anything ever happened to you. You're all I have." Hugging him to her chest, she closed her eyes. "I love you, baby. More than anything in this world. Don't you ever forget that."

It was moments like this Kenyon truly admired his sister-in-law. It had to be tough being a single parent but he knew no one was more important to Veronika than Terrance.

Checking the time, Veronika released her son and pulled out her cell phone from her jean pocket. "I'm going to go call my lawyer again."

Sighing, Kenyon drew a deep breath. "Don't you think you're blowing things out of proportion? Terrance is fine. He doesn't even have a scratch—"

"You're not a doctor," she pointed out, cutting him off. "He may have internal injuries for all you know. Why aren't you more upset? That woman could have killed him!"

"We don't know what happened."

"Terrance said Ms. Stevens pushed him and I believe my son."

"But his classmates said he jumped."

Her eyes narrowed. "Are you saying my child is lying?"

"I care about him, too, Veronika."

"You have a funny way of showing it. You weren't at his hockey game last week, now were you?"

Kenyon swallowed a retort. Every time something went wrong, Veronika reached back into the past and brought up his mistakes. His sister-in-law was hard to please, rarely satisfied and always angry. If she had not gotten pregnant, his brother probably never would have married her.

"I already apologized for that. It was a scheduling conflict that couldn't be changed. I had to work." Terrance was listening in and he hated arguing in front of him. If Kenyon wanted to, he could put Veronika in her place. Felix's insurance money had only gone so far. Once the funeral was paid for and a college tuition fund established for Terrance, there wasn't much left. Veronika didn't make much as a hairdresser and it would be months before her salon turned a profit. Kenyon had taken care of all of her financial responsibilities since Felix died. Mortgage, utilities and insurance were paid in full, on time, every month. Not because he had to, but because he wanted to make life as comfortable as possible for them. Because of his generosity, Veronika could afford to live in one of the best neighborhoods in Philadelphia.

Kenyon rubbed a hand over his head. "Let's hold off on hiring a lawyer until we know what happened. Once we know the truth we can—"

Veronika dismissed his suggestion with a flip of her hand. "Terrance wouldn't lie to me. There's nothing to discuss. Ms. Stevens hurt him. Case closed. I'm going to sue the skirt off her and there's nothing you can say to stop me." She brushed a strand of dark blond hair out of her eyes. "No one messes with my baby and gets away with it!"

Kenyon had heard enough of his sister-in-law's ranting for one day. He was just as upset as she was about what happened but he wasn't going to lose his head. Kenyon knew little about Ms. Stevens, but she didn't strike him as the kind of person who would intentionally harm a child. She was warm and nurturing and seemed to have a soft touch for kids. Then again, he'd learned a long time ago that looks could be deceiving. Kenyon turned to Terrance. "I'm going to the cafeteria. Do you want anything, li'l man?"

Absorbed in cartoons, Terrance shook his head.

"Veronika?"

"No, thanks."

Kenyon opened the door and strode down the hall to the elevators. As she reached out to press the down button, the elevator doors slid open and Ms. Stevens stepped off.

"Oh," she said, stopping abruptly. "Hi."

Kenyon took a deep breath. Her feminine fragrance sweetened the antiseptic smell in the corridor. "Hello, Ms. Stevens."

Makayla could tell by his subdued greeting that he wasn't

happy to see her. Still, she could see the deep brown flecks in his eyes more clearly under the fluorescent lights, as well as his flawless skin. The man was truly a sight to behold. "I came to see Terrance. How is he?"

"We're waiting on the X-rays."

"Can I see him?" She lifted the bag she was holding in her hand. "I bought him something to help pass the time. Nothing big, just some puzzles, a few coloring books and his homework."

Kenyon stole a look down the hall. Veronika was standing outside Terrance's room, talking on her cell phone. "Now's not a good time."

"When should I come back?"

"I'll tell Terrance you stopped by."

Makayla held out the bag. "Can you see to it that he gets this?"

"Sure."

"Do you have a few minutes? I was hoping we could talk about—"

"You bitch!"

Makayla froze. Storming down the hall, screaming obscenities marched Veronika Blake. Narrowly missing an elderly man in a wheelchair, she flung her hands and yelled, "How dare you show your face here after what you did!"

Eyes wide, Makayla looked helplessly at Kenyon. She shrank back like a panic-stricken child and frantically jabbed the elevator button. "I'll leave."

Kenyon felt for Veronika, he really did, but now was not the time for her to act out a scene from *A Thin Line Between Love and Hate*. He stepped forward, blocking her path. "We'll discuss this later."

"Like hell we will. I'm going to kick her ass!"

Kenyon gripped her shoulders. "No, you're not. You're going to go back to Terrance. He needs you, remember?"

The mention of her son's name momentarily calmed her. Her thin lips curved into an ugly sneer. She wagged a finger at Makayla. "If you ever put your hands on my son again, you'll be sorry. Trust me. You haven't heard the last of me, Ms. Stevens. This is only the beginning." Straightening her sweater, she shot Makayla an evil look and tramped off.

When Kenyon turned around, he was shocked to see Ms. Stevens shaking. Her eyes were heavy with tears and her bottom lip was quivering. As curious as he was to find out what had happened that afternoon on the playground, he didn't have the heart to question her. Overtaken by compassion, he put a hand on her back, steered her into the open elevator and said, "Let's go somewhere to talk."

The main-floor cafeteria was bright, modern and clean. There were dozens of round tables and several gigantic windows, which overlooked an open field. Hospital personnel occupied many of the tables.

Makayla plopped down on one of the cold plastic chairs and buried her face in her hands. This had to be the worst day of her life.

After recess, Principal Gibson had summoned her to his office. He'd stared at her for several minutes before he finally asked, "What happened outside at recess, Ms. Stevens?"

Since Makayla had nothing to hide, she told the truth. "I grabbed Terrance's arm, but he broke free and jumped off the play structure. Everything happened so fast I—"

"You do know the school's discipline policies, don't you, Ms. Stevens?"

"Yes, but—"

"School personnel are not supposed to touch children in an aggressive manner."

"I am well aware of that, Principal Gibson, but I had no other choice. Terrance wasn't responding to my orders and—"

"Terrance said you pushed him."

"He said *what!*"

"Is that true, Ms. Stevens? Did you hurt that child?"

"No, of course not. I would never—"

Principal Gibson leaned forward in his chair, his gaze strong and intense. "Have you ever heard of teacher burnout, Ms. Stevens? In my day, things like this happened all the time. Stressed teachers would rough up students and—"

Makayla tuned out. Images of being frisked and handcuffed in front of her students attacked her fragile mind. In one of her more lucid moments, she heard Principal Gibson ask if she was okay. She must have nodded, because he advised her to seek legal counsel and informed her the superintendent would be in touch.

Later that night, Desiree showed up with a tall, lean-faced man who smelled like new money. Impeccably dressed in a charcoal gray suit, shiny cufflinks and a designer watch, he strolled into Makayla's living room as if he had the deed to the house.

Desiree knew a host of white-collar men, everyone from plastic surgeons to city officials to restaurateurs, so Makayla didn't blink when she was introduced to Chancellor Hughes, attorney-at-law. Somewhere between serving coffee and telling her side of the story, Makayla remembered that she was innocent. She wasn't burned out, or stressed, or lashing out like Principal Gibson had implied. She was wrong for grabbing Terrance's arm but she wasn't responsible for his fall. Makayla listened politely to Mr. Hughes, but when he recommended she take a polygraph test to clear her name, she kindly showed him the door.

"Give it some thought," he told her, handing over a crisp white business card. "Don't hesitate to call if you need me."

After a quick stop at the school, Makayla drove straight to The Children's Hospital. Terrance could lie to the devil himself and make it interesting, but she had a hard time believing he could look at her, with his mother and uncle listening in, and say she pushed him off the jungle gym. On the drive over, Makayla had geared up for the inevitable confrontation with Mrs. Blake, but when the irate mother stormed toward her, with guns drawn, she lost her nerve.

Using a tissue to wipe her face, she contemplated whether to appeal to Kenyon. Her inner voice told her she could confide in him, but Makayla had faced enough hostility for one day and she couldn't handle him blowing up at her, too.

Kenyon returned to the table, handed her a cup of coffee and sat down. Sitting across from her, he couldn't help noticing how much prettier Kay looked with her hair down. She had thick, lustrous hair that his hands were anxious to touch. To keep from acting on his impulse, he sipped his coffee. "Are you okay?" he asked, keying in on her nervousness.

Her words came out in a painful whisper. "I didn't push Terrance off the play structure. He jumped."

Kenyon eyed her over the rim of his cup.

"I would never do anything to hurt one of my students. Never."

Scratching the stubble on his jaw, he slowly shook his head. He knew this was coming, but he was still shocked by her admission. His gut feeling was that Kay was telling the truth. Kenyon loved his nephew, but unlike Veronika, he saw the boy's devious side. Ms. Stevens wasn't the first person to complain about Terrance's defiant streak. Everyone from babysitters to other parents to relatives had labeled him a problem child and predicted a life of trouble if Veronika didn't lay down the law now. "I'll talk to Veronika."

"You will?"

"I had a feeling Terrance was lying."

"You did?"

Kenyon ate a curly fry. "Yeah."

"I'm sorry about all of this. It's my fault. I should have waited until all the kids went inside before I confronted him."

"I don't blame you. I should be the one apologizing. Terrance hasn't been the same since my brother died, but there's no excuse for what he did."

"Death is hard for kids to cope with. I was a teenager when my mom passed and it almost destroyed me. I was angry at the world but instead of lashing out at others, which I suspect Terrance is doing, I ate. I used food to fill the emptiness I was feeling inside."

"But at least you weren't hurting anybody."

"I was hurting myself." She toyed with her purse straps. "When I graduated from high school, I was almost two hundred pounds!"

"No way." Kenyon took in her appearance. He liked her jeans-and-blazer look. It was simple, pretty, casual. Kay had the face of an angel, a long, slender neck and eye-catching curves. It was hard to believe she had once been a candidate for an extreme makeover.

"Believe it. I have the pictures to prove it."

"I'd like to see them sometime."

Makayla looked away. She didn't know what had possessed her to tell Kenyon about her past. If she wasn't careful, she would jog his memory and he'd remember who she was. It was unlikely, but stranger things had happened. "I should get going."

"I'll walk you out."

"No, you're not finished eating."

She was right. He hadn't even tasted his cheeseburger yet. "Thanks for coming by. I'm sure Terrance will love the gift."

"It's the least I can do." Makayla could talk to Kenyon for hours. He was a good listener, understanding, and he didn't judge her. She didn't want to leave, but fear of seeing Veronika again pushed her to her feet. Dangling her keys between her fingers, she lifted her head and met his smile. "I guess that's it then."

"I guess so."

Kenyon concentrated on his burger. There couldn't be a worse time to put the moves on her. His nephew had blackened her name and there was a good chance she could lose her job. "I'll be in touch," he called, as she made her way through the cafeteria. Her jeans hugged the curves of her butt and her leather boots added several inches to her height. Kay was sexy in a natural, unprofessed way. His gaze followed her through the cafeteria doors and into the parking lot. Soon, she disappeared among the rows of emergency vehicles and police cruisers.

Kenyon finished his burger. Getting the truth out of Terrance wouldn't be easy. He had inherited his mother's stubbornness and even at the best of times, he couldn't be reasoned with. Glancing at his watch, he wondered if it was too late to call and set up a meeting with Principal Gibson. The sooner this situation was cleared up, the better. Standing, he collected his garbage and then dumped it into the trash bin.

As he got on the elevator, he couldn't help wondering who was waiting for Kay at home. She wasn't wearing a wedding ring, but that didn't mean she wasn't in a serious relationship. There was only one way to find out for sure. After he got the truth out of Terrance, they would pay Kay a visit at home. A bouquet of flowers and a small gift were sure to soothe her feelings. And once everything was sorted out, he would make his move.

Chapter 5

When Makayla arrived at school on Monday morning, Principal Gibson was waiting in her classroom. He greeted her warmly, said he was happy to see her and shared the details of his Friday-afternoon meeting with Terrance and his mother.

"I knew that boy was lying, Makayla. You wouldn't hurt a fly." Chuckling good-naturedly, he plopped down on the edge of her desk. "I suggested the boy be transferred to another class, but Mrs. Blake wouldn't hear of it."

Makayla shrugged off her coat. "But I made it very clear I didn't want Terrance to remain in my class."

"I know, but his mother made a stronger argument for why he should stay. He'd have to start over in a new class, he'd be separated from his friends and he's a strong student. You said so yourself."

Makayla couldn't think of a single student who considered Terrance a friend.

"Just so you know," Principal Gibson continued, "I let Terrance have it. I told him if he ever pulls a stunt like that again, he'll be asked to leave our school."

Makayla found that hard to believe. Mr. Gibson practically slobbered all over himself whenever Veronika was around, so she seriously doubted he had reprimanded Terrance in her presence. Rather than argue with her boss, she said, "I appreciate that, Mr. Gibson."

"Mrs. Blake was concerned you might penalize Terrance for the stunt he pulled, but I assured her that wouldn't be an issue. You're a professional and what happened last week is in the past." He smiled softly. "Terrance has a lot to deal with. You know, with his father's passing and all."

Makayla nodded. "I recently became aware of the situation."

"Maybe you could cut the boy some slack when he's out of line."

She'd tried being extra patient with Terrance, knowing he deserved understanding and sympathy. But the next time he hit a classmate or swiped something off her desk, she would demand he be transferred. Principal Gibson was extending his support, but Makayla had a feeling when push came to shove, he'd relent again. Mrs. Blake was very convincing, and Makayla's boss was easily swayed. At least where Veronika was concerned.

Makayla thanked Mr. Gibson for coming. When he left, she walked over to the window and stared outside. As she admired the soft, mellow light of the sun, her thoughts turned to her meeting with Brenda Van Buren. It wouldn't be long before a position in the travel department opened up at *The Philadelphia Blaze*. For now, she would pen her weekly column as Lady Sexpot and hone her writing skills. But when the opportunity presented itself, she would have no problems resigning and packing a suitcase for Rome. Or Singapore. Or Barbados. It didn't matter what the assignment was. As long as she was doing what she loved, she'd be happy.

* * *

A week after the incident on the playground, Veronika showed up in the middle of the afternoon, with cake, ice cream and soda. When she announced that it was Terrance's birthday and she wanted him to celebrate with his friends, Makayla slapped a smile on her face, told the kids to put away their math books and donned one of the glittery party hats. She'd hoped to review the subtraction lesson with the class before tomorrow's test but by the time they finished cleaning up after the cake, there were only ten minutes left in the day.

Makayla kept at least three kids between herself and Veronika all afternoon. It annoyed her no end that her desk was used to cut cake and dish out ice cream, but she kept her mouth shut. One run-in with Veronika was enough. Makayla was walking around the room, collecting garbage and wiping down desks, when Mrs. Blake called her name. "Where is the class going on Wednesday?" she asked from behind the lens of her digital camera.

"We're going to the zoo to observe the plants and animals in their natural habitat. It's an opportunity for the students to—"

"Do you still need volunteers?"

The thought of spending an entire day with Veronika made Makayla shudder. "Extra volunteers are always welcome." She injected her voice with a kindness she didn't feel. "Are you available on Wednesday from nine to two?"

"No, but my brother-in-law said he'd be happy to go."

"Great."

Veronika stared lovingly at Terrance, a wide smile on her lips. "Try not to let anything happen to my son this time."

Relieved that Mrs. Blake wasn't coming on the field trip, Makayla chose to ignore her last comment. "Can you remind Terrance that he has to be on his best behavior? If there are any problems, you'll be called to pick him up."

"It's not your place to tell me how to raise *my* child. And I don't appreciate you threatening him, either."

Makayla stood her ground. "I am not threatening anyone, I am merely asking you to speak to your son." To further underline her point, she added, "We don't want what happened at the museum to happen again, do we?"

Mrs. Blake made a sour face. No doubt she was thinking about what had happened last month. Terrance had tried to pin the blame on a classmate but the janitor had signaled him out as the one who wrote on the walls in crayon. The cleaning bill had set Mrs. Blake back hundreds of dollars and Terrance had been banned from The Philadelphia Museum for a year.

"If you'd rather I speak to Kenyon, I will."

Her lips were a tight line. "No. *I'll* talk to Terrance."

"Thank you," Makayla said with forced gratitude. Making a mental note to replace the sweatsuit she had been planning to wear with something dressier, she returned to her desk and added Kenyon's name to the volunteer list.

Kenyon chucked his jacket in the back seat, grabbed his camera equipment and slammed the car door. The fickle autumn weather had changed again, providing a surprisingly warm day, and he didn't want to be stuck lugging his jacket around the zoo.

Kenyon checked his watch as he searched the zoo parking lot. Springs Park Elementary should be here any minute. Instead of standing at the entrance among the crowd, he went inside the customer information booth and settled down on one of the wooden benches. He was engrossed in the morning paper until he heard Kay's voice, loud and clear.

Tossing his newspaper aside, he turned his attention to the eye-catching woman surrounded by a pack of restless first-graders. Sexy had never looked so good. From his vantage point, he had a clear, unrestricted view of Kay's delicious backside. Blue jeans outlined her strong legs and a teal-colored shirt hugged her lavish chest. When she tossed a fleeting look over her shoulder, Kenyon was sure he had been made, but just as quickly as she glanced around, she turned away. He allowed himself a few more minutes of quiet reflection. Or rather, lustful gazing.

Last night, he had driven Terrance to her Patterson Park home to apologize for what had happened on the playground. They hadn't stayed long, but Kenyon had gathered all the information he needed. Dinner and a movie wouldn't work with a woman like Kay Stevens. She didn't own a TV, VCR or a DVD player. In fact, the only piece of electronic equipment in the living room was an outdated stereo system. When Kenyon asked her what she did for fun, she motioned with her head to the numerous bookshelves lining the wall and said, "Read."

That had thrown him for a loop. Most women would have said shopping. Not Kay. She would rather stay home and read than go dancing. Kenyon couldn't remember the last time he had bought a book but he'd head to the closest bookstore and buy a whole stack of reading material if it meant getting close to Kay.

Kenyon had wandered around the living room, noting the simple decor and natural designs. Furnished with cozy sofas, armless chairs and overstuffed bookcases, it resembled a book-store. He had perused the shelves. The reading material she owned provided incredible insight into the shy but sexy teacher. Instead of educational resources, he found hundreds of books about sex, including the Kama Sutra, the *Woman's Gourmet Sex Book* and various issues of erotic magazines. The collection had left Kenyon short of breath. If Terrance had been at home, rather than in the kitchen with Kay making cocoa, Kenyon would have gone in there, pulled her into his arms and kissed her.

Kenyon settled back onto the bench, listening to Kay lecture the students gathered around her, enraptured by the soft, pleasant tone in her voice. For the last twenty-four hours, he had been trying to figure out why she would have so many books about foreplay, erogenous zones and aphrodisiacs. She couldn't be involved in anything as daring as escorting, could she? Kenyon examined her again. No, she just didn't give off that kind of vibe. In his presence, she was skittish, flustered, almost tongue-tied. Could it be an act? Was it possible she was really none of the things she appeared to be?

His face relaxed into a smile. It didn't really matter whether she was acting or not. Kenyon hadn't lived as a monk; he knew what was up. These days, women weren't at home waiting by the phone for a man to call. They were out in the clubs, seeking a good time, thirsty for some action and adventure. Kenyon liked experienced women. The more experience the better. He wasn't one of those men who had sampled all that life had to offer but wanted a good, clean girl to bring home to mom. A bad girl would suit him just fine.

Thoughts of making love to Kay plagued his mind. He saw them kissing, exploring, undressing. With all those naughty sex books at her disposal, she probably had moves he had never seen. Kenyon sighed in silent appreciation. It wouldn't be long before they were acting out their own private fantasies.

Draping an arm over the bench, he stretched his long legs out in front of him. His interest in Kay Stevens grew every time he saw her. The slender, dark-skinned beauty had a lot going for her. Not just physically, either. Making love to her was at the forefront of his mind, but he liked that she could also carry on an intelligent conversation and had a mind of her own.

"Shut up, Abe!" Terrance's voice carried around the park. "My uncle Kenyon *is* coming. He promised!"

Kenyon grabbed his camera bag and walked quickly to the

front entrance. His nephew had been disappointed a lot in his young life and he couldn't stand to see the wounded expression on the boy's face a second more.

Makayla stared at the iron gates, hoping to catch a glimpse of Kenyon through the crowd. If he didn't arrive in the next five minutes, she'd have no choice but to start without him. All of the students had been assigned to a group, but it would only take a second to reorganize the six kids standing behind Terrance.

A perky, dark-haired girl wearing a green park-ranger uniform emerged from the tourist information booth. "Good morning, Springs Park Elementary, and welcome to the Philadelphia Zoo, home of 2,200 exotic mammals, birds and reptiles. I'm Becky and I'll be your tour guide for the morning—"

Desiree gripped Makayla's forearm. "Who is that tall glass of *fine* making his way toward us?" she whispered out of the side of her mouth. "Please tell me that's *not* Terrance's uncle."

"I wish I could." It wasn't every day Makayla saw Desiree drool and she couldn't resist teasing her. "Close your mouth, girl. Flies are getting in."

"Uncle Kenyon!" Terrance took off running. He flung himself into his uncle's arms, his eyes shimmering with delight.

Kenyon tossed him high in the air. "Hey, li'l man."

"You're here!"

"I wouldn't miss this for the world. I used to live at the zoo, you know. I came to see my old friends!"

Terrance took his uncle by the hand and dragged him over to the group. "This is my uncle Kenyon!" He stuck out his tongue at a freckle-faced boy wearing glasses. "Abe, I told you he'd come!"

Makayla smiled. She couldn't remember ever seeing Terrance this excited. It wasn't her place to offer parenting advice, but someone had to tell Kenyon his nephew was desperate for more of his time and attention.

It took a few minutes for the kids to settle down and return their attention to the tour guide. "On to the lions!" Becky shouted, tiptoeing down the road. "We have to keep quiet. They have super-duper hearing and a strong sense of smell. We don't want anyone to get gobbled up by a jungle lion, do we?"

Kenyon approached Kay. "Sorry I'm late but traffic was insane." The lie rolled off his lips with ease. "I got here as fast as I could."

"No problem."

Their eyes did the tango. He stared; she looked away. She stared; he held her gaze.

Desiree stepped forward. "I guess I'll have to introduce myself since my co-worker here has forgotten her manners." She nudged Makayla with her elbow. "I'm Desiree Hill, the other first-grade teacher at Springs Park. I've heard a lot about you, Mr. Blake."

Kenyon turned away from Kay and shook Desiree's out-stretched hand. "Nice to meet you. I think you and I should talk." He read the confusion in her eyes and explained, "I want you to tell me everything you know about Ms. Stevens."

Desiree laughed and Makayla coughed.

"Are you all right?" Kenyon asked, a grin enveloping his lips. Kay looked like as if she was about to collapse. Her breathing was shallow and although it wasn't hot by any standards, she was fanning her face.

"Fine, thank you." In an effort to reclaim her poise, she cleared her throat. Handing him a yellow piece of paper, she said, "Every-thing you need to know is right here. Thanks again for coming. We really appreciate your taking the time out of your day."

"My pleasure." Something about the way he looked at her told her he wasn't talking about the field trip. Makayla's mind drifted back to last night. When she opened her front door and saw

Kenyon and Terrance on her doorstep, carrying a bouquet of flowers and a box chocolates, she had almost lost her footing and teetered off the steps. Thunderstruck, she could scarcely speak. In a short-sleeved shirt, a pair of tattered shorts and natty hair, she had been quite the sight but Kenyon didn't seem put off by her appearance. Her emotions had seesawed between excitement and all-out fear, but she had kept herself together during the hour-long visit. Terrance had been on his best behavior and surprised her by being incredibly polite.

Makayla spotted Terrance leaning toward the lion cage. If there was one thing she knew about the willful six-year old, it was that he had an eye for trouble. Heaving her backpack over her shoulder, she said, "Let's go. We'd better keep up with the kids."

Kenyon smiled at her, his gaze lingering on her full lips. "Lead the way, Ms. Stevens. I'm right behind you."

Chapter 6

For the next two hours, the group meandered around the zoo, snapping pictures, feeding the animals and playing in the sun. The children didn't want to stop for lunch, but Makayla ushered them into the cafeteria.

"I wish Mr. Blake was my uncle," she overheard one of the boys from Desiree's class say.

"Yeah, he's cool!" another said.

Makayla smiled. The kids were right; Kenyon was cool. Clearly, he had a way with women and children. She was impressed at how quickly he had developed a rapport with the kids. They clung to his every word, fought over who was his favorite and begged to hold his hand. At one point, Makayla saw Kenyon jump up on a bench and impersonate a gorilla. The kids had laughed hysterically. As the day wore on, she found herself looking for Kenyon's group. She told herself she was just checking in on the kids, ensuring that everything was going smoothly, but deep down she knew her interest in Kenyon was personal.

Makayla was in line, waiting for her order, when she noticed Desiree and Kenyon sitting on the far side of the cafeteria. They were an arresting pair. Both were tall, dark and attractive. A casual observer would have taken them for a couple and as Makayla stood off to the side, watching them, she couldn't help wondering if Kenyon was interested in her co-worker. It wouldn't be a shock if he was. Most men were.

"Number ten?"

Makayla stepped forward. She picked up her tray and walked carefully through the cafeteria. Since Terrance and most of her students were outside with the parent chaperones, she started toward the door. Terrance had been a model student all day but she knew how quickly things could change.

"Makayla, over here!"

Pretending she didn't hear Desiree, Makayla continued toward the doors. Desiree called her again, but this time, her voice was twice as loud. "Over here! By the window!"

"We were just talking about you," Kenyon confessed when she approached. He stood, took her tray and put it down on the table beside his own. "Here, have a seat."

"I can't stay." Smiling, she motioned toward the doors. "I'm going to eat outside with the kids."

"They're fine," Desiree told her, glancing outside the window. "There are tons of volunteers out there. Relax."

Careful to leave an adequate amount of space between them, Makayla took a seat on the bench. She directed her question to Desiree. "What were you guys talking about?"

"I didn't know your full name was Makayla." Kenyon cocked a brow. "Keeping secrets, are we?" When he grinned, his eyes literally shone.

To keep from saying too much, she focused on her salad. Shoveling lettuce into her mouth, she concentrated on not getting Caesar dressing all over her face.

"Have we met before?"

"No. Why?"

Kenyon frowned. "Makayla Stevens. Hmm. I'm sure I've heard that name before. I just can't remember where."

She reached for a napkin and inadvertently knocked over her cup. Orange juice spilled onto Kenyon's tray, dousing his plate of chicken wings. Apologizing profusely, she sprang to her feet and mopped up the mess with a stack of napkins. "I am so sorry," she said, wiping madly. "Wait here. I'll go get you some more."

Kenyon covered her hand. His touch was warm, pleasant, calming. "Don't worry about it. Besides, the wings weren't all that." He rose to his feet. "Be right back."

Makayla and Desiree watched him leave. When he was a safe distance away, Desiree said, "That man is something else. Fine and smart. Too bad I'm not single!"

"I can't believe I did that!" Makayla shook her head at her folly. "He probably thinks I'm a klutz!"

"I doubt that. Did you see the way he was checking you out?"

Makayla looked down at the bench to ensure it was dry before retaking her seat. "Kenyon Blake is way out of my league."

"You're crazy."

"I'm serious."

"You'd better get that man before some else does. Men like Kenyon are hard to come by. He's hot, down-to-earth and he has a kick-ass sense of humor." Desiree grinned. "Did I mention he was fine?"

Makayla laughed. "Okay, so he's a great guy, but that doesn't mean I want to date him. I'm in a good place right now and I don't need a man complicating my life."

"Go out with him."

"No."

"Why the hell not?"

"For starters, I'm his nephew's teacher. How would that look?"

"Like you were trying to get some!" Laughing, she took a healthy bite of her turkey burger. "Don't use that as an excuse. There's nothing in the school conduct manual that prohibits teachers from dating parents or family members."

Desiree made a valid point but not one that Makayla was willing to consider. "Do I have to remind you what happened with Jared?"

"No, thanks. I've heard that pitiful tale too many times to count."

"Good, so you of all people should understand my reluctance to get involved with another parent." Makayla picked up her fork and popped a crouton into her mouth. Against her better judgment, she had started dating Jared Lewis, a regular parent volunteer. The divorced father of two had swept her off her feet. Dinner at upscale restaurants, tokens of his affection and elaborate dates had been the norm. Within weeks, they were addicted to jalapeño pizza and talked endlessly about their future.

When one of her co-workers ran into them at a charity baseball game, the truth about their relationship had ripped through the school like a midafternoon snowstorm. Neither of his children were in her class, but when word got out that they were dating, Makayla had been shunned by her colleagues. It was as if she had broken some cardinal rule no one had told her about.

Much to her dismay, their relationship had ended disastrously and it was months before her co-workers spoke to her again. The whole incident had been a terrible embarrassment and Makayla had sworn never to make the mistake again. There were plenty of successful, eligible men in Philadelphia and when she was ready to date again, she would find one. Or two. With the way

brothers were juggling women these days, it ~~would be~~
for her to put all of her eggs in one basket. Now,
find a guy who looked, moved and sounded like
she would be in business.

"Here you go."

Makayla jumped at the sound of Kenyon's voice. She turned,
took the cup of orange juice he offered and said, "Thanks. How
much do I owe you?"

He wore a sly smile. "Nothing. Why don't you let me take you
out on Friday night and we'll call it even?"

She took a sip of her drink. As long as she kept the straw at
her lips, she wouldn't have to answer his question.

"Kenyon has tickets to the Comedy Cafe and he's invited us
to be his guests," Desiree explained. "What do you say?"

"I can't."

The smile slid from Desiree's lips. "Why not? It would be a
shame to let the tickets go to waste."

"Because, I, um, I, uh, have other plans."

"You don't want to go because I'll be there, right?" Kenyon
sniffed his shirt. "Do I smell *that* bad? Is it the cologne? It's the
haircut, isn't it?" He gave a deep rumbling laugh at his own joke.

Desiree giggled. "Come on, Makayla. It'll be fun."

"It's just a group of friends hanging out." Kenyon winked.
"That is, unless you want to ditch the pack so we can be alone."

Makayla stuck to her story. "Sorry, I'm busy. Maybe next time."

Kenyon didn't believe her. Her voice was shaky and she had
a hell of a time meeting his gaze. "What are you afraid of?"

"Pardon me?"

"You heard me. What are you afraid of?"

There was nothing Desiree loved more than a slice of gossip,
Makayla knew, but she left the table anyway. Picking up her
backpack, she said, "I'll catch you guys later."

before she could beg Desiree to stay, she was gone. Sighing deeply, she stared down at her salad. Now it was just her and Kenyon. There was no telling what he'd do. He wouldn't be happy until he got what he wanted. Back in high school, he would stop at nothing to get the girl. He had been relentless as a teen and he was even more aggressive now.

"I'm going to be honest with you. I'm attracted to you and I know you feel the same way."

His confession threw her for a curve. "How do you know?"

Kenyon's eyes moved across her face and settled on her lips. They were soft, moist, inviting. Her skin was flawless and her girlish features made her all the more appealing. Makayla Stevens was a sexy, brown-skinned angel and didn't even know it. "The eyes never lie. You want to be with me, but something's holding you back."

If anyone else had made that comment, she would have labeled him an arrogant fool. But Kenyon was anything but. He was supremely confident and there was nothing sexier than a self-assured man who knew what he wanted.

Makayla considered her options. If she denied his claim he'd see right through her, but if she told the truth, she'd be at his mercy. As far as her eyes could see, Kenyon had it all. Good looks, a successful career, an adventurous nature and she'd bet everything she owned he was a stud in bed, too. If Terrance wasn't her student, she would have yielded to Kenyon's advances a long time ago.

He spoke in a hushed tone, just loud enough for her to hear. "You're a private person and I can respect that. It's nobody's business what happens between us, and we don't need anyone's approval, either. But if you feel more comfortable with us keeping this private, I'll go along with it." Kenyon understood the delicacy of the situation. He wanted her in his bed, but he didn't want to cause problems for her. Underneath the table, he put a hand to her thigh. "What do you say?"

Startled by his touch, she looked nervously around the room. His words of reassurance calmed her, but she still wasn't convinced going out with him was a good idea. What if someone saw them together? What if it got back to her boss that they were dating? What would her colleagues think?

Kenyon wore his best smile. "It's just a date."

Makayla *was* attracted to him and what better way to spice up her writing than by having an affair with a deliciously handsome man? Just as she was about to give in, her good sense kicked in. No, dating Kenyon was a bad idea. Her present goal was to land a position as a travel writer, not have a fling with her old high school crush. "I'm flattered that you're interested in me, but—"

"I'm more than just interested in you, Makayla." The air was charged with desire, and the deep yearning in his voice was unmistakable.

"I—I don't know what to say," she stuttered.

Fueling his longing for this woman was her unwavering resistance. The more she refused him, the more he wanted her. "I want you and I'm not afraid to admit it."

Her mouth cracked open wordlessly. She thought back over her last few dates. Dating Kenyon would be a welcome change. In the last year, she had met nothing but whiny, immature boys who still lived at home with their mommas. Kenyon was a free thinker. He held back nothing and lived in the moment. That was just the kind of man she was looking for.

His hand traveled up her thigh. "One date, that's all I'm asking for."

There was something about being with Kenyon that made Makayla feel as if she were back in high school. Only this time she didn't tip the scales at two hundred pounds.

Unwanted memories showered her. There was a time when Makayla did nothing but fantasize about him. Sometimes, when they were studying and Kenyon had his head buried in his math textbook, she would imagine him making love to her. In her visions, the scent of orchids pervaded the air and Kenyon gazed down at her with adoration in his eyes. Their lovemaking was intense, filled with an uncontained passion. Her daydreaming had gotten so out of hand, her math teacher had called home to complain. It had taken Makayla a solid hour to convince her scripture-quoting father that she was suffering from sleep deprivation and not experimenting with drugs or alcohol.

She didn't dare admit it, not even to herself, but after all these years she still had a crush on Kenyon Blake. It was more than just his swoon-worthy looks. He put everyone around him at ease, had the ability to laugh at himself, and was truly one of a kind. Some people called it flair but Makayla called it charisma. And aside from all of his formidable characteristics, he was genuinely a nice guy. The leather jacket, his penchant for all-black clothes and his mischievous grin weren't fooling anybody. He was playing the part of a wild, untamable bad boy, but she had a feeling he was the same fun-loving boy she remembered from way back when.

"What's it going to be?"

"Thanks, but no thanks." Makayla glanced at her watch. "We should go. We have to meet the tour guide at the botanical garden in ten minutes and it's going to take a while to get the kids back into their groups."

"Can I call you?"

"I don't think that would be a good idea." She rose, emptied her tray in the garbage and exited the cafeteria at breakneck speed.

Chapter 7

"Lookin' good, teach!"

Makayla whipped around so fast, she almost fell off the wooden stool.

Kenyon stood with his back to the door, a smile on his lips. "Mornin'."

"Good morning."

Kenyon held out his hand, but Makayla braced herself against the wall and stepped down. Running a hand over her gray flouncy skirt, she tried to squelch the butterflies quivering in her stomach. "What are you doing here?"

"I came to see you, of course."

In the silence, Kenyon admired the art display. Underneath the orange banner that read Our Trip to the Philadelphia Zoo were dozens of paintings and short paragraphs about each animal. "Those look great."

"The kids worked really hard on them." She motioned with

her head to the bulletin board. "Thanks again for the pictures. You captured some amazing shots."

"I'm glad you like them."

"I do." Instead of channeling her gaze, which she had a habit of doing when Kenyon was around, she focused her eyes on his face. In the two weeks since she last saw him, his mustache had grown in and his chin was spotted with stubble. His rugged new look only added to his mystique. Makayla couldn't help noticing the thickness of his lips. They were full, well shaped, perfect for giving and receiving pleasure. A woman could get in a lot of trouble kissing him, she decided, sweeping a hand through her hair.

Kenyon unzipped his leather jacket and Makayla caught a whiff of his cologne. It was a subtle scent. Light, calming, cool; everything he appeared to be. "Did you get the thank-you card the kids made?"

"I have it in my office. I love it."

"I'm glad to hear it."

They stood in silence for several seconds.

Kenyon wondered what it would take to convince Makayla he was for real. He'd watched her at the zoo and marveled at how she interacted with the other volunteers. No timidity whatsoever. She was affable, genial and to his utter amazement, chatty. Studying her had verified his suspicions. She liked him—*a lot.* Why else would she be flustered in his presence? Why else would she avoid him? She was denying their attraction, pretending it didn't exist, but it was just a matter of time before he broke down her walls.

"Where's Terrance?" She picked up the stool and returned it to the closet.

"He won't be in today. He has the flu."

"Poor guy." There was genuine concern in her voice when she asked, "Is there anything I can do?"

"No. Veronika's taking good care of him."

She regarded him with a smile. "Was there anything else?"

"No."

"You came down here just to tell me Terrance is sick?"

Kenyon shrugged. "That's what any good parent would do."

"You could have called and left a message with the secretary."

"Then I wouldn't be able to see you. And my days aren't quite the same unless I see your smile."

Makayla giggled. It seemed her head and her heart disconnected whenever Kenyon was around. She wanted him to leave, but damn it if a bigger part of her didn't want him to stay. Somewhere in the distance tires screeched and horns blared. Vigorous chatter screamed through the windows. It wouldn't be long before the halls filled with kids. Much as she would love to continue flirting with Kenyon, she had to get ready for her class. "Thanks for coming by."

"Have you given any more thought to what I said?"

"No." The lie was off her lips with quickness.

Fired with determination, he stepped forward and captured her around the waist.

She made a small, frightened noise, much like the mewl of a kitten. "What are you doing?"

"Convincing you to go out with me."

Her eyes flared. She didn't know what to do. She had a rapid heartbeat and shortness of breath. Kenyon was trouble. Suave, cocky, debonair. He was a smooth-talking playboy who could easily sweep her off her feet. Sinfully sexy, he knew exactly what to say to turn her heart to mush.

"I think you know what's going to happen next."

Fear surged through her. Her palms were sweaty and her throat was tight. What if Mr. Gibson walked in? Would she be fired on the spot or given a chance to explain?

She tried to break free, which elicited a laugh from her captor. "If you don't let go of me this instant, I'm going to scream," she said, sounding more confident than she felt. "I mean it, Kenyon."

More laughter. "You're hot, Makayla. The kind of woman who turns me on."

She stared up at him wide-eyed. "What do you want from me?"

"Everything, but for now a kiss will do."

"We can't—"

"I'm going to kiss you and you're going to enjoy it," he boasted, lifting her chin to his mouth. "Now, try and relax and do what comes naturally."

Makayla could actually feel her heart beating. Every muscle in her body screamed out in protest. Her breathing thickened as his lips closed in on her mouth. Determined not to get sucked in by his smooth words, dreamy eyes and soft touch, she said, "Let go of me. I could get fired if someone catches us."

"Are we on for tomorrow night?" His voice was deep, smooth, sensual. "You, me, eight o'clock?"

"I already told you, I have—"

"Then you leave me no other choice." His head lowered over hers until their lips met in a kiss. Her reaction was unexpected. Tense shoulders, rod-straight back, arms dangling tightly at her sides. Undeterred by her response, he skillfully parted her lips with his tongue. When her shoulders softened, he deepened the kiss and caressed a forefinger along her cheek.

A tasty mix of lust and desire, the kiss engulfed her like a roaring wave. It did more than just heat her body; it touched the deepest part of her soul. Soft moans of pleasure soon filled the room. Caught up in the pure ecstasy of his touch, she didn't realize the noises belonged to her. She was in the moment. The kiss had lots of tongue, lots of heat and lots of passion. She enjoyed the thrill of wild, hungry lust. His impulsive act put her in a sexy state of mind, and her fears abated as his mouth feasted on her lips.

Kissing Kenyon was a hundred times better than all of the high school fantasies she'd conjured up in her mind. Makayla hadn't been pining away for him, but in the back of her mind she had always wondered if things would be different now. She wasn't the hefty girl with kinky hair and awful skin whom everyone poked fun at. Vibrant, attractive and intelligent, she had everything going for her now.

Affirmed by her moans, he allowed his hands to wander. The slight tingling of her body only fueled his need. Submitting to his inner craving, he trailed a finger up her thigh. The feel of her bare flesh in his hands solicited a staggered groan from his mouth. Pressing her against the door, he ravished her with his mouth and seduced her with his hands. He needed coolant or something equally persuasive to extinguish his raging hormones. Not even the high-pitched voices beyond the classroom door could stop him from drawing her closer to him. Pleased that he had had the prescience to lock the door when he entered the room, he ran his hands over her back.

A harsh knock on the door broke the spell.

"Hello? Hello?" The knocking grew louder, more impatient. "Ms. Stevens, are you in there?"

Makayla recognized Leilani's voice. The sixth-grader was on the student leadership committee and helped out in her classroom three mornings a week. When the voices outside the door grew louder, she wiggled out of Kenyon's grasp. "I'll be right out," she called. Her voice was a shy whisper when she addressed Kenyon. "You have to go. *Now.*"

He nodded but didn't move.

"Did you hear me?"

Kenyon knew he had behaved recklessly, knew he had put her in a compromising position, knew he had crossed the line, but that kiss had been building for weeks. "Are we on for tonight?"

"I can't."

"Makayla, I'm straight-up single. No baby-mama drama, no crazy exes, no girlfriend whatsoever." The look in his eyes changed from one of amusement to resolve.

"I'm flattered but—"

His mouth swallowed hers in another hungry kiss. This time, her body was warm and her lips sweet.

Makayla didn't try to escape. It felt good kissing him. Damn good. Anxious to feel his touch, she took his hands from around her waist and guided them to her breasts. Brazen had never been her style but being with Kenyon made her feel bold, nervy, reckless even. Kissing him made her feel indulgent and luxurious and she welcomed his touch. His hands caressed her until she was consumed with lust.

A violent thwack against the door snapped Makayla out of her stupor.

"Ms. Stevens, where are you?"

It was Leilani again. Makayla was going to give that girl a stern talking-to. She had no business banging on the door as if she were leading the fire brigade.

Kenyon reluctantly pulled away. "Sorry 'bout that. Guess I got carried away."

She didn't know what to make of his apology. If he was sorry, then why were his eyes skimming over her body the same way his hands had done just seconds earlier? "It's all right. Sometimes these things happen."

"I'll see you later, then?"

Overheated and tingly all over, she smoothed her hands over her face. "Thanks for coming. Give Terrance my best. Bye."

"I'll pick you up at eight."

She didn't dare protest. Who knew what he'd do if she turned him down again. Flattening the creases out of her blouse, she rehearsed what she was going to say to her students waiting in the hall. Leilani was a smart girl. If she sensed even a hint of wrongdoing, she would take the news back to her class, and it would eventually end up in Mr. Gibson's ear. Smiling brightly, she unlocked the door and said, "Good morning, class! Come on in!"

Francis Watkins's hand shot up. When Ms. Stevens didn't come to her aid, she quietly slipped out of her desk and marched across the room. Her teacher didn't like when she left her seat without permission, but this was an emergency. "Ms. Stevens! Ms. Stevens!"

Makayla blinked. Turning away from the window, she stared down at Francis. A look of displeasure framed her tiny mouth and her blond pigtails whisked about her face. "Lexus stole my Hello Kitty pencil sharpener!"

"Francis, didn't I tell you not to leave your seat without permission?"

"Yes, but I put my hand up and you didn't answer."

Sighing deeply, Makayla rested the water jug on the windowsill. It was hard being patient with Francis, especially after the stunt she'd pulled at lunch. Just thinking about how she had gone into her desk and helped herself to glow-in-the dark stickers made Makayla angry all over again. "Did you see Lexus take your sharpener?"

"No, but—"

"It's not nice to accuse people of things," Makayla said sternly.

"But she—"

"Enough, Francis. I will not have you making up any more stories about your classmates."

Hanging her head, she fiddled with her pink Hello Kitty bracelet.

Resting a hand on Francis's shoulder, she steered the tempera-mental five-year-old back to her desk. It wasn't until Makayla was halfway across the room that she noticed there was water everywhere. On the ground, pooling around the desks, flowing toward the carpet. Makayla groaned. If she had focused on watering the plants, instead of reliving the kiss she'd had with Kenyon in her mind, the flowerpots wouldn't be leaking and her classroom wouldn't resemble a wading pool.

"Francis, can you go to the bathroom and get me some paper towels?"

"Yes, Ms. Stevens." The girl left and returned in seconds.

After transferring the flowers to new pots and placing them back on the windowsill, Makayla moped and dried the floor. The class must have sensed her annoyance because they spent the period working quietly at their desks.

It took all of Makayla's strength to listen to the class reading eight different Robert Munsch stories, but after spending much of the day in a haze, she felt she owed it to the kids to give them some attention. She had been in a world all her own since Kenyon left. In math she had assigned the wrong homework, in language arts she forgot to collect the printing books and at recess she had been ten minutes late bringing her class back inside.

All day, her mind had been on Kenyon and that kiss. Her thoughts had induced a whole slew of visual images and try as she might, she couldn't get him out of her head. Hours had passed since the incident, but she still couldn't believe he'd kissed her. And more scandalous, she had kissed him back! And not just kissed him, but touched him, too! Where had that boldness come from? It was as if she had lost all self-control. If Leilani hadn't interrupted them, only God knew where things might have ended up. They might have taken off each other's clothes. Or worse yet, done the deed right there on the middle of her desk.

Makayla closed her eyes and thought back to the exact moment when Kenyon touched her. His hands were intrusive, needy, but it was the exigency of the kiss that had left her head spinning. No one had ever kissed her with such…such… Makayla was stumped. Words just couldn't describe it. The encounter was brief, but what had transpired was powerful enough to jar her emotions.

Maybe she had been wrong. Getting involved with Kenyon was a risk, but why pass up an opportunity to be with a gorgeous hunk just because she was scared of what people might say? No one had to know they were lovers. Kenyon understood her need for privacy. He could be trusted, couldn't he? When she was dating Jared, she had foolishly confided in one of her co-workers, and the blabbermouth had shared her business with everyone from the school nurse to the part-time janitor. This time, Makayla would be smart. No popular hangouts, no public displays of affection and no more kisses in her classroom. If she could conceal her identity as Lady Sexpot for all these years, surely she could keep her affair with Kenyon under wraps.

Her lips curved into a smile. Having a fling with Kenyon was sure to change her life. If the kiss was any indication, their coming together would be one hot, deliciously erotic experience.

"Did I do good, Ms. Stevens?"

Makayla blinked. "Pardon me?"

"Did I do good?"

It was the third time she had been caught daydreaming. She hadn't listened to Zacharias read beyond the first page, but she patted him on the head and said, "You did great!"

He beamed. "Thanks. I've been practicing."

"It shows."

The bell rang and once the room emptied, Makayla returned to her desk. She had marking to do and progress reports to complete but she didn't let that stop her from packing up her briefcase. It wasn't every day she had a date with Kenyon Blake and if she wanted to look her best, she had some serious primping to do.

Chapter 8

"My ex-wife was so fat, she was baptized at Sea World!"

Whistles, hoots and shouts of laughter filled the dark, smoky room.

"Lord, the woman can eat! I took Octavia out for dinner and almost lost my damn mind." Chucky J cocked his head to the right. "How the hell the check gonna come to a hundred bucks when all I had was water?"

Laughter flowed freely.

"You know when I knew she was going to be the death of me? The night she started sucking on my neck like it was a hotlink! Gnawed right through the skin, y'all!"

The audience roared.

Must be me. Makayla took a sip of her beer. Dabbing her forehead with a napkin, she reached into her purse and pulled out her compact. She stole a peek in the mirror. The room was stiflingly hot but her makeup was still flawless.

Makayla glanced around in search of their long-limbed waiter. The hole-in-the-wall comedy club was an eyesore and the teenage staff inefficient, but the laid-back vibe more than made up for it. Up-and-coming comedians kept the establishment packed day in and day out.

Crossing her arms under her chest, she turned back to the tiny, well-lit stage. Chucky J was no Chris Rock. And with lifeless eyes, crooked teeth and hairy arms, he had no business making fun of anyone else.

When the crowd burst into frenzied applause and Chucky J strolled off the stage, Makayla sighed in relief.

"Chucky J's a riot!" Kenyon wiped the corner of his eyes with the back of his hand. "What'd you think, Makayla?"

She shrugged a shoulder. "He was all right."

"All right? He killed it!"

"If you say so."

"Man, I laughed so hard my jaw hurts."

"Really?"

Kenyon studied her. Furrowed brows, pinched lips, rigid shoulders. Twenty minutes ago she was laughing; now she looked downright pissed. "Did I do something wrong?"

"No. Why?"

"You look angry."

"I didn't think Chucky J was funny, that's all. I found a lot of his jokes offensive."

"To who?"

"Overweight people, of course."

"But you laughed when he cracked on P. Diddy," Kenyon pointed out. "And you applauded when he said black men were cheap."

Makayla leaned forward, the swell of her cleavage clearly visible in her fuchsia lace-trimmed blouse. "And?"

Kenyon tried not to stare, but the sight of her smooth, brown skin was a turn-on. "Weren't those jokes offensive, too?"

A reluctant smile tugged at the corner of her lips. "Oh, shut up, Kenyon! No one asked you!"

Kenyon chuckled.

The sound of his laughter made Makayla warm all over. There was something tempting about being with someone who wasn't afraid to challenge her. And Kenyon had been goading her all night. When she confessed to disliking rap music, he enlightened her about its roots and encouraged her to give it a listen. He labeled her sexist when she said America couldn't handle a female president and laughed heartily when she announced that men were indeed the weaker sex.

"I don't know why you were offended by Chucky J's jokes. He wasn't talking about you," Kenyon said, watching her. "You're gorgeous." Tonight, her look was subtly sexy. A fitted top, a black miniskirt and light makeup gave her an older, more sophisticated look. When Makayla had opened her front door and welcomed him inside, words had escaped him. It had taken everything he had not to sweep her up in his arms and take her right then and there in the foyer.

"Trust me. I didn't always look this way. I used to wear size eighteen jeans," she confessed.

His jaw hit the table. "For real?"

"My weight problems started when my mom died and escalated from there. I tried everything under the sun but nothing worked."

Kenyon remembered her mentioning that she was a heavy teen but with those firm arms, trim waist and those sleek legs, it was hard for him to image her ever being overweight. "How did you finally lose the weight?"

"My dad had a heart attack when I was a freshman in university. Seeing him was a huge wake-up call." She paused to finish what was left of her drink. "It was just the kick in the butt I needed."

"Must have been hard," he said.

"It was, but I was determined. When I got home from the hospital that night, I cleared the fridge, dumped all the junk food and committed to eating healthy. A girlfriend of mine turned me on to the benefits of daily exercise and soon I was cycling, swimming, weight-lifting. I even took up kickboxing. By the end of the month I'd dropped twelve pounds and the weight just kept falling off."

Kenyon gave her a rich smile. "Good for you." He wanted to say more, wanted to tell her just how good she looked, but a redhead with a lissome frame and a sour expression approached their table.

"I'm your server. Would you like to hear the new additions to the menu?" she asked in a lifeless tone.

After the monotone litany, Makayla ordered a Cobb salad.

"Do you ever eat anything besides salad?" Before she could reply, he said, "Why don't you leave the ordering to me?" When he was done, he turned back to Makayla, his eyes settling on her lips. "Did I tell you how good you look?" he asked.

She flushed. "Thanks."

Another comedian took to the stage and the houselights dimmed. Makayla felt herself relax. Everything was going smoothly. She hadn't spilled anything, tripped or gotten tongue-tied all night.

She eyed Kenyon with interest. Six feet, lean and long, he still had the body of an athlete. It wasn't every day she went out with a gorgeous heartthrob and she had every intention of making the most of it. She had spent so much time looking over her shoulder at the past, she had let decent brothers and meaningful relation-ships pass her by. But not anymore. She wouldn't tense up if

Kenyon tried to kiss her and she wouldn't invent excuses for why she couldn't see him again, either. This was the beginning of one sexy relationship and she was ready for it.

Kenyon draped an arm casually around her shoulder. His fingers deftly grazed her collarbone and her breathing quickened.

Feeling confident, she scooted over on her chair. Impaired by the alcohol she'd consumed, she rubbed a hand over his leg. The aggressive move took Kenyon by surprise. He hadn't expected this. Could this be the same woman who'd turned him down repeatedly? Kenyon studied Makayla closely. There was no mistaking the naughty expression on her face. He wasn't the only one feeling frisky tonight.

He smiled and she smiled back.

Makayla put a hand on his thigh. What was it the divorced mother of three had told her about the art of seduction? *"Make the first move and don't hold back!"* Now was the time to put what she had learned into practice. Their table was at the back of the room, shielded by dim lights and safe from prying eyes. If they were quiet, no one would know what they were doing. *Tonight's the night.* Goodbye shy, sexually inexperienced woman; hello hot, sexually liberated woman! Inching up her skirt, she crossed her legs with the flair of Sharon Stone. Dangling her right shoe, she rubbed her heel against his shin. Then, she took his hand and put it on her thigh.

Kenyon stared at Makayla. If she didn't stop shoving her breasts against him they were going to have a serious problem. How could she expect him to behave when she was practically assaulting him with her hands? She was asking for it. Her eyes shone with cupidity and her lips were curved in a sumptuous smile. The woman was as fine as she wanted to be and far more adventurous than he ever gave her credit for.

His breathing was deep and even, but when her tongue flick-

ered lightly against his ear, he lost it. Kenyon crushed her lips
with his and she yielded to his touch. His mouth reached for her,
hungrily, robbing her of speech. He couldn't get enough of her
warm, supple thighs, and her hoarse, guttural moan urged him
on. He had a hand up her skirt when he felt the blinding stage
light on his face.

"Get a room!" a voice yelled.

Makayla's eyes flew open. Everyone in the club was staring,
pointing, laughing. In a feeble attempt to preserve her dignity,
she hid her face behind her hands. A band of teens sitting in the
front row made kissing sounds and if that wasn't bad enough,
the comedian jumped off the stage, chucked a wad of condoms
at them and said, "Here, tonight's on me!"

Kenyon pulled into Makayla's driveway. Snow flurries fell
from the sky and disappeared as they fell on the ground. The
wind howled, flinging tree branches back and forth. Oak trees
bordering the property sheltered the couple from the wind as they
approached the house.

It was freezing outside but Makayla could feel sweat dribbling
down her back. The drive home had been a guilt-ridden half
hour for her. If she hadn't pounced on Kenyon, they wouldn't
have been humiliated at the club. After they were busted making
out, the remaining comedians took cheap shots at them. Their
date had been a disaster and Makayla could barely bring herself
to look at him.

"Thanks. I had a nice time," she said, jamming her key into
the lock.

"It's still early. Why don't I come in and we can watch a movie
or something."

She glanced over her shoulder and smiled softly. "I don't
have a TV, remember?"

"Oh, yeah, I forgot." Kenyon chuckled. "I swear, you're the only person I know who doesn't own a TV."

"I hear that all the time. I never had one growing up so I got used to finding other things to do with my time."

"Did your parents think television was evil or something?"

"No, we couldn't afford one." Makayla faced him. "I think my dad did me a favor. I'd much rather read a book than watch TV, anyway. And if there's a movie I really want to see, I just go to the theater."

"Good, because I was thinking we should check out the new Samuel L. Jackson movie."

Her eyes bulged. "You want to go out with me again?"

"Why wouldn't I?"

She couldn't bring herself to answer. Back at the comedy club she had acted like a horny toad, but now that the alcohol had worn off, she was self-conscious.

Kenyon cracked a smile. Tiny snowflakes gleamed on her forehead and gave her soft, angelic glow. "Of course I want to go out with you again. I plan to be around for a while." He backed up his confession with a kiss. She tasted sweet. Kenyon pulled away before he lost control. "Are you free tomorrow night?"

"No, I'm going to a concert."

"Can I come?"

"I doubt you'd be interested."

He wore a grin. "Try me."

"Ever heard of Gretchen Wilson?"

"The country singer?"

"The one and only."

Kenyon hated country music, but the idea of being in a semi-dark arena with her was just too damn tempting. "Count me in."

Makayla couldn't believe her ears. Kenyon wanted to be her

date? He was a fan of Gretchen Wilson, too? This was bigger than
big news. Most of the men she dated broke out laughing when
she told them Shania Twain and Tim McGraw were two of her
favorite singers. "Are you sure?"

"Positive."

If Desiree didn't love Kenyon before, she'd love him now.
Under great duress, Desiree had agreed to go to the concert, but
now that Makayla had a willing partner in Kenyon, she didn't
need her friend's company.

"What time does the concert start?"

"Seven o'clock."

"Why don't I pick you up early and we'll grab a bite to eat first?"

A wave of giddiness swept over her. "Sounds good!" she said
in a too-loud voice. Makayla couldn't hold back her excitement.
Not only did she have front-row tickets to see Gretchen Wilson,
she had the best-looking man in all of Philadelphia as her date!

What exactly did one wear to a country music concert,
anyway? Kenyon wondered, examining himself in the mirror.
Something told him a FUBU sweatshirt, blue jeans and Timberland boots was the wrong look.

Kenyon ditched the sweatshirt, heaved it onto the bed and
pulled on a black sweater. He draped a gold chain around his neck
and put on his leather jacket and shoes. With a dash of his Nautica
cologne and a quick glance of himself in the full-length mirror
in the hallway, he was out the back door.

Five minutes later, he pulled out of the garage. He popped in
the latest Snoop Dogg CD and cranked up the volume. If he was
going to make it through the next two hours, he needed to get
his mind right. A Gretchen Wilson concert? Kenyon couldn't
remember the last time he'd done anything so stupid. If it weren't
for the photo shoot he'd done for *Rolling Stone* a few months

back, he'd have no idea who the woman was. The models had chatted nonstop about the newest "it" girl of country music. Kenyon couldn't name a single song on her album, didn't know how long she'd been in the business and would be hard-pressed to describe what the woman looked like.

But all of Philly must be going to the concert. Cars were lined up in all four lanes. Since he had time to spare, he opened his cell phone and punched in Veronika's number.

His tone warmed when he heard his nephew's voice. "Hey, li'l man, what's up?"

"We're having a party!" Terrance said, his voice brimming with excitement. "Mom bought a bucket of chicken and she rented *Bride of Chucky.* Can you come? Huh, can you?"

"Sorry, li'l man. Uncle Kenyon has plans tonight."

"Are you taking me to my hockey game tomorrow?"

"I wouldn't miss it."

"Yay!"

"Where's your mom?"

After a brief pause, he said, "Ah—she's in the bathroom, I think."

"Okay, li'l man. Tell her I called and I'll talk to you later."

"Bye, Uncle Kenyon."

As he disconnected the call, lines creased his forehead. What was Veronika thinking? *Bride of Chucky?* If Terrance was a teenager he wouldn't mind. But he was a young, impressionable kid who scared easily. Kenyon thought of calling back, but talking to Veronika would inevitably spoil his mood. And the last thing he wanted to do was start his date off on the wrong foot. Everything had to be perfect tonight. If the night went according to plan, he'd have Makayla in his bed by the end of the night. He licked his lips in anticipation. The traffic cleared and Kenyon took off down the freeway. The sooner he picked up Makayla, the better.

Chapter 9

Kenyon flipped on the hallway lights. "Let me," he offered, helping Makayla out of her jacket and hanging it in the closet. He admired the way her jeans cupped her butt and elongated her legs. Her short-sleeved T-shirt bearing Gretchen Wilson's face was a size too small, but it showcased her flat stomach. The humidity of the arena had loosened her curls and now her hair hung freely over her shoulders, giving her a softer, prettier look.

Kenyon put an arm around her waist, feeling an instant connection. He ran a hand over the gentle contours of her body. "Can I interest you in something to drink?"

"Sure, I'll have a diet cola."

"Come on, you can do better than that."

"What do you recommend?"

Kenyon winked. "I'll surprise you."

Makayla ran her tongue slowly over her lips. A string of deep breaths did little to calm her. This wasn't the first time

Kenyon had touched her so why was she on the verge of hyerventilating?

"Make yourself at home," he said, relinquishing his hold. He'd only had her in his arms for a moment but it was enough to make an impression on him. Before the night was over, he would know if she was every bit as sexy as he thought she was. Kenyon took her hand. "Take a look around. Tell me what you think."

She surveyed the room. There were pictures on the walls, perched on tables, displayed on the mantel. She recognized the more famous monuments—the Taj Mahal, the Great Wall of China, Edinburgh Castle—but she needed Kenyon's help in identifying the others. As she listened to him describe the staggering beauty of the Amazon falls, she decided in her heart that one day soon she'd see them for herself.

There was a framed family portrait above the fireplace and Makayla was struck by the similarities between Kenyon and his late brother. Terrance stood between them, a wide smile on his face. It was hard to believe that such an adorable boy was capable of creating such mayhem.

The look and feel of Kenyon's home made Makayla wonder if there wasn't a woman living there, too. Cool blue walls blended easily with silk drapes, crystal candle chandeliers and contemporary area rugs. Deep, oversize armchairs and an eight-seat sectional sofa were dressed with fluffy cushions. Either Kenyon had taken tips from a Martha Stewart magazine or a woman had helped decorate his house.

"I love the decor. Did you do this all by yourself?"

"No, a friend helped me out."

A friend? Makayla wanted to ask about the gender of this "friend," but decided against it. She had a strong feeling the friend was Veronika. Later, when the time was right, she'd find out exactly what was going on between them. Dating

Kenyon was one thing, but being one-third of a love triangle was plain stupid.

She watched Kenyon fix their drinks. With his light eyes, quick smile and strong arms, he was gorgeous with a capital *G*. They shared an intense connection, a love of country music and had grown up in the same neighborhood. He was her dream man, but Makayla knew she didn't have a fighting chance with him. Men like Kenyon dated supermodels, not women like her.

"Ice?"

"Sure." She smoothed the sides of her hair. She'd acted a fool at the concert—yelling, screaming, jumping like a preteen girl—but she'd had the time of her life. What made the evening even more special was having Kenyon beside her. "Did you have a good time at the concert?"

Kenyon came over to the couch and handed her a glass. "Yeah, it was fun."

Tasting her drink, she watched him closely. For someone who claimed to be a Gretchen Wilson fan, he'd been rather subdued when the singer leaped off the stage, grabbed his hand and danced with him. Makayla didn't know if his lack of response was due to shock or disinterest.

"You know what the best part was?"

"No."

"Watching you dance."

Her laugh was shaky. "You must have been watching someone else, because I'm a horrible dancer."

Kenyon gave her a long, searching look. "I bet there are a lot of things I don't know about you." His eyes were smiling but his gaze was intense. "Follow me. There's something I want to show you."

As they walked through the main floor, Makayla caught glimpses of the rest of the house. Gleaming floors, big rooms, lavish furniture. Pictures were displayed on every wall, and the entire house reeked of style and elegance. "You have a beautiful home."

"Speaking of beautiful, did I tell you how great you look tonight?"

She laughed lightly. "Yeah, about a dozen times."

A disarming smile claimed his lips. "What can I say? I'm a sucker for a pretty girl." He opened a door and led her down a short flight of stairs.

The basement was a stark contrast to upstairs. The masculine ambiance of the room was enhanced by recliners, arcade games, a pool table and another fully stocked bar. Framed basketball jerseys hung on the tan-colored walls.

Kenyon picked up the marble structure above the fireplace. At first glance, it looked like a replica of an elderly man. "I got this in Ghana from a local I befriended. Do you know what it is?"

Did she ever. In her studies she had read hundreds of articles about fertility gods and the unconventional practices of tribal people. She took it from him and studied the intricate carvings along the base of the sculpture. It was smooth to the touch and far heavier than it looked. "This is an Udoka. The African God of passion, right?"

"In Western Africa men still believe sexual prowess is a gift from the gods. What do you think?"

Makayla swallowed. "I don't know."

"Do you think women can teach men how to be good lovers?"

"Definitely."

"I was hoping you'd say that." Kenyon took the sculpture from her hands and returned it to its rightful place. The close quarters of the basement and the enticing scent of her perfume made him feel as if he were going to combust. "Come here."

A combination of reasons kept her feet firmly planted. One, she was too nervous to move. And two, there was no telling what she would do if he kissed her. The last time she had acted on her feelings, she had embarrassed them both.

Kenyon bent down and kissed her cheek. Her manslayer scent tickled his nose, and the delicious warmth of her smile made his pulse soar. "I'm really feeling you, Makayla. I want you *bad*."

Her mind spun. If someone had told her a month ago she would be on the verge of making love to Kenyon Blake, she would have laughed herself silly. In high school, she had followed him around shamelessly, and now he was the one pursuing her. For the first time, she was in control and it was an empowering feeling. Kenyon wanted her and she was going to enjoy his attention for as long as it lasted. "You do, huh? What do you have in mind?"

"A little bit of this—" He pressed his lips behind her earlobe and then twirled the tip of his tongue in circles. "A little bit of this—" He moved his hands down the slope of her hips and cupped her butt. "And a lot of that!"

Makayla laughed. In the silence, she thought about their growing attraction. A feeling of bliss surrounded her whenever he was near, and she thought of nothing but kissing him. But she had to know if he had feelings for Veronika. "Can I ask you something?"

"Ask away."

"Is there anything going on between you and Veronika?"

"No."

"Are you sure?"

"Positive. We're family. We both want what's best for Terrance. That's it." Kenyon motioned to the couch and they sat down. "I'm not going to lie to you, Makayla. I haven't been a Boy Scout. I've been with a lot of women."

"And—"

"And I'm not looking to settle down."

"Me, neither."

He was startled by her response. Most of the women he knew were anxious to get married, build that white-picket-fence dream house and start a family. He reflected on her collection of X-rated books. She was stunning, sexually adventurous and could have any man she wanted. Kenyon wasn't in the market for a wife, but he wanted the woman in his life to be faithful. "Are you dating other guys?"

"Nope, I'm all yours."

His smile returned. "Now that we got that out of the way, where were we?"

She leaned in, closed her eyes and kissed him.

Inspired by her boldness, he stretched out on the couch and pulled her down on top of him. His lips deserted hers to nibble on her earlobe. He gently circled her neck with a series of soft kisses, moving from her throat to her breastbone.

There was something intensely sensual about not knowing where he was going to touch her next.

He took off his shirt and Makayla moaned. His chest should be bronzed, she thought. Flawless skin, smooth to the touch, a ripple of tight muscles. One kiss was swallowed by another and soon, they were lost in the magic of it all.

He stroked her flesh with one hand and unzipped her jeans with the other. She had fantasized about him undressing her, but now that it was actually happening she couldn't stay still. He slipped a hand inside her panties and she quietly exhaled. Breathless with anticipation, she closed her eyes and parted her legs.

Lost in the moment, Kenyon didn't hear the phone ringing or the answering machine click on. When he heard his nephew's voice, he broke off the kiss and jumped to his feet. "Sorry, I've got to take this call. It could be important." Kenyon snatched up the phone. "Terrance?"

Feeling exposed, Makayla put on her shirt and swung her feet over the side of the couch. Standing, she zipped up her jeans and readjusted her clothes. She didn't need to look in the mirror to know her hair was a mess and her makeup was smudged.

"Don't worry, li'l man. I'm on my way." Sighing deeply, he replaced the receiver and returned to the couch. "Terrance had a nightmare. I have to—"

Makayla shook her head. "No explanation necessary."

Kenyon didn't want the night to end. He thought of asking her to stay until he came back, but swiftly rejected the idea. There was no telling when he'd return and he had a feeling Makayla would turn him down, anyway. Allowing himself a wry smile, he took her hand and gave it a light squeeze. "Thanks for being so understanding. I promise to make it up to you."

Feeling playful and flirty, she said, "I'll hold you to that, Kenyon."

"Please do."

The Pier was the place to be on a Friday night. Located in downtown Philly, the trendy restaurant catered to a young, hip clientele. The personification of wealth, The Pier boasted a world-class menu, top service and a lively atmosphere. Makayla couldn't afford ten-dollar cocktails, twenty-dollar salads or fifty-dollar steaks, but she wanted to impress Brenda Van Buren. The senior editor at *The Philadelphia Blaze* had hiring power and Makayla was desperate to get on board as the newest travel writer.

She glanced around at the surrounding tables filled with patrons eating lamb, lobster and caviar. A middle-aged woman wearing a hideous sky-blue fur was devouring a crème brûlée. Makayla sighed. Coming here suddenly seemed like a bad idea. Maybe she should have sent Brenda flowers and called it a day.

But if treating the senior editor to an expensive meal would give her an edge over the other applicants, it was worth every penny.

The well-dressed European man sitting alone to her left smiled. He wasn't nearly as handsome as Kenyon but he had kind eyes and a strong, sturdy build. If he wasn't wearing a wedding band, Makayla would have struck up a conversation with him.

She didn't know why she was thinking about chatting to the stranger. She had Kenyon now. They hadn't spoken since the concert, but he hadn't been far from her thoughts. In fact, he had been the inspiration behind her last article, "Sexin' Him on the First Date: To Be Or Not To Be?" The article had triggered an enormous response from her male audience and Makayla was hard at work on a follow-up. According to readers, sex on the first date was not only welcomed, but strongly encouraged. Makayla wondered what Kenyon's opinion was on the subject. Their first kiss had turned into a full-blown make-out session in her classroom, with her students only a few feet away. Kenyon had pushed a hand up her skirt and kissed her with an almost savage intensity. If that wasn't evidence enough of his feelings, she didn't know what was.

To keep her mind off Kenyon, she studied her reflection in the butter knife. She didn't look half-bad considering she had worked a full day and come to The Pier straight from work.

"Sorry I'm late."

Makayla dropped the knife. "Hi, Brenda."

"I had a meeting that ran longer than expected," the editor explained, unzipping her multicolored trench coat and draping it behind her chair. "I don't know about you, but I'm famished. I haven't eaten a thing all day."

A quick-moving waiter approached, presenting a bottle of wine. "This is a 1998 Zinfandel," he said, lifting the bottle.

"We didn't order this," Makayla told him, covering her glass with her hand.

He stared down at her, his thick eyebrows raised halfway up his forehead. "It's the house special, ma'am. Free of charge."

Makayla felt her skin prickle. To cover her embarrassment, she buried her eyes in the menu.

The waiter pulled out his notepad. "Are you ladies ready to order?"

Brenda nodded. "I'll have the clams, with sautéed mushrooms, a side of steamed broccoli and—"

Makayla couldn't believe her ears. Stick-thin Brenda was ordering enough food to feed a cheerleading squad. When she ordered the most expensive cocktail on the menu, Makayla forced a smile. Biting down on her bottom lip, she kept a running tab of the bill. By the time her turn came to order, she had exactly thirteen dollars to spend on her meal. With few choices, she ordered the soup of the day.

The waiter collected the menus and left.

Makayla smiled at Brenda. The forty-something senior editor had a dark olive complexion and her short, layered haircut flattered her high cheekbones. "I love your hair and the color's great, too."

"Thanks. The stupid thing was taking too much time out of my day so I asked my hairdresser to chop it off and to give me a brighter shade of brown." Brenda tasted her wine. "Enough about my hair. Let's discuss your future with *The Philadelphia Blaze*."

Makayla cleared her throat. It was time to convince Brenda she was the right person for the travel writer job. "I want to thank you for giving me an opportunity to work at one of the most respectable and trusted newspapers. Writing a weekly column has given me more confidence as a writer."

"That's good to hear." She laughed lightly. "And here I was thinking we'd have to triple your salary."

"Excuse me?"

"You're a hit!"

Makayla gulped. "I am?"

"My boss wants more! More provocative articles that will set tongues wagging and get readers talking. If you agree to the terms of the contract, your column will run three times a week and you'll have complete creative control. What do you think?"

Makayla didn't want to sound ungrateful, but being a travel writer was a lifelong dream that she wasn't ready to give up on just yet. "I'm glad readers are enjoying the Sexpot Files, but I came here to discuss the travel writer position. I'd like to be considered for—"

"The travel writer position? Oh no, it's not right for you."

"I'd like to give it a try."

"But your column is doing so well! Men love you, women want to be you and you're the talk of the town." Brenda patted Makayla's hand in a motherly fashion. "I've been in this business a long time, hon. Take it from me, you're not cut out to be a travel writer. It's a taxing job with crummy pay, no benefits and little recognition."

"I know I have what it takes to—"

"Being a travel writer is not as glamorous as it seems," she snapped. "I know what I'm talking about. I was stuck doing it for almost five miserable years. Jet lag is a killer, the locals are ignorant buffoons and the hostels are filthy."

Makayla watched her good mood walk out the front door. Brenda wasn't going to recommend her for the job and there was little she could say or do to change the woman's mind.

The waiter arrived with their entrées but she was too upset to notice. Practicing her speech had been a waste of time. Brenda had dominated the entire conversation and every time she tried to speak up, she was interrupted. In a last ditch effort to win the editor's favor, she retrieved her résumé from her bag, inflected her voice with confidence and said, "Could you pass this on to Mr. Izzorio? I understand he's in charge of hiring. You're a highly respected editor and I know a recommendation from you would be taken very seriously."

Brenda wore a pained expression. "Sorry, hon, but the position's been filled. He made the final decision yesterday. Hired a friend of the family, I think."

Makayla didn't believe her. Five seconds ago Brenda said she wasn't cut out for the job and suddenly she remembered the position had been filled? With damp eyes and a sore throat, she shoved her résumé back into her bag.

While Brenda devoured her meal and gulped down her twelve-dollar cocktail, Makayla replayed their conversation in her mind. Who was Brenda to decide she didn't have the resilience to be a travel writer? Writing the Sexpot Files was a great gig, but she wanted more. She had written all she could about aphrodisiacs, sex toys and erogenous zones. It was time for a change.

"Will you have time this week to read over the contracts?" Brenda asked, heaving broccoli into her mouth.

Makayla nodded absently.

"My boss is anxious to close the deal," she confessed between bites. "I think she's nervous about you being lured away by the competition."

"I'll courier them over by the end of the week."

"Great. I look forward to receiving them." Brenda finished her cocktail and stared down at the empty glass. "I'm going to have to get another one of those. They're tasty!"

Chapter 10

Makayla slammed the door with such force the entire house shook. Propping herself against the wall, she yanked off her boots and hurled them into the closet. Her stomach growled, reminding her of what a disaster the night had been. Not only had she wasted a hundred bucks wooing Brenda, she'd received a parking ticket, as well. In her haste to be on time, she'd failed to put her receipt on the dashboard and now she'd have to dip into her savings to square the seventy-dollar fine.

Twenty minutes later, she was in her room, sprawled out on the bed, munching on trail mix. The light on the answering machine was blinking but she wasn't in the mood to talk. Besides, the messages were probably from Cordell. She should call him back and tell him she wasn't interested in going out with him anymore, but right now she needed some time alone.

Why didn't I stand up for myself? Why wasn't I more assertive?

Because she was petite, people often told her what to do. As a teen, she had learned it was better to go along with what her father said than to argue. He was a bully and Makayla had made sure to stay out of his way. Like Brenda, he thought she wasn't cut out to be a travel writer. But she was going to prove them wrong. If she wanted to travel halfway around the world and stay in roach-infested hostels no one had the right to stop her.

She sat up. If she was going to land the travel writer job, she needed a plan and a damn good one. Desiree would help her think of something. Her best friend was a great sounding board and always full of fresh ideas. Filled with renewed hope, she picked up the phone and dialed Desiree's number. Popping a peanut into her mouth, she cradled the receiver to her ear.

"Hello?"

She instantly recognized Kenyon's voice. Swallowing, she propped the snack bowl on her lap. "Hi."

"That was weird. The phone didn't even ring."

"I picked it up and there you were."

"Is this a bad time?"

"No, I'm not doing anything." She smoothed a hand over her rumpled hair. *What am I doing? He can't see me through the phone!*

"How've you been?"

"I'm all right."

"What's wrong? You don't sound like your usual self."

"It's been a rough week, that's all."

"Want some company?"

Makayla checked the time. "Now? It's almost midnight!"

"I don't have a curfew. Do you?"

"Well, no, but—"

"I want to see you," he confessed.

"I guess it would be okay." She tossed a pretzel into her mouth and dusted the salt from her hands. "How long will it take you to get here?"

"I'm already here."

Makayla coughed. The pretzel was lodged in her throat. Tears filled her eyes as she rubbed away the burning sensation in her chest. Not only did his admission catch her off guard, it would be the death of her, too. "You're outside?" she finally managed.

"On your doorstep," he told her.

"Are you serious?"

"Come see for yourself." The line went dead.

She leaped off the bed, sprinted down to the living room and pulled back the curtains. The sensor lights were on. Someone was definitely on the porch.

After a quick stop in the bathroom, she went into the foyer and turned on the lights. She opened the door and Kenyon smiled down at her. "Hi" came out in a whisper.

"I hope you're hungry." He motioned to the box in his hands. "I brought pizza."

"What kind?"

"Jalapeño, pepperoni and extra cheese."

Makayla rubbed her stomach. "Mmm. My favorite."

"Me, too." His eyes held her captive. For several seconds, they stood on the porch, staring at each other. When the silence became too much, Makayla stepped aside and said, "Please, come in."

He grinned broadly. "Thanks for having me."

Inside the kitchen, she cleared the table of flyers and old newspapers and wiped down the glass surface.

Kenyon watched her move around the room retrieving plates, napkins and glasses. He couldn't help noticing the outline of her bra through her pink V-neck shirt.

"Is Sprite okay?"

Kenyon blinked. He was so busy checking her out, he missed the question. Not wanting to look foolish, he took the glass she offered and said, "Thanks."

The phone rang and Makayla put down the bottle. "I'll be right back."

His gaze followed her out of the room. Kenyon didn't know why he was drooling. He was surrounded by beautiful women on a daily basis. That was one of the many perks of being a photographer. Just last month, he did a photo shoot for *Black Beauty Magazine* with five of the most stunning women he had ever seen. But not one of them had piqued his interest like Makayla did. Not even Alexandria.

Kenyon was looking for someone completely different from his ex, and Makayla was it. The two women were like night and day. Just the thought of Alexandria made his head throb. He couldn't figure out for the life of him why he hadn't given his head a good shake when the former beauty queen strutted over to him at the end of the photo shoot a few months ago. She had handed him one of her business cards, ordered him to call and also been the one to suggest dinner later that week. Kenyon knew why he'd yielded to her advances. She was Alexandria, the supermodel who could bring midday traffic to a commanding halt. It was her creamy, smooth-to-the-touch skin, size-four waist and long legs that made men lose their minds. She had a smile so bright it could light up Manhattan. Not only did the world think she was breathtaking, she did, too. Alexandria had never failed to remind him that she was a highly sought-after supermodel, and after three weeks of her egocentric ways, he'd called it quits.

Makayla returned to the kitchen. As soon as she sat down, the phone rang again. Smiling sheepishly, she put down her napkin and said, "I'm going to go turn off the ringer."

Several minutes later, she rejoined Kenyon at the table. "Sorry about that."

"You're a popular girl."

"Hardly. That was my dad."

Kenyon knew both calls weren't from her old man, but he didn't push her for details. "Are you guys close?"

"Not really. He remarried shortly after my mom died, and his new wife and I don't get along. We see each other a few times a year. Mostly holidays and stuff."

"Does he live in Philly?"

"Yeah, over in Melrose Park."

"What a coincidence. I grew up in that neighborhood. Hey, where did you go to high school?"

Makayla gulped down her soda so fast, she was overtaken by a vicious, throat-burning cough.

Kenyon stood. "You okay? You're coughing up a lung over there."

Her eyes filled with tears, but she waved him away. "I'm fine. I drank too much, too fast," she explained, thumping a hand on her chest.

A roguish smile claimed his lips. "Do you want to lie down? I could carry you into the bedroom if you need to catch your breath."

"Thanks for the offer, but I'll live."

He laughed.

Makayla took a bite of her pizza. "Oh, this is good!" she said, wiping the grease off her hands. "Thanks, Kenyon."

"My pleasure." He stared down at her. Her lips were glossy, her smile wide, her eyes bright. A week had passed since he last saw her but it wasn't until she opened the door that he realized how much he'd missed her. Kenyon wanted to kiss her, but if he gave in to his impulse there would be no turning back. This was his first real meal of the day and if he was going to make love to her, he needed his energy. Kenyon sat down and took another slice of pizza. Dinner first, romance second. "Tell me about your week."

"There's not much to tell. The kids were pretty good and last night after class, Desiree and I went out for drinks."

"Class? Are you taking university courses?"

"No, karate."

His eyes flared. "Really?"

Makayla studied him. Why was his tongue hanging out of his mouth? Was it so hard to believe she was interested in martial arts? She wondered what Kenyon's reaction would be when he saw her tattoo. She struck the idea from her mind. The only way he would see the butterfly was if she was naked from the waist down, and the chance of them ever getting that close was unthinkable. Bringing her a hot meal was a caring gesture, but there would be no show-and-tell tonight. "I'm working toward my black belt."

"Wow! That's the last thing I expected you to say."

She resisted giving Kenyon a crash course on the twenty-first-century woman and said, "Why is it so hard to believe? Because I'm a woman?"

"No, because you're soft and delicate and pretty and I couldn't imagine you hurting anyone."

Makayla didn't know what to say. It wasn't every day a man of Kenyon's caliber paid her a compliment, and she wanted to go outside and shout it from the rooftop.

"Where do you train? Maybe one day I can come and watch you do your thing."

Makayla liked Kenyon, but she didn't want him to sit in on her class. She was liable to twist an ankle or fall flat on her face if he was around. But not wanting to be rude, she said, "I study at King Bonk Institute of Martial Arts."

"Cool." Satiated, he wiped his mouth with a napkin. "I called earlier, but there was no answer. Hot date?"

"No. I had a business meeting of sorts."

"Oh?" He smiled. "I know Terrance is a handful, but I hope he hasn't driven you to find another teaching job."

"No, no, nothing like that. I write a column for *The Philadelphia Blaze*. I had a meeting with the editor."

"What do you write about? Entertainment? Books? Health?"

Makayla had been afraid he would ask that question. She took a sip of her drink, then said, "Sex."

His eyes lit with surprise and his mouth shaped into the most delicious smile. "Damn, Makayla! You're just full of surprises, aren't you?" He stared at her, a look of pure admiration on his face. "That explains why you have so many erotic books."

Kenyon wanted to know more about her side job, but he sensed something was wrong. Later, when the time was right, he would find out more about her naughty sex column. "What did you meet with your editor about?"

Makayla had no intention of telling Kenyon about the details of her dinner with Brenda, but when his face softened with concern, everything came tumbling out. "I just sat there like a lump, listening to her tell me why I was completely wrong for the job. I was so angry, I didn't know what to say," she finished.

"Do you want to know what I think?"

"Sure, why not."

"Screw them."

"Come again?"

"*The Philadelphia Blaze* isn't the only paper in town," he told her. "I have a friend who writes for *Travel and Entertainment* magazine and he's always complaining about how short-staffed they are. I can give him a call and see if there are any available positions."

Makayla swallowed. "You'd do that for me?"

"Why not?" Kenyon loved to see the sparkle in her eyes and the animated expression on her face. She looked as if she was about to do cartwheels around the room. "Roman is covering the African-

American Film Festival, but he'll be back from L.A. tomorrow. I'll get him to call you next week. How does that sound?"

"I don't know what to say."

"Say I'm the nicest guy you've ever met." Kenyon pulled her to her feet and took her by the waist. It was a perfect fit. Like a hand to a glove.

Words escaped her. His cologne tickled her nose, but she wouldn't have moved out of his arms if her life depended on it.

"I've been dreaming about holding you all day."

"That's sweet."

"It's the truth." Then, "Do you want me to kiss you?" he asked, stroking his thumb across her cheek.

Makayla blinked in awe. *What do you mean, 'do I want you to kiss me'? Of course I want you to kiss me!* She licked her lips and hoped that was answer enough.

It was. Kenyon parted her lips with his tongue and tasted her. His mouth covered her lips, cheek and ear. Like a bottomless cup, he sought to have his fill of her. As he kissed her with a savage intensity, his hands roamed freely over her body. He pressed his mouth to her ear and whispered, "I want you."

The urgency in his voice made her palms sweat. She was confident that Kenyon would be a good lover. He had a strong, masterful body and she loved the feel of his hands on her bare flesh. "I want you, too, Kenyon."

"Then what are we waiting for?" Making love to her had been at the front of his mind since the day they met and now that the opportunity presented itself, he couldn't wait a second longer. He bent down and sucked her nipples through her T-shirt. She arched her back, and he used his finger to draw light circles around her stomach. Backing her up against the table, he continued caressing her skin.

Makayla forced her eyes open. As much as she liked the spontaneity of the moment, she couldn't have sex on the kitchen table. She smelled like garlic, her lounge suit had sauce stains and she needed a warm shower. No, if they were going to make love everything had to be perfect. "Why don't you wait in the living room while I go freshen up."

"You're not having second thoughts, are you?"

His penetrating gaze unnerved her. "No, it's just—"

"We aren't going to do anything you're not comfortable with. I promise."

Makayla had been fighting her feelings for Kenyon ever since he knocked her off her feet. But no more running. If there was one thing she had learned from her father's heart attack it was that tomorrow wasn't promised to anyone. She didn't want to look back on tonight and wonder what could have been. Kenyon wanted her, at least for the night, and that was enough for her.

Smiling seductively, she patted his chest. "All I need is ten minutes." She added, "I want to look nice for you."

Kenyon liked the sound of that. Her sex kit was loaded with treats and she wanted to go set the mood. Tonight, he'd sit back— or rather lie back—and enjoy the show. Envisioning Makayla in one of her sexy lace getups, brandishing a leather whip, he kissed her hard on the lips, then strolled into the living room.

Chapter 11

Makayla cracked open the bathroom door. City lights twinkled in the distance, casting a fair glow around the bedroom. The room was cool, light, airy: the perfect setting for making love. Two wineglasses sat on the nightstand and music was playing on the stereo. Makayla listened. Kenyon must have gone out to his car, because she didn't own any rap CDs. If it were up to her, Trisha Yearwood would be serenading them.

A smile found her lips. Kenyon was in bed, propped up against the headboard by a stack of pillows. His eyes were closed but he was drumming his fingers on his thighs. Seeing him bare-chested reminded her of all the times she'd snuck into the gym and watched him lift weights. In high school, he was long and slender, nowhere near as defined or muscular as he was now.

I can't go through with this, she told herself, backing away from the door. *What if he doesn't like my body?* She turned toward the mirror. The fuchsia-colored baby-doll nightgown, heels and full makeup had transformed her from a schoolteacher to a very desirable woman. The lace material clung to her curves and veiled every flaw. Confident that Kenyon would be pleased, she dabbed perfume on her wrists and added more body shimmer to her legs.

She breathed in deeply, exhaled her fear and cut the lights.

The scent of her perfume danced toward him in the air. The sweet, slightly sexy fragrance was tempered with a fruity smell. Kenyon opened his eyes. Makayla was a visual delight. Sweeping curls, smoky lashes, moist lips. There was no mistaking her beauty, but tonight she was a certified knockout. The gentle curves of her body were clearly visible through her nightgown. He couldn't take his eyes off her bountiful cleavage. Kenyon didn't know what to do first—commit her image to memory or rip off her nightgown and bury himself inside her. The latter was an all-too-consuming need but he had to be patient.

Makayla took small steps into the room. "Sorry I took so long. I—"

"You're perfect."

She melted like the wax from the glowing candles. "Thank you."

"Come closer. I want to get a good look at you."

Honoring his request, she came from around the foot of the bed. Facing each other, they entwined their fingers and came together in the sweetest embrace. Her exposed thigh goaded him into touching her. Reaching out, he stroked her flesh, fingered the intricate detail along the bodice of the nightgown and around the deep but flattering neckline. He pulled her down on his lap and swept her hair off her shoulders.

Crippled by his smile, she stared down at her hands. His reaction was more than she could have hoped for. For the last half hour, she had been hiding out in the bathroom, scared he would take one look at her and bolt.

Kenyon handed her a glass of wine. He spoke in a low, almost sedate voice, but his eyes held the promise of a passionate night. "To us."

She took the glass and sipped slowly. His eyes explored her body and his smile bolstered her confidence. Back in high school, Kenyon was the guy everyone wanted—including her. She had heard the stories. According to legend, Kenyon could take panties off with his tongue, had a voracious sexual appetite and could make love for hours. Tonight, she would find out if those rumors were fact or fiction.

He reached for Makayla and her body went stiff.

"Are you okay?"

Self-conscious about her stomach, or rather the thick pad of fat around it, she covered her hands across her midsection. "Could we turn off the lights? I've never done it with the lights on before."

"You mean make love?"

Her lips quivered and she couldn't meet his gaze. The last thing Makayla wanted to do was relive the painful experience of her first time, but the expression on his face told her he wasn't about to let it go.

"It only happened once, a long time ago, and it was anything but love."

The hardness of her tone unsettled him. He'd never heard her sound so bitter. "Go on, I'm listening."

She closed her eyes in an attempt to block out the memory but it didn't work. Makayla had been a sophomore in university with just three dates under her belt when her roommate's older brother, Quency, asked her out. They had lunch a few times and although they didn't have much in common, they got along well. No sparks, no romance, but she felt comfortable with him. One night after too many free cocktails, they had ended up in a two-bit motel on the outskirts of the city. From the time they'd stumbled onto the bed to the time the deed was done, seven excruciating minutes had passed. Makayla had hobbled into the bathroom, locked the door and taken a long shower. Her tears had mingled with the warm water and she had decided if that was all there was to sex, she could live without it.

Quency had dropped her back at the dorm, promised to call in a few days and then tore out of the parking lot like the police were in hot pursuit. She never heard from him again. Makayla didn't blame him. As disgusted as she was with the whole experience, she felt fortunate he'd wanted to sleep with her. No one had ever tried before.

"That brother was a jerk. I'm not that kind of guy. Don't deprive me the joy of seeing the pleasure I bring you. Half the thrill of making love is *seeing* your reaction." The fear in her eyes was still there. Kenyon got up, turned off the lights and flipped on the bedside lamp. "Better?"

Makayla nodded.

"Here, have some more wine. It'll help you relax."

In seconds, the wine had its desired affect and Makayla could feel the tension in her body recede. She put her empty glass on the nightstand. Hoping she hadn't spoiled the mood, she smiled down at him and touched a hand to his face. Her lips trembled slightly as she reached up and kissed him. She abandoned his mouth and laid soft kisses along his jaw. He moaned when she licked the length of his ear and the side of his neck. "Is that okay?"

"I like that, babe. Don't stop."

The more he moaned, the more confident Makayla felt.

Kenyon stretched out on the bed, and she straddled him. Just because she didn't have much experience didn't mean she couldn't take the lead. She had read enough books and interviewed enough couples to know what worked and what didn't.

What she liked most about Kenyon were his lips, so she started there. Outlining his lips with her tongue elicited a deep moan. The warmth of his mouth was an incredible turn-on. As she stroked his arms she noticed the bold, edgy tribal band tattoos on each arm. On the upper right-hand corner of his chest was elaborate calligraphy writing. It read, Don't be about it, do it!

Makayla nipped at his ear, licked the side of his neck. Slipped a hand inside his boxer shorts. Either the music was messing with her head or she had finally found her inner vixen. The relentless, rhythmic beat of the drums and the roaring pulse of the electric guitar gave her a courage she'd never known.

Kenyon couldn't speak. His eyes blazed with passion and his lips were wet with desire. Like a seasoned pro, she stirred his loins and pulled him back before he could reach his peak. Tortured by her mouth, he moaned from the depth of his soul. He didn't know what he'd done to deserve such treatment but he was loving every wicked minute of it. Makayla was as good as a girl could be, except in the privacy of her bedroom and that was damn hot.

The more she stroked him, the more he moaned. Groaning, he cupped her shoulders and brought her to him. He loved that her eyes were bright, her hair ruffled and her body warm. She belonged on the cover of *Maxim* magazine, surrounded by the sun, the coral blue sea and the sky.

Covering her body with his own, he tasted her lips. He was in her mouth, on her chest, then between her thighs, punishing her with his mouth and his tongue and his hands. His tongue dipped into her navel as if it were a goblet filled with chardonnay.

A whirlwind of emotions filled her heart and a warmth she had never known engulfed her. Makayla felt as if Kenyon was drawing out her very heart and soul. The slow circular pattern of his tongue traced along her skin, immobilizing her. She was drowning in his love, powerless to resist.

Kenyon paused to protect them. When he returned to bed, she took his hand, guided it between her legs and let him feel her wetness. He entered her then, slowly and carefully, as if it were the first time for them both. For a split second, he thought he felt her flinch. But when he looked down at her, her face was a portrait of ecstasy. He savored the moment. Relished the feel of her. The sound of her. The taste of her. Her scent.

Kenyon needed to slow down. It wasn't about his needs tonight. It was about pleasing Makayla. Thrusting forward, she matched his intensity, stroke for stroke.

Everything Makayla had ever heard about sex echoed in her ears. Yes, it was amazing. Yes, it was unlike anything she had ever known. Making love to Kenyon was the best thing that ever happened to her and she would cherish this moment for the rest of her life.

Her ultratight grip increased his pleasure. She spread her legs and he felt every delicious inch of her. Her breasts jiggled in perfect rhythm to the music, teasing him, taunting him, pleasing him. The feel of her mouth on his neck triggered his orgasm. Kenyon dropped his chin into his chest, hiked up her right leg and plunged into her with all of his strength.

The move was electrifying. Unbelievable pleasure radiated throughout her body. She focused her mind and body on the experience, desperate to preserve the beauty of it. As she climaxed, she grabbed the bedpost for support and screamed out his name.

A car horn blared, interrupting Makayla's sleep. Bleary-eyed, she stumbled out of bed, closed the window and crawled back under the covers. She lay snug and warm amid the blankets, reliving every moment of the last five hours. Had they really made love on and off all night? Had she really poured chocolate syrup on his chest and licked it off? Makayla inspected the linens.

Dark, gooey spots stained her once-pristine blanket. Giggling, she flopped back down on the bed and screamed into the pillow. An overwhelming sense of joy flooded her heart as she remembered what Kenyon had said before he left.

"Last night was incredible," he'd said, drawing her to him. "Sorry I have to rush off, but Terrance and I have a standing appointment at the barbershop every Saturday morning."

"It's okay. I understand."

Kenyon nibbled on her ear.

"Um—I like that."

"Good, 'cause there's a lot more where that came from."

"I can't wait." She kissed his cheek. "Call me later?"

"I'll do better than that. Be ready by eight. We're going out."

"Where?"

"Just be ready," he told her, in an authoritative tone. After another toe-curling kiss, he jogged down the steps, got into his truck and sped off.

Makayla stretched her hands over her head. The idea of spending the rest of the day in bed was tempting, but she had a house to clean, an article to write and calls to return. She rolled onto her side, hit Play on the answering machine and got out of bed.

Stripping the sheets off the bed, she listened to her messages. Desiree wanted to meet for lunch and was offering to spring for manicures. Frowning, she replayed the message. Her co-worker rarely called on the weekend. The only time she did was when Elliot couldn't fly in to see her. At times, it grated on her nerves that Desiree didn't make more time for her, but whenever she found herself complaining, she tried to be more understanding. If she had a boyfriend who lived out of town, she'd probably ditch her friends when he was around, too. Besides, after spending five days a week together, they needed a break from each other.

Makayla tugged off the pillow covers and pitched them on the pile of dirty sheets. She was surprised to hear Gemini's voice on the answering machine.

"Hey, Makayla. I know you're going to think that I'm a knob, but I need directions to your house again. The last time we met at your place was months ago and I drank a lot of wine that night. I know you live in Patterson Park near Willow Oaks Plaza, but I don't know how to get there. Call me!"

Confused, Makayla abandoned her task and picked up her purse. She pulled out her planner and flipped to the date. November seventh was circled in red and the word HOST was written in bold black letters. Slapping her forehead with her hand, she plunked down on the bed. *How could I forget I'm hosting tonight's book club meeting?* Because ever since she started dating Kenyon, she had become absent-minded.

Makayla considered her options. She wanted to go out with Kenyon, but canceling the book club meeting at the last minute was rude. For some, book club meetings were the only time they got away from their husbands and kids. And for others, it was the opportunity to hang out with friends. Before meeting Kenyon, book club meetings had been the highlight of her week.

Meetings normally ran three hours, but if she kept the group on course they could be finished in two, then she could see Kenyon. Convinced she could pull it off, Makayla picked up the phone and dialed his cell phone number.

He answered on the first ring. "Kenyon Blake."

"Hi. It's me."

"Hi, you."

Her heart bounced in her chest.

"Is everything okay?"

"I'm calling about tonight."

"I hope you're not calling to cancel." His voice was low, teasing, playful.

"Not exactly." Makayla told him about the book club meeting. "I was hoping we could get together later."

"No problem. Why don't you give me a call when your guests leave?"

"Or, you could just be here at nine o'clock."

"Sounds good. And, Makayla?"

"Yes?"

"Buy more chocolate syrup."

Chapter 12

The Erotic Woman's Book Club boasted a hundred members but only a handful attended monthly meetings. Founded in the early nineties by a disenchanted housewife, the all-women group consisted of professional urbanites between the ages of twenty-five and forty.

Makayla had stumbled upon the group's Web site when she was a junior in college. Tired of being alone on the weekends, she had registered online, paid the membership fee and attended her first meeting a week later. But now, as she listened to Jo relay a story she had heard about Denzel Washington having a tryst with his female makeup artist, Makayla wondered if the eighty-five-dollar annual membership was worth it.

It was seven-thirty and no one had even mentioned *Sins of a Co-ed.* Were they going to discuss celebrity gossip all night?

Sydney popped a cheese puff into her mouth. "Enough about Denzel. Let's get into the book."

Makayla couldn't agree more. "Yeah, let's." As the night's host, it was her job to facilitate the discussion and ensure everyone had equal speaking time, so she opened *Sins of a Co-ed* to chapter one and said, "First things first. What did you all think of the plot?"

"What plot?" Dallas waited for the laughter to die down before she continued. "The book was a series of long, gratuitous sex scenes and the heroine was so busy shaking her ass in everyone's face she couldn't get her shit together."

"I disagree."

Makayla wasn't surprised. Kewanda loved a good argument. Narrow-minded, outspoken and abrasive, she had a way of making everyone around her feel inferior. Makayla didn't know how such an intolerable woman could have a thriving medical practice. Kewanda had an ugly edge that only the love of a good man could smooth over and members were hoping her Prince Charming would come soon. "I loved the heroine. Simone knew what she wanted and she went after it. There's nothing wrong with that. I think we can all learn from her."

Someone snickered. "What, how to be a ho?"

Kewanda sighed dramatically. "It's time for sisters to stand up and be heard, and not just in the workplace, either. We can persuade a room full of executives to invest in our company but we can't tell our men what we want in the bedroom. If you ask me, that's pathetic."

Makayla hated to admit it, but Kewanda had a point. The women she interviewed often complained men were more interested in getting off than meeting their needs. As she sipped from her wineglass, her mind wandered back to the previous night. A smile lit the corners of her lips. Kenyon was a very generous lover. Her only complaint was that he had a limitless amount of energy. Before she could catch her breath, he was eager to make love again.

"I hear you, Kewanda, but the scene in the club was a little too far-fetched, even for me." Rhandi flipped her wavy hair over her shoulder. "I don't care how fine a man is, I'm not about to get it on in a dingy public bathroom."

Jo laughed. "You's a damn lie! If Terrance Howard propositioned you, you'd hop up into the sink and hike up your skirt."

"You know that's right!" Rhandi shrieked, slapping hands with Dallas.

Makayla could do without Rhandi. She dated married men, accepted expensive gifts and had never worked a day in her life. Desirous of fame, the yet-to-be-discovered actress used men to finance her extravagant lifestyle and didn't care who she stepped on to get ahead. The twenty-five-year-old starlet had the morals of a shark and there was nothing she wouldn't do to advance her career.

Desperate to stay on track, Makayla forged ahead. "Do you think Simone's past made it difficult for Weston to trust her?"

For the next hour, the group discussed the highs and lows of *Sins of a Co-ed*. Makayla ensured no one dominated the conversation and curtailed arguments before they got out of hand. The only time she spoke was to correct Gemini, a single mother of three, who had a habit of embellishing scenes.

Makayla checked the time. She had half an hour to wrap up the discussion, see her guests off and change into something more casual. Since she didn't know where Kenyon was taking her, she'd keep it simple. Jeans, a blouse and some nice jewelry.

"Earth to Makayla."

Makayla shot Kewanda a noxious stare. "I'm listening."

"No you're not. You've been quiet all night."

"I'm always quiet."

Sydney wagged her finger in Makayla's face. "No, it's something more. The only time you're spaced out like this is when you have a guy on the brain. Who is he? Anyone I know?"

Makayla ignored the question. "Would anyone like some tea or coffee before we wrap up?"

"Wrap up?" Jo refilled her glass with wine. "But we haven't discussed the shower scene yet and I think it's the best part of the book. What did you think, Makayla?"

What shower scene? Makayla wiped the frown off her face and replaced it with a smile. The last thing she needed was Kewanda attacking her again. How would it look if she confessed that she'd been too busy daydreaming about Kenyon to read the last three chapters of the book? She had picked *Sins of a Co-Ed,* e-mailed the discussion questions and sent weekly reminders to keep the stragglers on track. Feeling trapped, she said the only thing she could. "I loved it. You?"

Sydney fingered the buttons on her blouse. "I was so inspired I tried it out on my husband."

Makayla didn't know what "it" was but she was dying to know. Fortunately, she wasn't the only one.

Gemini finished her beer. "Don't leave us hanging. What did you do?"

"Yeah, inquiring minds want to know!" Dallas added.

A cell phone hummed. "Sorry, but I have to take this call," Rhandi said, hurrying from the room.

"Come on, we're waiting," Kewanda prompted.

"First, I shipped the kids off to my mother's for the weekend. Can't have them breaking up our groove."

"I heard that," said a bank manager.

"I took a bath, put on my red do-me pumps and met Curtis at the door with nothing but a smile." Sydney closed her eyes, threw her head back and moaned as if she was reliving the moment. "One look at my *outfit* and it was on like Donkey Kong!"

Laughter ricocheted around the room.

Makayla admired the real-estate agent's confidence. Medium

height with fair skin and light eyes, the mother of two did things for her husband most men only dreamed of. Spirited, outgoing and humorous, she made friends easily and excelled in the business world. Three years ago when Makayla was in the market to buy a house, she had sought Sydney's advice and they had become close friends.

Jia patted Sydney's thigh. "Damn, girl, you're bold!"

"Just because I'm not a size two doesn't mean I can't do something sexy for my man. Besides, Curtis loves the waggin' I'm draggin'!"

"Amen!" and "That's right!" and "I heard that!" followed.

Makayla shook her head in awe. She couldn't imagine meeting Kenyon at the door naked. Leaning forward in her seat, she directed her question to Sydney. "Is there anything you haven't tried?"

Sydney thought a moment, then snapped her fingers. "Sex in public. I'd love to go at it in a deserted movie theater or on a park bench underneath the stars but Curtis won't go for it. Said it would ruin his bid for governor if we ever got caught."

Like a boomerang, the poignant question came back to her. "Have *you* ever done the nasty in public?"

Kewanda snickered. "Now I know you're drunk, Syd. Makayla's too straitlaced to do anything that wild. She's never even had phone sex."

Makayla opened her mouth but her mind went blank when Rhandi burst into the room and said, "Look who I found outside."

All eyes were on the stranger Rhandi was clinging to. His rustic cologne underlined his presence in the room, and his megawatt smile traveled all the way up to his eyes. "Good evening, everyone."

"Good God, he's fine!" hollered a full-figured woman of forty.

A manicurist waved her hand in the air as if she was showing reverence to God. "It should be a crime for a man to look that good!"

"My, my, my, who do we have here?" Dallas asked, sticking out her chest.

Makayla beamed like the light from a torch. She had never felt so proud. Kenyon looked like a piece of sexual chocolate in his casual yet attractive attire. All across the room women licked their lips, tossed their hair and crossed their legs, but Kenyon only had eyes for her.

Makayla was all smiles when she stood up. "Hi."

He greeted her with a kiss. Her body temperature soared when he put a hand on her waist and slipped his tongue into her mouth. Makayla could feel the heat of a dozen eyes on her. Behind her, someone cleared her throat. Reluctantly pulling away, she turned and addressed the group. "Everyone, this is Kenyon. Kenyon, this is everyone."

"Do you care to join the discussion?" Dallas asked, crossing her long, trim legs.

"What's the topic?"

"Sex." The word came out of her mouth like liquid honey. "Sex in public places to be exact. Ever done it?"

Kenyon stared over at Makayla. "No, but the night's still young."

Cheers, shrieks and applause exploded across the living room.

Laughing, he bent down and kissed Makayla's cheek. "I'll wait for you in the bedroom." To the group he said, "Nice meeting you, ladies," then strolled down the darkened hallway and out of sight.

Questions came fast and swift.

"Hot damn! Where did you meet him?"

"Is he a stripper?

"Does he have any cousins? Brothers?"

"Is he well endowed?"

"Is he good in bed?"

"Of course he's good in bed! Look at him!"

Conversation swirled around the room and it took several

minutes before Makayla could quiet the women down. "Thanks for coming, everyone. Syd will e-mail the next book selection sometime next week."

Jia grinned. "Are you trying to get rid of us?"

"Hell yeah!"

The women laughed as they thanked Makayla for hosting, wished her luck with Kenyon and gathered their belongings.

Makayla saw her company to the foyer. One by one, guests trickled out of the house. Waving, she leaned against the door, reflecting on the night. Kenyon's arrival had been the highlight of the evening. The look on Kewanda's face had been priceless.

When the last car drove off, she closed the door and turned the lock.

"I like your friends," Kenyon said, coming up behind her. He was standing so close, she could feel his erection pressing against her butt. Makayla's heart leaped in her chest when he brushed his lips against her ear.

"I think they like you, too." Makayla turned to face him, a smile overwhelming her lips. Overcome with gratitude, she reached up and kissed him.

"Not that a brother's complaining, but what was that for?" he asked when they parted.

"For making me look good in front of my friends."

Kenyon chuckled. "I do what I can."

Makayla patted his forearm. "I'm going upstairs to change."

"Why? You look great." He smoothed a hand over the delicate sway of her back. His eyes beat down on her, his gaze strong and intense. "I'm going to miss you."

Giggling, she rolled her eyes in an exaggerated fashion. "You'll survive. I'll only be gone a few minutes."

Makayla moved out of his arms, but he gently pulled her back in. "I'm going to New York on business."

Her smile withered. "You are?"

"I'm doing a photo shoot for *Modern Bride* magazine."

"When do you leave?"

"The day after tomorrow."

"For how long?"

"A week or two."

The light in her eyes dimmed. "I'm happy for you. Congratulations."

"I'll call you every night."

"You don't have to."

Kenyon cupped her chin. "I know. I want to. Besides, I can't have another man horning in on my territory. You're my woman now and don't you forget it." He sealed his declaration with a kiss. He sucked on the much-neglected outer rim of her lips, as his hands moved down the slope of her hips. The heat of his tongue spread through her. His touch was pure heaven and when they parted, Makayla was wearing an odd, dreamy smile.

Kenyon being gone wouldn't be so bad. Since they'd started dating, Makayla had been slacking on her responsibilities at home and it had been months since she'd seen her dad and stepmom. Maybe she'd go see them tomorrow. The rest of her free time would be used to prepare for her upcoming meeting with Roman Douval. She wanted the travel writer job at *Travel and Entertainment* magazine but she had to nail the interview first.

Kenyon smiled down at her. "Are we cool?"

Makayla nodded. Then, she picked up her purse from off the end table and said, "Are you ready to go?"

"We're staying in tonight."

Her eyes flickered, then opened wide. "We are?"

"Damn right! All that sex talk got me riled up!"

Chapter 13

Kenyon called Makayla every night. Their conversations were private, intimate affairs and often lasted until the first light of day. Aware of the staggering long-distance rates, Makayla tried to keep their conversations short, but Kenyon wouldn't hear of it. He asked about school, bombarded her with personal questions and told her sidesplitting stories about the models he worked with. Kenyon exhibited all the signs of a concerned boyfriend. He sent long, sappy e-mails, told her he missed her and reminded her to double-check the locks and windows before she went to bed.

When he didn't call on Sunday at his usual time, Makayla assumed he was working late and sent him a short e-mail letting him know she was thinking about him. Confident he would phone the next day, she climbed into bed and fell into a peaceful sleep. But Kenyon didn't call or respond to any of the e-mail messages. By Wednesday, Makayla was in panic mode. There had to be a reason why he hadn't been in touch. Was he sick? Did he get hurt on the set? Had he been in an accident?

It was unthinkable for him to miss three consecutive days without calling, so when Makayla didn't hear from him on Wednesday, she took matters into her own hands. She knew Kenyon was staying at the Sheraton, but she didn't know which one. Three clicks of the mouse and Makayla had the phone number to the illustrious downtown hotel.

As she dialed the phone number, she rehearsed what she was going to say. It was fine for Kenyon to say he missed her, but Makayla knew from experience that men freaked out when women got emotional. Their relationship was still in the early stages and she didn't want to scare him off. The last time they spoke, Kenyon had asked her to clear her schedule for Friday. They were going to spend the entire weekend together but if she acted jealous, he might call the whole thing off.

The receptionist greeted Makayla warmly, then put her through to Kenyon's suite.

"Hello?"

Makayla stared down at the phone. Who was this woman with the heavy accent and where in the world was Kenyon? Worried that the receptionist had inadvertently dialed the wrong room number, she asked, "Is this Kenyon Blake's room?"

"Yes. What can I do for you?"

The stranger spoke eloquently, like someone who had experienced the very best that life had to offer. Her rich, haughty tone of voice lead Makayla to believe she might be from somewhere in the United Kingdom. "Is he there?"

The woman's voice took on a seductive edge. "He's in the shower."

Makayla felt a heaviness in her chest. Steadying her breathing, she tightened her grip on the phone. There was nothing to worry about. The woman could be the maid or room service or an employee of the hotel. But even as she mulled over the possibilities of the stranger's identity she realized none of her thoughts made sense. *Don't be naive, Makayla! Hotel employees don't answer phones.*

"Do you care to leave a message?"

"Can you tell him Makayla called?"

"Very well. Good night."

Hanging up the phone, she took slow, deep breaths. Her hands were shaking, her mouth was dry and her eyes watered. A blend of hurt and anger tore through her. She was sick to death worrying about him and he was spending time with another woman. Makayla wouldn't be surprised if his new love interest was one of the models he was working with. Kenyon often complained the fashion industry was full of shallow, insecure women who had a distorted view of life, but Makayla found it hard to believe he wasn't enamored by their jaw-dropping beauty.

Makayla spent the rest of the night moping around the house. Every few minutes she picked up the phone to ensure it was working. The endless ticking of the clock reminded her that she had nowhere to go and nothing to do. To keep her mind off Kenyon, she organized her closet, cleaned out the refrigerator and scrubbed the kitchen floor. When she ran out of chores to do, she sat back down at the computer. Her next article wasn't due for several days, but she revised the first draft and sent it off to Brenda.

At ten o'clock, she shut down her laptop and plodded into the kitchen for a hot cup of tea. It would calm her nerves and clear her mind. While she waited for the kettle to boil, she replayed her conversation with Kenyon's lady friend in her mind. Was there something she'd missed? Was she reading too much into the ten-second conversation? Makayla considered the facts: Kenyon hadn't called in days, didn't respond to any of her e-mails and when she called him, she discovered him alive and well and living it up in a luxurious suite with some sexy-sounding woman. What else was she supposed to think?

Pouring water into her mug, she added three scoops of sugar and a touch of cream. Glancing at the clock, she wondered why Kenyon hadn't called back yet. Three hours had passed. Makayla wanted answers and she wanted them now. Kenyon couldn't just walk into her life, make her fall for him and then disappear. Despite her protests, he had pursued her relentlessly. Dinners, kisses, lovemaking. Makayla was a strong-willed woman, but even she couldn't resist his charms. If Kenyon had found someone else, he needed to tell her. He owed her that much.

Walking into her bedroom, sipping her cup of ginger tea, she started to feel herself relax. Maybe she was overreacting. The woman could be a friend, or a relative or a business associate. Kenyon would call with a reasonable explanation and they would laugh about the whole thing. What they had was real. Kenyon may have looked the part of a bad boy but he was a stand-up guy.

Makayla picked up the book on her nightstand. She would read the next chapter of *What's a Bad Girl To Do* while she waited for Kenyon to call. Settling against the pillows, she started reading. But she couldn't concentrate. Memories of the last time she'd seen Kenyon assailed her mind. He had spent the night at her house and the next morning she had driven him to the airport. His flight was delayed an hour, so they'd sat in a tiny coffee shop, watching travelers pass by. Before he boarded the plane, he'd wrapped her in his arms and kissed her passionately for all the world to see.

Makayla blinked hard. Thinking about Kenyon was a distraction she just didn't need. Sydney was hosting the next book club meeting and this time, Makayla had to be prepared. But when she realized she'd read the same paragraph three times, she put the book on the nightstand and shut off the lights. Except for the distant sounds of traffic outside her window, the night passed quietly.

Makayla patted back a yawn. She was trying to follow Olga's story, but it was like putting together a puzzle with missing pieces. And it didn't help that she was listening to her student with half an ear. Kenyon had been on her mind all day. Last night, she had waited up for him to call but he never did. Makayla had had a fretful sleep. She'd tossed and turned for hours and by the time she finally fell asleep, her alarm clock went off.

Every time she thought about Kenyon, she felt a twinge of sadness. She had been wrong to get involved with him. He was way out of her league when she was in high school and the same was true today. Kenyon had found someone better and moved on. She couldn't fault him for that.

Makayla forced herself to concentrate on what Olga was saying, but when the girl scratched her head in an attempt to remember the name of her neighbor's German Shepherd, Makayla pried the toy microphone out of her hand and said, "Thanks for sharing, Olga. I hope you get your own dog very soon."

Weekly circle time gave students the opportunity to share something special in their lives with the class, but after listening to three incoherent stories, Makayla was beginning to wonder if circle time was such a good idea. "Would anyone else like to share?"

Terrance spoke up. "I went to the Chubby's Arcade last night and I played air hockey for two hours!"

Makayla silenced him with her eyes, then addressed the class. "Are we allowed to talk out of turn?"

"No!" they yelled in unison.

"What do we do if we have something to say?"

"We put up our hands!"

"Terrance, I don't pick students who don't follow the class rules."

The light in his eyes dimmed. "Sorry, Ms. Stevens. I forgot." His smile returned. "I'm just really excited about meeting my uncle's girlfriend. She's famous!"

The room erupted in chatter. Several minutes passed before Makayla was able to quiet the students down. "I didn't know your uncle had a girlfriend, Terrance."

"But, Ms. Stevens, you said he couldn't share," Antonia stated matter-of-factly. "He's not following the class rules."

Makayla looked at her sharply. "Are *you* following the rules?"

The judicious six-year-old hung her head.

Terrance, who was clearly in his element, recounted last night with astounding detail. "First, we went to Chuck E. Cheese for dinner. Alex said she wanted to go somewhere quiet and intimate but Uncle Kenyon said no."

Out of the mouths of babes, she thought, clinging to his every word.

"Alex gave me fifty dollars and told me to play as many games as I want!"

Diego tapped Terrance on the shoulder. "Who's Alex?"

"Her real name is Alex-and—Alexand…"

Makayla's eyes popped. "You mean Alexandria? The supermodel?"

"That's it!"

"Are you sure?" This wouldn't be the first time one of her students had gotten a story mixed up. But when Makayla gave it some thought, she realized his tale wasn't that far-fetched. Kenyon worked with a number of fashion houses and magazines. Alexandria was the world's most famous model and her face was plastered across billboards and posters everywhere. Everyone knew who she was. It was very likely Terrance had met her last night.

Makayla ignored the tiny hands waving in the air. She had

some questions of her own. "Did your uncle play air hockey with you?" she asked, hoping it was an innocent outing misconstrued by Terrance.

"No. He was too busy talking with Alexandria about their wedding."

"Wedding!"

Eighteen pairs of eyes stared up at Makayla.

Forcing a smile, she clasped her hands in front of her. Was Alexandria the person who answered the phone? The woman with the sexy voice? Kenyon was dating Alexandria? The woman was perfect in every way. Her skin, her eyes, her smile. Multi-talented, the Egyptian-born model had recently starred in her first feature film and was set to release an album at the end of the year.

Makayla felt as if a thousand stallions were trampling on her heart. *Just last week he'd said he was falling for me....*

"I like Alex," Terrance said. "She gives me toys and money and other cool stuff."

"Did you hear your uncle say they were getting married? I mean, did the words actually come out of his mouth?" Makayla knew she was grilling Terrance but she couldn't stop herself. "Are you sure that's what he said?"

"Oh, yeah, right before she—she—kissed him!" Covering his mouth, he dissolved into a fit of giggles. Soon the entire class was laughing. Makayla gripped the plastic microphone so hard, sweat dripped down her arm. No wonder she hadn't heard from Kenyon. He'd forgotten all about her. He was romancing a centerfold and flaunting their relationship in her face. *Wait until I get my hands on him!*

Chapter 14

"Do you want to drive with me to class or should I go on without you?" Makayla glanced up from the mound of notebooks on her desk. Desiree stood in the doorway, decked out in a purple yoga suit and runners, gym bag over her shoulder.

"Is it five o'clock already?" Makayla dropped her pen and rubbed the sleep from her eyes. She'd been anchored in her chair for the last hour and was finally starting to make a dent in the pile.

"You look like you've had a rough day." Desiree walked into the room. She dropped her bag on the floor and plopped down on one of the desks. "What did Terrance the Terror do this time?"

"Actually, aside from a few outbursts here and there, he's been a model student."

"Terrance? The short black kid who can't sit still?"

"Yup."

Desiree cocked her head to the right, her eyes wide with fright. "Are you beating him?"

Makayla rocked with laugher. "No, nothing that extreme."

"Tell me your secret."

"I don't have one."

Desiree gave her a long, searching look. "Well, you must have done something, because that boy was one afternoon special away from juvee."

Makayla's lips relaxed into a smile. "Remember a few weeks ago when Terrance wrote on all of the desks with permanent marker?"

"How could I forget? I was here when Principal Gibson came tearing into the room. I thought he was going to have a heart attack."

"I sent Terrance to Mr. Zadowski to clean the desks. But what was supposed to be a punishment turned out to be a blessing in disguise. At the end of the day, Terrance came strutting into the room wearing a cheeky smile. He told the class that Mr. Z. let him wax the floors and even showed him how to unplug the toilets."

Desiree laughed. "That little liar."

"That's not all. He told the kids he climbed a ladder and retrieved all the soccer balls on top of the roof. The boys were so impressed, they shook his hand!" Makayla laughed at the memory. "Now Terrance is a junior janitor and if I even threaten to call Mr. Z. he snaps back into line quick."

"Wow! You're good."

"I wish everyone shared your confidence. Principal Gibson paid another visit to my classroom this afternoon. He told me Veronika doesn't want Terrance helping out Mr. Z. anymore."

"Why? You'd think she'd be happy her son isn't getting into trouble."

"She told Principal Gibson I'm setting Terrance up for failure. Said I put him in the janitor's room because I don't think he can succeed."

Desiree groaned. "Oh, brother. There's just no pleasing that woman, is there?"

"Who are you telling? I know she's going through some things, but I honestly don't know how Kenyon puts up with her. Sometimes she's just plain ol' mean."

"Speaking of Kenyon, I heard about Alexandria."

"You did?"

"She was the talk of the playground. A bunch of sixth-grade girls practically mobbed Terrance at lunch. I wouldn't be surprised if that boy grew up to be famous one day. He loves the spotlight." Desiree smiled softly. "Do you want to talk about it?"

"There's nothing to talk about. Kenyon made his choice and I'm fine with it."

"You're not going to speak to him?"

"About what?" Makayla riffled the papers on her desk. She opened her bottom drawer, rummaged around for several seconds and pulled out a staple gun. With precise accuracy, she stapled the sheets together and pushed them off to the side. "I'm fine, Desiree. Drop it."

"You're going to take the word of a six-year-old and end a perfectly good relationship with a great guy? Kids exaggerate, they twist the truth, they misconstrue the most innocent things, and you and I both know Terrance is a masterful storyteller. How do you know he's not lying?"

Her words strung together. "I haven't heard from Kenyon since Saturday night. If he calls I'll ask him about Alexandria. If he doesn't, he doesn't. Oh, well. Life goes on. It's not the end of the world. Besides, I am too busy to think about him. I have an article about sexual fantasies due on Monday, spelling tests to mark and—"

"Why don't you call him?"

"Because."

"Because what?"

"Because he said he'd call me."

Makayla didn't realize how childish she sounded until the words reached her ears. Grateful Desiree didn't point out the obvious, she leaned back in her chair and considered the past few weeks. Life had become richer since she had started dating Kenyon. He was sensitive and thoughtful, but that didn't mean he wasn't playing games with her heart. If he cared about her, he wouldn't have had another woman in his hotel room. Another woman? It was *Alexandria!* "Desiree, I can't compete with a fashion model!"

"No one's asking you to. If I were you I'd call him, because from what I've seen he really likes you."

"It's an act. Kenyon has a master's degree in seduction. Trust me, I know."

"Don't be so negative, Makayla. If he didn't have feelings for you, he would've hit it and quit it. There's a reason he's sticking around."

Makayla grew quiet. She didn't want to compete with Alexandria for Kenyon's affection, but ending things abruptly held even less appeal. He was high-energy, always up for an adventure and he knew how to make her laugh. Makayla liked that. "I guess I could call him later."

"Do dinner and a movie," Desiree suggested, her voice cheerful. "I'll tell Instructor Chang that something important came up." She picked up her bag. "Leave tomorrow's lesson plans on your desk."

Makayla made a face. "Why?"

"I hear the twenty-four-hour flu is a killer." Desiree winked. "Have a good weekend. See you on Monday, girlfriend!"

The paper bag rested in Makayla's hands like a pound of coal. She stood on the sidewalk, staring at Kenyon's house, debating whether or not to return home. The sky was a dark shade of gray and there was a strong, bitter wind blowing snow flurries in the night. Her heart was racing, her hands were numb with cold and she had a strong premonition the evening wasn't going to go as planned. *Maybe I should have called first.* What if he wasn't home? Or worse yet, what if Alexandria was there? What if they were... Makayla struck the thought from her mind. Calling would have negated the surprise. Weeks ago, Kenyon had showed up at her door with pizza. Tonight, she was returning the favor. What man didn't love a home-cooked meal? The scalloped potatoes were fresh and tangy, the Caesar salad was dressed with bacon bits and croutons and the steak was grilled to perfection.

Confident she had made the right decision, Makayla slammed the car door with her left leg and hurried up the steps. Aside from a single light on the second floor, the entire house was bathed in darkness.

Makayla rang the doorbell. Once, then twice. Seconds later, the house lit up and she heard footsteps on the other side of the door. Her heartbeat raced. Taking a deep breath, she smoothed out the stubborn wrinkles on her dress. Wanting to look pretty for Kenyon, she had re-straightened her hair, touched up her makeup and put on her favorite dress. The neckline was a bit low and it was too tight around the hips but Makayla felt sexy in the slinky burgundy dress.

"Who is it?"

She swallowed twice. "It's me, Makayla."

The door swung open. Kenyon stared down at Makayla. Bundled in a thick scarf, a heavy coat and fur gloves, she looked like a chocolate snow bunny. Despite the frigid temperature, her skin had a warm, vibrant glow. Tiny snowflakes were gleaming on her forehead and pert nose. He wished he had his camera nearby. A picture of Makayla, surrounded by fresh, white snow flurries would look great in his office. His smile broadened into a full-fledged grin. "This is a *very* pleasant surprise."

"It is?"

"Yeah, I was just thinking about you."

Heat rushed to her face. "You were?"

"I was planning to come by your place later tonight." He opened the door and stepped aside. "Where's my head? Come in, it's freezing out there."

Makayla peeked inside. "Are we alone?"

"Yup. It's just us."

"No one else is here? You're sure?"

"I'm positive. Terrance is at home with his mom." Kenyon put an arm around her shoulders and brought her inside the foyer. His touch made her feel welcome and sent tiny ripples down her back.

"I'm not interrupting anything, am I?"

"Nothing at all." His voice was deep, low. "I'm glad you're here."

"You are?" Confused by his reaction, she searched his face for clues. His eyes had their familiar shine and he was wearing a hearty smile. She could be wrong but he seemed genuinely happy to see her.

Kenyon sniffed the air. "Something smells good."

Makayla lifted the bag. "I brought dinner. Steak, potatoes, salad, bread."

"What did I do to deserve all this?"

"I thought you might like a home-cooked meal, that's all."

"You thought right."

Kenyon brushed a stray hair back in place. Affectionately kissing her cheek, he unzipped her jacket, stuffed her accessories into one of the sleeves and hung it up in the closet. He soaked all of her in. The deep V-neck dress hit her curves and the color played up her eyes. She was wearing little makeup, no jewelry and her perfume was a light, airy scent. Her simple style was very sexy. Casting an admiring glance over her dress, he released a low whistle. "I like—a lot."

Makayla acknowledged his compliment with a smile.

"Let's eat." Kenyon took the bag from her hands and led her down the hall. The kitchen was redolent with garlic, and dishes and utensils were piled in the sink like a mountain of garbage. "Sorry 'bout the mess," he said, placing the bag on top of the stove. "My cleaning lady couldn't come in this morning."

"Why don't you go choose a wine to go with dinner while I straighten up in here."

The request hung in the air for several minutes. Kenyon made a small noise in his throat, then said, "I owe you an apology."

She cut him short. "You don't owe me anything."

"Yes, I do. I'm an ass. I said I'd call and I didn't. I don't want you to think you're not important to me, because you are."

Makayla looked away. Her calm demeanor hid the conflict she was feeling inside. His words touched her deeply, but she still didn't know where they stood. Did he want to break up? Was he dating Alexandria? Makayla couldn't come right out and ask him what happened in New York, but she wanted to know the truth. Her lips parted, but when Kenyon touched a hand to her cheek and asked if he was forgiven, she said, "Yeah, everything's fine."

"Great. I'll be right back."

Ten minutes later, they were sitting at the dining room table, eating. They discussed the weather, their plans for Thanksgiving and Makayla's upcoming interview with Roman Douval. Kenyon didn't mention Alexandria and Makayla didn't ask.

"How did the photo shoot go?"

Kenyon talked at length about New York. He spoke about the vibrancy of the people, the lights, the extraordinary collection of museums and galleries and the fast-paced lifestyle of the residents. The more he talked, the more inspired Makayla was. One day soon, she would be living out her dream, too.

"We should go to New York and check out the Yankees."

"I'm not much of a sports fan."

"We can take in a show or a gallery or a club. There's lots to do in the Big Apple. It's the city that never sleeps, remember?" His smile embraced her and his eyes held her captive. He was mentally undressing her, but doing a formidable job of keeping up his end of the conversation. "What do you say?"

"I don't know. I'll have to think about it."

Kenyon put down his napkin. "I almost forgot. I brought you something." He left the room and returned minutes later, carrying a shiny red gift bag. "I was going to wrap it, but I might as well give it to you since you're here."

Makayla stood. "That's okay," she said, accepting the gift. "I'm sure I'll love whatever it is." She peeked inside the bag, pushed aside the tissue paper and pulled out a white bag with the Barney's logo. Inside was a short, midthigh ruby-colored dress. Soft ruffles flattered the hem and there were slits on the sides. A look of wonder crossed her face. "You brought me a dress?"

Kenyon shrugged. "What can I say? I have an eye for fashion. I was going to buy you shoes to go with it but I didn't know your size."

"It's so short."

"All the girls are wearing it in NYC. You'll look great."

"No one has ever bought me a dress." She held it at arm's length. "I like it. Thanks, Kenyon."

"Don't thank me yet," he told her. "There's more in the bag."

By the time Makayla was finished taking everything out, the table was covered with a Yankees mug, an *I love NY* T-shirt and a book. Makayla laughed when she read the title. "*The Single Woman's Guide to Traveling Alone*?"

"You never know when it will come in handy. Sisters are always complaining that black men are aggressive, but wait till you get to South America. I once saw a Brazilian man follow a woman around for hours in the hopes of getting her phone number."

"I'll keep that in mind."

"You forgot something." Kenyon put his hand in the bag and dug around. He pulled out a package of tea bags four times the regular size. "Here you go."

Makayla closed her eyes and inhaled the sent. "Mmm—lavender. Is this for drinking?"

Kenyon chuckled. "It's Body Tea. A blend of herbs and scents that's supposed to work wonders. Fill the tub with warm water, drop one of these inside, close your eyes and escape."

"Sounds like quite an experience. I've never heard of these before."

"European women swear by them," he told her. "It's supposed to calm the mind. I figured after a long day with a bunch of rambunctious first-graders, it's just what the doctor ordered."

Makayla reached up and pecked his cheek. "Thanks, Kenyon." She tucked the bag under her chair and retook her seat.

"Speaking of rambunctious first-graders, is Terrance still giving you a hard time?" Kenyon eased the cork out of the second bottle of wine and refilled her glass.

"He's getting better. In fact, he got a perfect score on his last social studies test."

Kenyon raised his glass in the air. "That's my boy!"

Makayla chewed her food slowly, then drank some wine. The light, sweet flavor tickled her nose. Two glasses were her maximum, but Makayla was already working on her third. A quick glance at Kenyon brought a smile to her lips. A feeling of bliss surrounded her whenever he was near. Articulate, down-to-earth and worldly, he found a way to bring out the very best in her. Spending an entire weekend in New York with Kenyon would be a dream, but how could she go away with him when there were secrets between them?

Kenyon pushed away his empty plate. "That's just what I needed. Good food, great company. I owe you one, Makayla." When she didn't respond, he took her by the hand and sat her down on his lap. Wrapping his arms around her, he nuzzled his face against her ear. "Are you still mad at me?"

"I'm not mad."

"Yes, you are."

"No, I'm not."

Kenyon stared up at her, his gaze strong, intense, penetrating. "Be honest."

"Okay," she conceded. "Maybe a little."

"I thought a lot about you while I was gone."

"No, you didn't."

"Why would you say something like that?"

Makayla shrugged. "You spent the last week with gorgeous centerfolds. Why would you be thinking about me?"

"Because you're sweet and kind and caring. I don't know too many women who'd surprise their men with a home-cooked meal, especially on a night like this. You're special to me and there's no one I'd rather be with tonight than you."

Makayla suppressed a smile. "Really?"

"Really."

"I called you in New York."

"You did? When?"

"On Wednesday. A woman answered the phone and said you were in the shower. Didn't you get my message?"

The question hung in the air for several painful seconds. He looked contrite and his eyes begged for forgiveness. Makayla stood, but he forced her back down.

"I didn't get your message. I swear."

"Sure."

"It's true."

"Are you dating Alexandria?"

"No, we broke up a while ago."

"When?"

Kenyon coughed.

"When?" she repeated.

"I can't remember."

"You're lying."

He muttered a string of curses. His eyes darkened like storm clouds rolling in on the horizon. His face hardened, his jaw clenched and his breathing was ragged. "I'm telling you the truth. Why does it matter, anyway?"

"Because I have a right to know if you're dating me on the rebound." Makayla would have given her right arm to have a quarter of Alexandria's beauty. Last year the model-turned-actress had been voted by *GQ* as the celebrity most men would like to date. *I'm way out of Kenyon's league. Always have been, always will be,* she thought, her shoulders slumped in defeat. Now everything made sense. Kenyon was dating her on the rebound. He'd broken up with Alexandria and now he was consoling himself with her. In high school, Kenyon had always dated the tallest, thinnest, prettiest girls, and clearly not much had changed. He had led her to believe he was attracted to her, desired her, but the truth was he was biding his time until he got back together with Alexandria. Then Makayla would be strung out in the cold.

"It's not like that."

"Then what's it like?" She stared down at him, her face an angry mask. "Do you still love her?"

"It was never love."

They locked eyes. Kenyon took her hands, but she steeled herself against his touch. Trust was the foundation of every good relationship. She cared about Kenyon and wanted him in her life, but she didn't want to be with someone who lied to her. A stab of guilt pricked Makayla's conscience. He wasn't the only one keeping secrets. If she wanted him to be up front with her, shouldn't she do the same? Makayla swiftly rejected the idea. Her identity wasn't a betrayal, but Kenyon cheating on her with his ex-girlfriend was. "You still haven't told me why she was in your hotel suite."

"I ordered room service and the crew came up. We were never alone."

"Did you kiss her?"

"No, she kissed me."

Her voice was sour. "What a convenient excuse."

"It's not an excuse. I'm telling you the truth." Kenyon dragged a hand down his face, a weary look in his eyes. "Where is all this coming from?"

Makayla couldn't tell him what Terrance had said in class and furthermore, she didn't want him to think she had pumped his nephew for information. "I'm going home. It's been a long week and—" The rest of her sentence fell away when Kenyon kissed her. She melted under his touch. Her body was warm and she was hungry for more. Rattled by her body's reaction, she pulled away.

Under her heated stare, he felt compelled to confess. "I didn't tell you about Alexandria because I thought you might feel insecure if you knew I dated a supermodel."

Her laugh was shaky. "I'm not insecure."

"Good. You have no reason to be." Kenyon tightened his hold around her waist. "You're every bit as beautiful as she is."

"Right. The only thing Alexandria and I have in common is that we're both black." Her voice was small, plaintive, quiet. "She's stunning and I'm, well, average."

He cupped her chin, his mouth a stern line. "Makayla, you're not average. And I'm not just saying that 'cause you're my girl."

"Alexandria's stunning. She's tall and thin and she has big boobs and—"

"Makayla, a good body is earned, not bought. Fake breasts are about as attractive as a toupee on a balding man."

She laughed. "I hear what you're saying, but I'd still kill to look like her. I—"

Kenyon cut in again. "It takes a team of professionals to make Alexandria look the way she does. I'm talking makeup artists, hairstylists, manicurists, nutritionists, trainers and a personal consultant at her beck and call 24/7.

"I have the most expensive camera on the market, use the highest quality of film available and there's also lighting, props and a ton of other factors that go into capturing the perfect shot. And despite my best efforts, they still airbrush the hell out of the pictures."

Makayla's eyes widened. "They do?"

"Yup, it's pretty brutal. They airbrush the lines near her mouth, erase the bags under her eyes, thin out her face and shave off five, sometimes ten pounds. Don't get me wrong, Alexandria's a gorgeous girl, but the images you see on posters and in magazines are misleading."

"But…she always looks so amazing. Like one of those porcelain dolls." Makayla leaned into him, inhaling his dreamy-smelling cologne. "I guess you're really good at what you do."

"I try."

Makayla rolled her eyes and Kenyon chuckled.

"So, you guys aren't getting married?"

"Married!" His voice exploded across the room.

"I'll take that as a no."

"Damn right it's a no!"

"Then why does Terrance think you are?"

Kenyon laughed. "Because he's a nosy kid with bad hearing. Alexandria is doing a photo shoot for an Italian boutique and she wants me to be the lead photographer. I told her I needed some time to mull it over. The shoot's in Venice and I'm not sure I can fit a week into my already hectic schedule."

He kissed her cheek and coaxed a smile from her lips. "Are we cool now?"

"Yeah, we're cool." Makayla couldn't hold back her smile. For as long as she lived, Kenyon would always be her first love. It wasn't one thing about him or even a bunch of little things she liked. It was everything. Makayla closed her eyes, moved in close and kissed him gently on the lips.

When they parted, Kenyon was wearing a smirk. "Now, that's what a brother's talkin' 'bout! That's how you're supposed to greet me when I come back home!"

Makayla laughed.

"By the way, I loved last week's article about fruit and foreplay."

"You read my article?" she asked, swiveling on his lap to get a better look at him.

"Sure did. In fact, I've been checking your column ever since you told me about it. Sometimes the guys on my crew diss me, but I've caught some of them reading it out, too!" Remembering the suggestions in the titillating article, he nibbled on her ear and trailed a hand up the slope of her legs. "Let's go for a drive."

"Where?"

"I know a place that makes the best banana floats in the city."

"But it's cold outside."

Kenyon curled an arm around her. "I'll keep you warm."

"Are you serious?"

"It's the least I can do. You brought me dinner, so it's only fair I buy you dessert." His smile spread up to the corners of his eyes. "Let's get out of here."

Makayla patted her stomach. "I'm stuffed. I couldn't eat another bite."

"You'll work up an appetite during the drive. I know I always do."

"But the kitchen's a mess. I can't leave it looking like this!"

"I won't take no for an answer." Kenyon stood. He put his hands on her hips and steered her out of the kitchen. "You'll thank me later."

Chapter 15

The Stardust Drive-In was the length of a football field, and the neon sign marking the entrance was visible from the I-95. It had the traditional look and feel of a fifties drive-in, complete with a malt shop and diner. Cars, trucks and motor homes were scattered across the wide-open space. The wind had died down to a whisper, and thousands of stars glittered in the night sky.

Kenyon turned off the main road and parked his Escalade on a desolate part of the field. "We're here."

"You drove all this way for a banana float?"

"Like I said, they're the best in the city."

"How did you find this place?"

"My stepdad used to bring me here during the summer for a movie and ice cream. It's still one of my favorite spots."

Makayla leaned forward in her seat. She couldn't believe the movie on the screen was one he'd been dying to see. She told him.

"I know. You've mentioned it at least ten times. It took me a while but I finally got the hint."

"You're just full of surprises, aren't you?"

"I try." Kenyon brushed his eyes across her face. He put a hand on her leg and squeezed. "Are you warm enough?"

"Yes, it's nice and cozy in here."

Kenyon adjusted the heat, then clicked off his seat belt. "Do you want a banana float or should I bring you something else?"

Makayla stared out the window. The sign in front of the malt shop listed the menu and the prices. Since meeting Kenyon, she'd abandoned her low-calorie diet and found a multitude of reasons for not going to the gym. Makayla wanted to get back on track, but it wasn't every day she came to an old-fashioned drive-in. "I'll have a vanilla milk shake with lots of sprinkles and some of those mini doughnuts, if they have them."

"Coming right up." He opened the door and closed it behind him.

She watched him stroll across the parking lot, marveling at just how handsome he was in a sable-brown jacket, jeans and Timberland boots. The simple, urban look worked for him. His collar was up, his swagger bold and there was an aura about him.

Releasing her seat belt, she kicked off her shoes. Since they were going to spend the rest of the night watching movies, she might as well make herself comfortable. Makayla shrugged off her jacket and put it in the back. Settling into her seat, she tucked her feet under her bottom. If she had known they were going to the movies, she would have worn jeans and a T-shirt instead of a dress.

There was a loud tap on the window. Makayla shrieked, but when she recognized Kenyon's silhouette, she unlocked the door and pushed it open.

"Sorry 'bout that. I didn't mean to scare you."

Makayla stared at the tray he was holding. It was loaded with milk shakes, doughnuts, popcorn, cookies and an assortment of candy. "That's a lot of food for two people."

"I know, but it's a double feature. We're bound to get hungry." Kenyon motioned with his head to the side door. "Let's sit in the back. There's more room there."

Kenyon was right. It was roomy. "This is quite the car," Makayla said, taking in the fine wood paneling. "It must have cost a fortune."

"It did. Took me a year to save the down payment, but it was worth it."

Makayla couldn't imagine spending a year's salary on a car, no matter how trendy it was. "You must get a lot of female attention driving around in this," she teased.

"Some." Kenyon twiddled with a button on the center console.

Seconds later, Makayla felt a warm, tingling sensation on her back. "These seats heat up fast. This feels like a massage."

Kenyon draped an arm around her shoulder. An electrical charge zipped through her body as his hands glazed her skin. "I meant what I said about keeping you warm."

For the next hour and a half, Makayla and Kenyon laughed at the absurdity of the movie and its larger-than-life characters. When she dug her hand into the tub of popcorn and came up with a fistful of kernels, her eyebrows crinkled. *Where did all the food go?*

Lately, she couldn't seem to get enough junk food. Extra-cheese pizza, cheeseburgers, doughnuts. Makayla blamed Kenyon. He was always plying her with food. If she wasn't careful she was going to gain back the weight she had worked so hard to lose. Her pants were snug, her sweaters tight and her only pair of low-rise jeans didn't fit anymore. *I'll get back on track tomorrow,* she decided, polishing off the rest of her soda.

"Should I make another trip to the concession stand before the next movie starts?"

Makayla grabbed a napkin and wiped the grease from her hands. "No, I've eaten enough junk for today."

"In that case, come here."

She went into his arms and softened when he kissed her, but she was stunned by what came out of his mouth next. "Take off your dress."

Her eyes shot open. Makayla's head was dizzy with excitement, her mouth dry, her hands trembling. "I—I can't do that."

His smile stretched the length of his mouth. "Of course you can. I know you don't think I brought you all this way to watch movies all night."

She wasn't persuaded by his grin. If Makayla was going to resist him, she had to keep her head. "Kenyon, this is wrong."

"Says who? I want you and I'm going to have you. *Now.*" His voice was passionate, his eyes ablaze. The look on his face spoke volumes. It was going to happen, right here, right now. Kenyon kissed her again. His touch was laced in urgency and sprinkled with need. "Sex is like real estate, baby. It's all about location."

"W-we can't do it here!" Makayla glanced outside the window, half expecting the police to pop up and shine their flashlights into the car.

Kenyon slipped a hand up her dress and traced the lace trim of her panties. "We can and we will. Now, relax and let me love you."

Voices whirled in her brain.

You can't have sex in the car. What if someone sees you? What if they call the police? Do you want to be the lead story on the evening news?

Makayla rolled her head back, inaudible moans trapped in her throat. Now they were right in the thick of it. Lips feasting, hands stroking, bodies rubbing. The decision should have been an easy one to make, but Makayla grappled with what to do. *How could something that feels so right be so wrong?* It took an army of self-control, but she managed to speak through her haze. "I want you, too, but not like this. What if someone—"

"Don't worry, no one can see us."

"What if kids—"

"It's almost midnight. Trust me, there aren't any kids around here."

"But—"

He stole another kiss.

"What if we get caught?"

"You worry too much, Makayla."

Light flooded the car, illuminating the apprehension in her eyes. "Are you sure? I don't want to go to jail, Kenyon."

Chuckling, he nuzzled his face against her chin. Shifting to the middle of the seat, he pulled her down on his lap. With unerring accuracy, he untied the knot on her dress and unhooked the clasp on her bra. He took his time kissing her, caressing her, exploring her. His fingers caressed her inner thigh, then slipped between her legs. It was an exhilarating sensation. Her unvoiced desires consumed her when he traced his lips down her neck and along her collarbone. Making love to Kenyon in his car was outrageous. Scandalous. Unconscionable. Shame seized her. She shouldn't be doing this. Or enjoying this.

"W-we can't." Makayla stood up and stuck her head on the roof. "Ouch!"

Kenyon looked up at her, his face showered in concern. "Are you okay?"

Embarrassed at her clumsiness, she nodded.

"Come here." Kenyon held her against his chest. For several seconds, there were no words between them. He cupped her face and placed soft kisses on her forehead, nose, lips. "Better now?"

"Yes."

Kenyon inched down her panties and positioned her on his lap so she was straddling him. Gripping her hips with one hand, he unzipped his jeans with the other. Smiling up at her, he gently cupped her bottom. "Want me to stop?"

Her breathing grew shallow. Makayla couldn't bring herself to lie. No, she didn't want him to stop. This was like a scene out of one of her erotic books. Only, Kenyon wasn't some over-sexed stud looking for his next sexual conquest. They were a couple, fully committed to each other.

The perfume of their love heightened the excitement in the air. Her adrenaline was pumping, her lips moist, her desire high. Makayla pushed aside her fear. Giving him a naughty grin, she tilted her head to the right and parted his lips with her tongue. She darted the tip of her tongue in and out of his mouth. Arching her back, she clutched the seat and lowered herself onto him. Her thighs trembled as he entered her.

Makayla pressed her eyes shut and explored his mouth with her tongue. She brought her hands to his face and traced the outline of his jaw. His skin was smooth, his scent dreamy, his grunts rousing. She draped her arms around his neck, pulling him in. Her breasts grazed his lips in a sensual tease.

Kenyon reached up and took a nipple in his mouth. He lightly caressed the swell of her breasts, rubbing his finger around the edge.

His touch made her feel good all over. Made her feel sexy, confident, feminine. It had taken some convincing, but she had finally given in. Not because she felt pressured, but because she wanted him just as much as he wanted her. *Wait until the next book club meeting!* she thought, biting down on her bottom lip to keep from screaming out. *Do I ever have a story to tell!*

Her orgasm stole her breath. Left her feeling delirious and spent. She held her rigid, arched-back pose for several minutes before her panting subsided.

"Are you good?"

Makayla managed a nod. The dreamy smile on her face brought a grin to his lips.

"Good." Kenyon flipped her on her back. "Now, it's *my* turn!"

Giggling, she wiggled out from underneath him only to be caught seconds later. Kenyon pinned her down. He kissed her slowly, tenderly, reminding her just how gentle he could be. Lost in the moment, Makayla didn't see the well-built security guard until he was at the side window, shining his flashlight into the car.

Makayla propped a leg up on the toilet seat and hiked up her skirt. "Great, just great," she mumbled, inspecting the damage. The run in her nylons wasn't more than an inch, but it was the width of her index finger. She unscrewed the top of the clear nail polish bottle and applied a generous amount of the liquid to the tear.

She dropped the nail polish back into her purse and exited the stall. Now was not the time to fuss. Focus and poise were key. In twenty minutes, she'd have the most important interview of her life and only a fool would blow this opportunity.

Makayla faced the mirror. She was pretty in a pink, crochet-knit cardigan and black pencil skirt. Her hair was in a sleek ponytail and the makeup Desiree had advised her to buy looked soft and natural. If it weren't for the run in her nylons, she wouldn't be so nervous. Makayla examined the tear, unsure of what to do. If she crossed her legs when she was seated, Mr. Douval wouldn't see it. Her experience and qualifications were in question, not whether she was a stylish dresser, but Makayla didn't want the magazine editor to think she was a slob. In this business, appearance counted almost as much as ability. She put back on her blazer, but left the top three buttons undone. After touching up her lipstick and washing her hands, she left the washroom.

The offices of *Travel and Entertainment* magazine looked sophisticated. Glass windows, decorative floor tiles, bright lights.

Makayla had expected to find clutter, casually dressed staff and the scent of stale coffee in the air, but instead found tidy cubicles, friendly employees and vibrant flower pots.

She stopped at the reception desk. "Hello. I'm Makayla Stevens. I have a five o'clock appointment with Mr. Douval."

After pressing a button on her switchboard and speaking quietly into her headset, the receptionist led Makayla down a short hallway.

The door at the end of the hall opened, and a well-dressed man in a midnight-blue suit emerged. "Ms. Stevens."

Roman Douval was a surprise. Six feet, with stunning brown eyes and a confident smile, he exuded a type of energy that few men possessed. He had a slender build and his dark brown hair fell lightly across his forehead. Makayla liked him immediately. "It's nice to finally meet you."

They shook hands.

"We've been playing phone tag for so long, I feel like I already know you." Roman led Makayla to his desk. "Please, have a seat."

"Thank you." Makayla sat down. She flicked a speck of fluff off her skirt and drew a deep breath. Straightening her shoulders, she clasped her hands in front of her.

"I was very impressed with your CV, Ms. Stevens." Roman paused to open the file in front of him. "May I call you Makayla?"

"Please do."

"I enjoyed your article on the Philadelphia Zoo. What inspired you to write the piece through the eyes of a child?"

"Most of the students I teach are first-generation immigrants. Many of them have never been to the zoo and as newcomers they often notice things adults ignore, such as the sway of the trees, the scent of the grass, the sounds the animals make. I drew on some of the experiences I've had with my students and tried to write the article with a childlike innocence." Makayla watched his eyes soften and sensed he was impressed. She felt a surge of confidence and said, "I love teaching. I have a great team, an inquisitive group of students and I've grown tremendously as a teacher the last ten years."

"Please don't take offense to my question, but if you love what you do, why are you here?"

Makayla knew the question was coming, and had practised what she wanted to say. "I'm ready for a change. Teaching is all I've ever known and though I'm happy with my career, I'm passionate about writing. I'd like to see what else I have to offer."

"But aren't you passionate about teaching?"

Is this a trick question? "I'd like to think I'm passionate about a lot of things."

He eyed her with interest. "Are you married?"

Makayla pitched a brow. What did her marital status have to do with her ability to do the job? Roman must have read the bewildered expression on her face, because he was quick to explain. "The last travel writer I hired spent exactly nine days in New Zealand before bailing on me. Seems she missed her fiancé and couldn't handle the separation. I'm leery about hiring someone in a long-term relationship. You understand."

"Yes, and in response to your question, no, I'm not married. Or engaged."

Roman dug deeper. He leaned back in his chair, his hands folded across his chest. His eyes zoomed in on hers. "There's no special man in your life? No one at all?"

Uncomfortable with the line of questioning, she said, "I'm not sure I understand what you're asking."

"You're an attractive woman. I'm sure you have a lot of admirers."

"Thank you." Makayla leaned forward. "Mr. Douval, I am resourceful, hardworking and I have an intense desire to succeed. I can do this job. All I need is a chance."

"So there's no one you might have trouble leaving behind if I should offer you this position?"

Shifting in her chair, she unclasped her hands. Kenyon cared about her, that she was certain, but he didn't include her in all areas of his life. And outside of her friends, no one knew they were dating. This was the chance she was waiting for. She couldn't allow her feelings for Kenyon to cloud her judgment. They were lovers. They had a good time together. They made each other laugh. But she had known the score from day one. No strings. No promises. No commitments. Makayla loved Kenyon but she couldn't put her life on hold for anyone. She dismissed Roman's concerns by saying, "There's nothing that will prevent me from taking this job. And as far as my teaching career goes, I can always find a job when I come back."

He nodded eagerly. "When can you start?"

Makayla smiled. "That depends. Do I have the job?"

Chapter 16

Arranging the resource books on her desk, Makayla stole another glance at her watch. *His flight is just taking off.* She thought of calling Kenyon, but struck the idea from her mind. They had plans for tomorrow and if she could handle not seeing him for the last two weeks, surely she could handle a few more hours.

God, I miss him, she thought, her gaze drifting to the classroom window. Thanksgiving had been a quiet affair. Dinner with her dad and stepmom, home by six, in bed by ten. Kenyon had called from Miami and they had talked so long, she ended up falling asleep on the phone. He was in Florida on business, and each day they were apart, she missed him even more. He had come to mean so much to her. It was more than just his good looks. The playfulness of his laugh, his cool, me-against-the-world swagger and his hip, urban style were just a few of the things she loved about him. In recent weeks, they had begun spending more time together and the Barbecue Kitchen had become their new hangout. On cold nights, they'd spend hours sitting in their favorite booth, talking, laughing, joking. Makayla had become a permanent fixture at his house and Kenyon had even joked that she should move in and start paying half the mortgage.

Rolling her neck from side to side, she closed her eyes and replayed their last night together. The tenderness of his hands as they glided down the slope of her back had heightened her desire. His hands, so strong, yet smooth; his mouth, so gentle, yet urgent. *God, I must have it bad,* she thought allowing her fingers to caress the delicate slope of her collarbone.

"I hope you're thinking about me."

Makayla's eyes flapped open. Kenyon stood at the back door, wearing a mischievous smile. His hair was shorter, his mustache trimmed and he was wearing a chocolate-brown suit. Swallowing, she tried not to drool all over her dress. "Kenyon, what are you doing here? I wasn't expecting you until much later."

"I caught an earlier flight." He approached her desk. "Happy to see me?"

"Of course, but I thought you were coming in at—"

He lowered his head and kissed her.

Overwhelmed, giddy and basking in the feel of being back in his arms, Makayla stood and wrapped every inch of herself around him.

Kenyon broke off the kiss. "It's good to be home."

"Things just weren't the same here without you."

"I did a horrible job on the travel brochure."

"I'm sure it's not that bad."

"It is. I'll have to do the shots again."

"You're being too hard on yourself," Makayla said, hoping to comfort him.

"I blame you." The sparkle in his eye could not be hidden. "I spent so much time fantasizing about you I took crappy shots."

Her smile brightened the room. "You're not the only one pre-occupied. This morning I knocked the jar of pennies onto the carpet. We had coins all over the place." Makayla giggled at the memory. "Loving you is turning me into a klutz."

Kenyon lifted a brow. "Pardon me?"

"I inadvertently knocked over the jar of pennies and—"

"No, the part after that."

"I, uh, well—"

The door swung open and Desiree poked her head inside. "I'm ready to go whene—" She stopped midword. "I am *so* sorry. I didn't mean to interrupt. I'll catch you guys later."

"No, wait!" Stepping out of Kenyon's arms, Makayla smoothed her hands gingerly over her face. "Y-you weren't in-terrupting. Come in. Kenyon and I were just—um—chatting."

Desiree's eyes darted between the two guilty parties. "I just wanted to know if you were ready to go."

Makayla addressed Kenyon. "Desiree's car's in the shop so she's driving with me. The girls are taking me out for a celebra-tory dinner."

"That's cool. Lucas and I are going to the Sixers game. I'll come by after I drop him off." He leaned over and whispered, "Then we'll finish what we started."

Suppressing a smile, Makayla grabbed her jacket and picked up her purse and tote bag from off the back shelf.

Outside a strong wind was blowing. The evening sky was the darkest of blues, blanketed with fluffy clouds piled on top of each other like chunks of snow. Despite the gravel scattered about, the parking lot was a sheet of ice. Makayla held on to Kenyon with one hand, and gripped her jacket collar with the other.

"I can't believe Christmas is only a few weeks away!" Desiree said as they approached the car. "Seems like the first day of school was just yesterday."

"Do you have anything planned for the holidays?" Kenyon asked.

"No, unfortunately my boyfriend has to work. If I get desperate I might go visit my grandparents. But that's only if nothing else comes up." Laughing, she opened the passenger-side door and put down her belongings. "I love them dearly but ringing in the new year playing bingo is not my idea of a good time."

"I'm throwing my annual house party. You're more than welcome to come."

"A house party?" Desiree wore a skeptical look. "I thought house parties went out with the high-top fades, acid-washed jeans and Spandex."

"Not to mention those stupid parachute pants," Makayla chimed in. She gave Desiree a high five and the two women laughed.

"They're alive and well where I come from. I'm an eighties kid to the bone," Kenyon thumped his chest with his hand. "It starts at nine and it's semiformal attire. Come with an empty stomach because there'll be tons of food."

"Sounds good to me. Count me in. Thanks for the invitation, Kenyon."

"No problem. If you need directions to my place you can always get them from Makayla."

Desiree addressed her co-worker. "We'll just drive together, right?"

"I—I don't know if I'm going." Makayla unlocked her door, heaved her bags into the back seat and turned back to Kenyon. "I kinda have other plans."

"Then break them." His voice was firm. "I want you there. I want all my friends to meet the woman who's got my head in the clouds." He tugged on the belt of her coat, a sad, forlorn expression on his face. "Say you'll be my date."

Desiree got into the car, leaving the couple alone.

The wind slapped Makayla's face. She turned her back on the wind, which brought her that much closer to Kenyon. "I promised my dad and stepmom I'd come over."

"I thought you said they were going on a couples' cruise."

Makayla forgot she'd told him about their holiday plans. "I have to go by and collect the mail and I promised to water the plants and stuff."

Kenyon pulled her to him. "I need you there."

"You'll be fine without me."

"No, I won't."

"Don't be silly."

"Why don't you want to come?"

How can I tell him I'm scared of seeing Lucas? If she went to the party there would be no avoiding Lucas-the-jerk Shaw, one of the many who'd made her life hell back in high school. Makayla had gone to great lengths to conceal the fact that she and Kenyon were dating, plus she wasn't about to blow her cover now. She couldn't take the chance that Lucas would remember her. Whenever Kenyon suggested getting together with his friends, she turned him down. They had been dating for months and she'd been spared a reunion with Lucas Shaw. Kenyon came to her house most nights, and when they did go out, they avoided popular hangouts. To her knowledge, not even Veronika knew they were dating, and that's how Makayla wanted to keep it.

Desiree leaned across the driver's seat and stared out the partially open door. "Don't listen to her, Kenyon. We'll be there. Besides, with Elliot working, I have nothing to do but wash my hair." She added, "Or play bingo."

Makayla shot her co-worker a look. Desiree would have to drag her out of the house because she wasn't going anywhere on New Year's Eve.

Kenyon drew a deep breath, his eyes focused on her face. He

slipped a hand around her waist and nuzzled his face against her cheek. "I won't take no for an answer, Makayla."

Normally, she loved being in his arms, loved being in kissing range, but showing this much affection in front of her school was a definite no-no. There were only three other cars in the parking lot, but there was no telling who was watching. "Can we talk about this later?"

"Sure." Kenyon maintained his hold. "What time will you be home?"

"Around ten, maybe eleven."

"Cool. I'll call you when I'm on my way."

"Okay."

"Say yes, Makayla. Veronika and Terrance will be out of town and I'll need you by my side to play hostess." Kenyon pushed further, his voice smooth and silky. "Think about it, babe. I'll be miserable without you." His lips were just inches from her face and the tantalizing smell of his cologne was turning her on.

I'll have to give it some serious thought, she decided as his mouth lowered for another kiss.

Ultraposh dining rooms, faultless service and live music flittering in from the adjacent cocktail bar made All that Jazz the place to be on a Friday night. The slightly upscale and refined decor of the establishment with its white walls, lined tables and six-person booths made it the spot for after-work drinks.

Brandi raised her martini glass high in the air. Eyes focused on Makayla, she asked the other women at the table to join her in toasting the newest writer at *Travel and Entertainment* magazine. "Congratulations, Twinkie. No one deserves this more than you!"

"Thanks you, guys, but you didn't have to go to all this trouble." Smiling sheepishly, she glanced around the room. "It's a bit much if you ask me."

"Well, we didn't," Desiree said, nudging her playfully in the ribs. "Aren't you glad I convinced you to go home and change?"

"Yeah, I would have felt like a bum walking in here in my old cardigan and loafers." When Makayla entered the private dining room and saw the faces of her closest girlfriends, amid balloons, streamers and an enormous chocolate cake, her eyes had pooled with tears. For the last hour, she had eaten and drunk so much she'd need a trolley to make it outside to her car.

Desiree smiled at Makayla. "You deserve to be spoiled. You work hard."

"I've finally stopped waiting for a man to do for me what I deserve," Jia told the group. "I go to nice restaurants, send myself roses and if I'm really hard up for some company, I have a list of men on standby!"

Sydney nodded. "I hear you. Sisters need to learn to do for themselves. I love my husband and I wouldn't trade him for nothin', but I don't expect him to take care of me. What's that famous line from Aretha?"

"Take care of me first, better to love you," Jia and Desiree sang, their voices reaching a squeaky pitch.

Makayla laughed. Surrounded by love, laughter and joy, she reflected on just how great her life was. She had landed her dream job, her friends and family believed in her and soon she'd be traveling the world. Dating Kenyon was the icing on the cake. Their relationship wasn't going to last forever, but she would always cherish the time they had spent together.

"When do you start?" Sydney asked.

Makayla couldn't hide the excitement in her voice. "I'll be writing monthly pieces about various U.S. cities until the end of the school year. Then in July, I'll be off to Barcelona to do a special one of the world's best cities."

Jia tasted her chicken. "What's your first assignment?"

"It's a piece about Wyoming."

Desiree laughed. "Wyoming? What the hell is in Wyoming?"

"The Amangani Hotel has been voted the most romantic place on earth five years running. I'm going to go check it out for myself."

"You'll be a terrific travel writer, Makayla, because you can find the beauty in almost anything," Sydney noted, taking a sip of her wine.

Brandi helped herself to another slice of cake. "What did Kenyon say when you told him you got the job?"

"He wished me luck."

Jia's face registered surprise. "That's it?"

"What else was he supposed to say?"

"Did he seem happy?" Sydney asked.

Makayla shrugged. "I guess so."

Her friends exchanged looks.

Desiree spoke next. "His reaction didn't seem odd to you?"

"No." It was a bold-faced lie but Makayla didn't want her friends to know she'd been confused by his response, too. His smile was forced, and although he congratulated her, something in his eyes made her uneasy.

"I almost forgot to tell you guys what happened at school this afternoon!" Desiree's mouth flared into a smirk. "You should have seen Makayla and Kenyon all hugged up on her desk!"

Makayla shot her co-worker a simmering look. "You're exaggerating. We were *not* hugged up on my desk. It was just a kiss."

"He had his hands up your skirt!"

"No, he didn't!"

Desiree giggled. "Sure looked that way to me."

Anxious to change the subject, Makayla turned to Jia. The graduate student was a semester away from graduation but always made time to hang out with her girlfriends. "How is your thesis coming along? If you ever need an extra set of eyes to look it over, I'm available."

Brandi wagged a finger in Makayla's face. "Don't change the subject, Twinkie."

"That's right," Desiree said. She went on to tell the group about Kenyon's New Year's Eve party. "Can you believe she turned him down?"

Jia gasped. "No, she didn't!"

"Now I know she's trippin'," Sydney said, shaking her head.

"I'm not."

"Then why won't you go to his party?" Brandi asked.

Makayla didn't want to talk about her feelings; her heart was already a cauldron of mixed emotions. Confiding in her friends would only leave her more confused. "It's complicated."

Desiree rolled her eyes. "Complicated my foot! Kenyon was practically begging you to be his date and men like him don't beg."

"I'd be careful if I were you," Jo added. "Another woman might just swoop in and steal him away."

To silence her critics, Makayla spoke about the bullying she'd endured at the hands of Lucas Shaw. She left nothing out, revealing secrets she'd never even told Brandi. "Lucas made my life a living hell in high school. He smeared chocolate syrup all over my locker and wrote the word *pig*. Another time, he put a whoopee cushion on my chair. The day of graduation pictures he gave me a Halloween mask and said it would be an improvement."

"What a bastard," Desiree said. "I would have cleaned his clock."

Sydney agreed. "Same here."

"Now do you guys understand why I can't go to the party?"

"Lucas was a creep, but this is not about him. It's about you and Kenyon." Jo smiled softly. "He wants you by his side and that's gotta matter more than your fear of seeing Lucas again."

Sydney added, "Kenyon can have any woman he wants.

Remember the last book club meeting? Rhandi and Dallas practically threw themselves at him, and you were sitting right there. Don't leave room for another woman to come in and take your place."

Brandi gave Makayla a one-armed hug. "You have every right to be afraid, Twinkie. He picked on me, too, remember? Lucas terrorized you but you're not a seventeen-year-old girl anymore. You're pretty, outgoing and smart. Don't let the man you love, especially one as fine as Kenyon, slip away."

Makayla fiddled with her napkin. "Who said anything about being in love?"

"Don't play dumb with me, Twinkie." Brandi squeezed her shoulder. "You've loved that man since high school."

"I admit I once had a crush on Kenyon but that was almost fifteen years ago. I don't—"

Desiree cut her off. "You forget I've seen the two of you in action. Thank God I walked in your classroom when I did. Five more minutes alone and you guys would have been buck naked on your desk!"

The women chortled, clapped and shrieked.

Makayla ignored them. Her relationship with Kenyon was nothing to laugh about. She'd been living life in the slow lane until she met him. His spontaneous, get-up-and-go attitude had definitely rubbed off on her and she counted herself lucky that he was her man. Even if it was only for now.

Brandi was the first to sober up. "I wish I could go with you to Kenyon's party but Jamaal won't be happy if I skip dinner with his family."

"Makayla, don't worry," Desiree told her. "Lucas won't hurt you again, I promise. I'll be by your side the whole night and there's no way in hell I'll take any of his crap."

Hours later, Desiree's words still echoed in Makayla's mind.

As she drove toward home, she was struck by the truth of her friend's words. Kenyon was a good catch, and although she'd be traveling after the end of the school year, she didn't want to lose him to someone else. *But what if Lucas recognized her? What if he humiliated her in front of Kenyon and his guests?* Makayla wanted to face her fears, wanted to come to terms with her past. But was she strong enough?

Chapter 17

Kingsley Shopping Mall had hundreds of stores, a twenty-theater Cineplex, a dozen high-end restaurants, cafés and the state's largest indoor park. Situated on the edge of south Philly, the shopping complex attracted residents and tourists on even the most treacherous weather days. With Christmas only a week away, the plaza was swarming with fretful shoppers in search of the perfect last-minute gift.

Makayla and Kenyon took their time browsing stores, strolling casually side by side, their hands weighed down by shopping bags.

"Are we finished?" Kenyon asked as they approached the food court. "Everyone on your Christmas list covered?"

Makayla caught sight of the fifty-percent-off sale sign hanging in the Victoria's Secret window. She motioned with her head. "My stepmom wants a robe. I'm sure I'll be able to find something nice in there."

"Cool, I see something you should try on."

Resting a hand on his chest, she stopped him midstep. "Wait right here, lover boy. Give me ten minutes."

Kenyon propped his elbows up on the railing, a wide grin on his lips. "Fine, if that's the way you want it. But holler if you need me."

Laughing, she walked briskly into the store and smiled at the buxom saleswoman greeting customers. Makayla carefully shopped the racks and after some deliberation selected a silk ankle-length robe for her stepmother and a sheer, zebra-print teddy for herself. It was ridiculously expensive, but she wanted something special for Christmas Eve dinner with Kenyon.

"Are you going to model that for me?"

She glanced over her shoulder and sent Kenyon a smile. "I thought you were waiting outside?"

"I saw you admiring that sexy number and thought you might need a second opinion." Kenyon came up behind her and nuzzled his chin against her neck. He wrapped an arm around her waist, pulling her close. His rich, lubricious voice induced thoughts of what would happen when they were finally alone. "Look around. This place is packed. We could slip into a fitting room and nobody would even notice."

Kenyon was right. The place was a zoo.

"We'll be in and out in ten minutes." A grin hugged his lips. "No pun intended. Are you up for a little role play?"

"What if someone sees us?"

"It'll be cool. I promise. Trust me."

Before she could decide either way, Kenyon steered her toward the back of the store. Makayla felt her temperature rise with nervous excitement. She visualized them making love, imagined how the thrill of possibly being caught in the act would increase their passion. Kenyon took breaking the rules to a whole new level. He wasn't a flowers-and-champagne kind of guy, but he sure knew how to keep things interesting.

With his index finger he motioned to the left. "Let's use that room over there."

Giggling, she stopped in front of the intended dressing room door and gripped the lock.

"Ms. Stevens, is that you?"

Fear coated Makayla's stomach. She knew that voice and she knew it well. Her first impulse was to pretend she didn't hear her principal's wife calling her and rush into the changing room. She turned around, a look of genuine surprise on her face. "Mrs. Gibson, how nice to see you again."

"I almost didn't recognize you," she said, her eyes laced with disapproval. "You sure don't look like a teacher in *that* outfit."

Makayla tucked a hand into her pocket. It wasn't every day she wore a cropped jacket, a halter tunic sweater and skinny jeans. Her outfit wasn't appropriate for school, but it was the perfect look for a night out on the town with her man. She felt young, sexy and vibrant and Kenyon had been touching her all night. "Is Mr. Gibson shopping with you, as well?"

"Yes, he's trying to find an electric car for our oldest grandson. He's probably waiting outside as we speak."

Makayla felt warm all over. Not only had she been busted trying to sneak into a fitting room for a quickie, but she was about to be exposed for the whole world to see. Principal Gibson was a genial, soft-spoken man but was rumored to have a brutal temper. Thankfully, he had never unleashed his wrath on her.

Mrs. Gibson turned toward Kenyon, her eyes flickering up and down, her mouth a flat line. The woman was on the wrong side of sixty, and from the creases on her forehead it was obvious she had spent most of those years frowning. "I don't think we've met. Do you teach at Springs Park Elementary, as well?"

Worried Kenyon might divulge personal information, Makayla spoke up. "No, Mrs. Gibson, this is Kenyon Blake. He and I are old friends. We go *way* back."

Kenyon stared down at her, a humorous gleam in his eyes. "That's right. We're old high school sweethearts."

Makayla gulped. He was joking, right? Unless he'd finally remembered her! She washed the thought from her mind. No way Kenyon knew who she was. If he did, he would have said something by now. Her bottom lip quivered but her voice came out even. "Did you receive the card I sent?"

Her tone was ice. "We receive so many cards this time of year it's hard to remember who sent what."

"Principal Gibson mentioned how much you enjoy the dinner theater, so I included two tickets for the New Year's Eve show."

Mrs. Gibson's face came alive. "Yes, yes, now I remember! That was very thoughtful of you, Ms. Stevens. Very thoughtful indeed!"

Every year Makayla bought the couple a gift. Nothing flashy, usually a box of chocolates or a holiday gift basket. But a chance meeting with a local actress led to an interview for her column and two free tickets to the theater. *Thank God for small miracles,* she thought. "I'm glad you like it."

"I do, very much." Her face radiated joy. Smiling, she patted Makayla's shoulder. "I have to go but it was lovely running into you. Happy holidays!"

"Please give my regards to Principal Gibson and season's greetings to you and your entire family."

"God knows I have the worst memory. These days I can't even remember where I put my keys. Don't hold it against me if I forget to tell my husband we ran into each other."

"No problem at all. Forget I mentioned it."

"Goodbye." Mrs. Gibson turned and walked away.

Makayla released a heavy sigh when the woman disappeared

around the corner. Kenyon was watching her, but she couldn't bring herself to look at him. *That's the first and last time I do anything that stupid!*

"That was a close call."

"I'd say." She cleared her throat. Aflame with curiosity, she asked, "Of all the things you could have said, why did you say we're high school sweethearts?"

"It sounded good. And if I'd known you back then you definitely would have been my girl." Kenyon opened the fitting room door, pulled her inside and dropped the bags. Unzipping her jacket, he said, "Now, where were we?"

Popping grapes into her mouth, Makayla jogged upstairs and pushed open the bedroom door. She wasn't in the mood to clean but Kenyon was coming over for Christmas Eve dinner and she didn't want him walking into a messy house. Flipping on her stereo, she padded into the bathroom, singing at the top of her lungs. The funky divas of En Vogue engulfed her room with their distinctive blend of funk, rock and soul. Makayla rummaged under the sink until she found what she was looking for. Kenyon wouldn't be in her bathtub but that didn't stop her from scrubbing the tub with every ounce of her strength. The shrill of the phone beckoned her but she ignored it. Whoever was calling would have to catch her later. She had work to do.

Once the bathroom smelled piney fresh, Makayla clogged the tub with a stopper and turned the water on full blast. She peeled off her sweat suit and covered her hair with a plastic shower cap. Dipping her foot into the water, her eyes caught sight of the pink gift bag poking out of her top drawer. *The Body Tea.* Ambling back into the bedroom, she retrieved the package and ripped it open. *I hope this works,* she thought, *because right now I couldn't be more stressed.*

As she soaked in the tub, her thoughts drifted to Kenyon. *Why does life have to be so complicated?* she wondered, propping her feet on the side of the tub. Things had been strained between them ever since Makayla told him she couldn't go to his party. He had played it cool, but she could tell by his rigid posture and the stiff expression on his face that he was upset. He had been distant all week and there was an undercurrent of tension whenever they spoke. They had spent little time together since her announcement and the only reason he had agreed to come over was because she insisted. Tonight, they'd have a fine meal, exchange gifts and hopefully make up.

Glancing at the clock, Makayla calculated exactly how much time she had before he arrived. An hour tops. She wanted to relax longer but the water was cold, her hands were shriveled prunes and En Vogue was gone. Stepping out of the tub, she toweled off and released her hair from the elastic band. She plodded into the bedroom, the sweet scent of lavender trailing behind her.

Thirty minutes later, she was in the kitchen, putting the finishing touches on the lamb. The doorbell chimed, pulling her attention away from the stove. The time on the microwave said it was five-fifteen. Makayla wasn't expecting Kenyon yet.

By the time she reached the foyer, Brandi had the front door wide open.

Makayla shivered as a bitter wind swept into the house. "I gave you that key to use in case of an emergency."

"This *is* an emergency," Brandi insisted, breathing heavily. She was huffing and puffing as if she had run a mile. "It's freezing outside!" Slamming the door, she stooped down and retrieved the plastic bags at her feet. "I thought you weren't home. I called from the store, but you didn't pick up."

"I must have been in the bathroom." Laughing, she tugged at the sleeve of Brandi's jacket. "What's with the outfit? By the way you're dressed, you'd think it was minus thirty out there." The bulky parka, which Makayla could swear was the same ugly thing Brandi's boyfriend wore when he shoveled the snow, could fit a linebacker. A brown toque concealed her hair, a wide, burly scarf sheltered her neck and earmuffs covered her ears.

Peeling off her gloves one finger at a time, she said, "It's brutal out there. Forecasters are predicting this to be the coldest winter in Philadelphia history. Twenty inches of snow on New Year's Eve alone."

Makayla rolled her eyes. "They say that every year." Returning to the kitchen, she opened the oven, set the lamb inside and programmed the timer. "*Please* tell me you remembered to get the cheesecake."

"I did." Brandi slid onto a stool. "I know you don't like hard liquor, but I also took the liberty of buying you a little something for the occasion. I bought a bottle of this—" she modeled the pink, eye-catching bottle "—for Jamaal's birthday, and by the time he finished his second glass, he was all over me."

"Then I will definitely *not* be serving Kenyon any." Laughing, she took the bottle from Brandi's outstretched hands and buried it in the fridge on the bottom row behind a head of lettuce.

Brandi whistled. "Girl, you're working your ass off in that dress. Kenyon's going to have a lot on his plate tonight—a tasty dinner, you in that hot number and after a glass of the strawberry tequila he'll be drooling at the mouth!"

Makayla giggled. "I doubt that, Brandi. He's dated Alexandria for God's sake! I hardly think he'll be impressed with me."

"I still can't believe you're dating him! No one has ever seduced, duped, cajoled or bedded more women than Kenyon Blake. Everything we've ever heard about that man is true, trust me. I had girlfriends who knew him in college." She shook her head slowly, her voice laced with admiration. "Remember the Sadie Hawkins dance senior year?"

Makayla groaned, covering her face with her hands. "How can I forget? We spent the entire night watching everyone else dance because—"

"No one wanted to dance with us," Brandi finished, a wistful expression in her eyes. "You damn near fell off your chair when Kenyon came over and asked you for the last dance."

"He was just being nice because I tutored him in math."

"Well, my night wasn't a total bust. Shakeesha Mooris clocking Lucas in the mouth was the highlight of the evening. He had blood gushing down his nose and everything!"

"Serves him right for grabbing her butt!"

Makayla and Brandi laughed so hard their eyes filled with tears.

The doorbell rang, interrupting girl talk.

"He's here!" Ripping off the apron, Makayla cleaned the invisible specks on her dress and wore a confident smile. "How do I look?"

"Like a sista who's gonna to be gettin' some tonight!" Makayla tried to swat Brandi's arm, but she dodged the blow. "I'll hide out in the bathroom and then slip out while you're in the living room."

"Why? Don't you want to meet him?"

Brandi shook her head. "Don't worry, I'll meet him before the wedding."

Laughing, Makayla hurried down the hall toward the front door.

Chapter 18

By midnight, Makayla and Kenyon were sprawled out on the couch, too full to move, too tired to talk. Soft music floated out of the speakers and it wasn't too long before Kenyon was fast asleep, snoring soundly beside her.

Content simply lying in his arms, Makayla reflected on how much life had changed. Kenyon had turned out to be everything she thought he'd be. Lively, energetic and fun, he made her feel like a teenager again, only this time, she wasn't overweight with bad skin and hair. Drawn to his impeccable sense of style, and his larger-than-life personality, Makayla had been swept off her feet and had fallen hard for her old high school crush. Why couldn't she have her career *and* Kenyon? Surely there was a way to keep their relationship going while she was away. Who said things had to end? They were committed to each other, Kenyon made it known that he cared about her and with his open schedule, they could squeeze in regular visits. During dinner, Kenyon had mentioned he would be in Europe over the summer and had hinted to them hooking up. He wouldn't travel halfway around the world to see her if he wasn't serious about her, would he?

Kenyon wasn't the kind of guy who talked about his feelings. If she waited for him to open up, she'd be eighty years old pushing a walker. His actions spoke loud and clear. The way he kissed her, the tone of his voice when he said her name, the look in his eyes when they made love all testified to his true feelings. Kenyon Blake was a man of many contradictions. He was educated, articulate and cultured, but very street. He liked living on the edge, but he was also responsible and trustworthy. Definitely her kind of man.

They'd been sneaking around for months and Makayla was tired. Tired of going out late, tired of keeping their relationship under wraps, tired of constantly having to look over her shoulder. They didn't hold hands, didn't cuddle in public, kissing was out of the question. She wanted to date like other couples. Her teaching career was standing in the way of her happily ever after, but it wouldn't be long before she handed in her resignation and packed her bags for Europe.

Makayla stared up at Kenyon and giggled. His mouth was open, he had a small gravy stain on his cheek and every few minutes he scratched the side of his face. She'd watched him eat two hearty plates of food, drink several rounds of strawberry tequila and polish off an enormous slice of cheesecake, marveling at how he could eat so much in one sitting. They'd retired to the living room, dimmed the lights and flopped down on the couch. Makayla had been hoping they'd cap the night off by exchanging gifts, but she had a strong feeling Kenyon wouldn't open his eyes until morning.

Makayla basked in a sense of peace and well-being. She could cuddle with him like this for hours. Snuggling up to him, she closed her eyes and rested her head in the crook of his arm.

There was something so comforting about eating together, cuddling on the couch and then hitting the sack together like an old married couple. Who knew love could be this sweet?

She was drifting off to sleep, envisioning an elaborate fairy-tale wedding, when she heard a loud humming sound. At first she ignored it but when the noise persisted, she opened her eyes in search of the source. Kenyon's cell phone sat on the coffee table, vibrating.

Makayla shook his shoulder. "Baby, wake up. Your phone's ringing."

Kenyon didn't move. If it wasn't for the rise and fall of his chest, Makayla wouldn't even know he was alive. In the time they had been dating, Terrance had had two trips to the emergency room, nightmares so frightening Kenyon had left her bed in the middle of the night and several emotional breakdowns after visiting his father's grave. At midnight, Terrance should be in bed, but sometimes the six-year-old called when she least expected it. Worried that it might be an emergency, Makayla reached for the phone and flipped it open. A text message popped up on the screen. Then another.

Makayla's eyes narrowed as she read the first message. She was midway through reading the third when she felt Kenyon stir beside her. Turning her eyes on him, she threw down his phone, pelting him in the stomach. "You asked Alexandria to be your date for your New Year's Eve party?"

Kenyon yawned. His eyes had the blankness of a man half-asleep. "Only after you turned me down." He tucked an arm behind his head. "You don't expect me to be the only one at my party without a date, do you? I have a reputation to uphold. It's nothing personal. Alexandria and I are just friends."

"It's nothing personal?" she repeated, her voice a roaring wave. "And when were you going to tell me you invited her?"

He shrugged. "I don't know. When it came up."

"I thought we agreed not to see other people?"

"It's not a date. It's a party, remember? There'll be lots of other people there. Friends, associates, family."

"How would you feel if I spent New Year's Eve with an ex-boyfriend?"

"I wouldn't care." His tone was indifferent, but there was no mistaking the smoke in his eyes. "Especially if I refused to be your date."

Makayla's lips flared. In high school, Kenyon had dated the tallest, thinnest girls and not much had changed since then. She wanted to believe he was attracted to her, desired her, cared about her, but the truth was he was still a playboy, always on the prowl for another pretty face. She should have trusted her instincts. Kenyon wasn't over his ex and this latest stunt proved it. "If you go with Alexandria to your party then—then—"

"Then what?" he prompted, swinging his feet out in front of him. He closed his eyes and let out a big, slow yawn. "Don't make threats, Makayla. Especially ones you can't keep. You and I both know you don't want things to end."

He was right. She didn't. They'd made so many plans for the new year. There was the three-day weekend in New York. The overnight at a renowned bed-and-breakfast in nearby Malvern. Valentine's Day at the Couples' Masquerade Party. But if Kenyon thought she was going to let him get away with dating Alexandria—even for one night—he was crazy. Trust, loyalty and respect were the basis of any good relationship. Was it too much to ask that he be faithful and true?

Kenyon stood and stretched his hands high above his head. "I'm going to the kitchen to grab a beer. You want one?"

"No."

He touched a hand to her lips and stared down at her. His eyes shone brighter than a blue strobe light, and his broad grin couldn't be any more enticing. "When I get back we'll start unwrapping our gifts."

Makayla resisted the urge to slap his hand away. Kenyon thought sex could fix everything. The only way he could make things right was by uninviting Alexandria to his party. But when she voiced her thoughts, he laughed out loud.

"It's not going to happen, Makayla."

"You haven't changed one bit."

"What's that supposed to mean?"

"Forget it."

Kenyon could tell Makayla was about to cry by the telltale redness in her eyes. In an attempt to diffuse the situation, he gently rubbed his hands along her shoulders. He lowered his mouth to kiss her, but she turned her face away. "Are you going to let this ruin the rest of our night?"

"I'm not the one who caused the problem. *You* did."

"Do you want me to leave?"

"I don't care." It was Christmas Eve and she'd rather argue with him than be alone. She wanted him to stay, but she wasn't about to admit it. If she excused what he did, it wouldn't be long before he was mistreating her.

"All right, suit yourself. I don't want to be where I'm not welcome." Kenyon strode out of the living room. She heard the closet door squeak open, some rustling, then seconds later the front door slammed.

Makayla told herself she was happy to see him go. To prove to herself she didn't care that he'd left, she went over to the window and pulled back the curtain. As she watched Kenyon get into his car and pull away, she wondered if and when they would make up.

* * *

On Saturday mornings, Uptown Hair and Nail Salon resembled the DMV at the end of the month. Angry-looking women stood rigidly against the wall, staring at the clock, those lucky enough to snag a seat thumbed through fashion magazines and the handful of men in the establishment watched college basketball on the flat-screen TV.

It had been snowing heavily all morning, as predicted for New Year's Eve, but Desiree, Sydney and Makayla had a standing appointment every Saturday afternoon. They drove the thirty miles to Uptown's no matter what Mother Nature was whipping up outside.

Sydney rolled up her sweat pants and submerged her feet into the tub of warm water and closed her eyes. "Nothing like a good soak to clear the mind." She stole a look at the front door. "I'm surprised Makayla isn't here. She's always on time."

Desiree smiled at Sydney through the haze of steam. "I told her our appointment was pushed back an hour. I wanted us to talk. *Alone.*" She unzipped her jacket and pretended not to notice one of the male stylists watching her. Desiree liked men who looked like men and though the thirty-something man had deep, soulful eyes, everything about him screamed "pretty boy." The shoulder-length braids, dainty hoop earrings and glossy lips told her everything she needed to know. A meterosexual if she had ever seen one. "I don't know about you, but I do not intend to spend New Year's Eve at home watching Dick Clark. I love Makayla and all, but the last time I spent New Year's Eve at home I was eighteen. Not a good year."

"I hear you. Curtis is home sick and the girls are with their grandparents. I love my man but I refuse to take care of him another night. Men are such babies when they're sick!"

"Who are you tellin'? Elliot broke his foot last year and whimpered for weeks. You would have thought they amputated his leg!"

Sydney's laugh was a cross between a cackle and a squeal. "Well, Curtis told me to go out and have a good time and that's what I'm going to do. There's got to be something we can do to change Makayla's mind about going to Kenyon's party."

"There is but it's underhanded and sneaky." Desiree added, "But it's for her own good. Kenyon is the perfect guy for her, she just doesn't know it yet. It's up to us to show her the light. What kind of friends would we be if we sat back and did nothing?"

"Not very good ones."

"Exactly!"

Sydney thought a moment. Desiree was right. Makayla had all the classic symptoms of a woman in love. The shortness of breath when Kenyon entered a room, the flushed skin, widening eyes, gasps of delight when he touched her. They were doing her a favor, right? But what if their plan backfired? What if Makayla caught on and…

"So, are you in?"

"I don't know, Desiree—"

"You don't know what?"

"Maybe we shouldn't get involved. Last time I talked to Makayla she was still pretty upset about Kenyon inviting Alexandria to the party."

"That girl doesn't know what's good for her." Desiree wore a mischievous smile. "Thank God we do!"

This plan had *scandalous* written all over it, but there was no doubt in Sydney's mind it would work. She leaned over so their shoulders were touching. "What's the plan, Desiree?"

"Tell me, Syd. How do you feel when you catch your husband eyeballing a younger, more attractive woman?"

Sydney's mouth twisted into a frown. Her husband's penchant for flirting was a sore spot for her, but she didn't speak on it. Tonight was about mending Makayla's broken heart, not her issues with Curtis. "I want to smack him upside the head. He makes me feel so jealous. Like he should be looking at me that way."

"Exactly!"

Sydney was stumped. "I don't get it."

"It's quite simple, my friend. If we want Makayla to go to Kenyon's party, we have to make her insanely jealous."

"But she's already jealous of Alexandria."

"Then it's our job to push her over the edge! And if that doesn't work, we'll drive her to boredom. By the time we sit down to eat, she'll be begging us to go to the party!"

Sydney let Desiree's words sink in. It sounded like a good idea. They'd bring Makayla and Kenyon back together and she'd have the opportunity to meet her favorite star.

"If we're going to do this we have to go all the way. No backing out. No flaking. No second thoughts. When Makayla comes over, we've got to force her hand, got it?"

Sydney nodded, her smile growing. They'd convince Makayla to go to the party or take her against her will. Either way, they were going to the party.

"Leave everything to me. I know just what to do." Desiree looked pleased.

"Girl, I like how you think!" Sydney said, holding up her right hand. "Here's to Project Makayla!"

Laughing exuberantly, the two women slapped hands.

Chapter 19

We shouldn't have come, Makayla thought as Desiree turned onto Aberdeen Road. It was only ten o'clock but the streets in front of Kenyon's house were lined with cars. After driving around for several minutes, the trio agreed to park on a nearby street and walk up to the house.

Desiree and Sydney got out of the car, but Makayla didn't join them on the snowy sidewalk. She sat in the back seat, toying with the hem of her dress.

Desiree opened the back door. "We're here," she sang, no doubt hoping to coax a smile from her friend. "Let's get in there before I freeze my butt off!"

"I don't know about this." In her mind's eye she could see Kenyon and Alexandria talking and laughing. They stood under the mistletoe, their eyes shimmering with desire. "Things have been awkward between me and Kenyon ever since we argued. How do I know he even wants to see me?"

Makayla had seen little of Kenyon over the last week. And when they talked on the phone, neither one of them had much to say. He didn't mention his New Year's Eve party, and Makayla didn't ask. Last night he'd promised to stop by after he took Terrance to the festival of lights, but he never did. When he finally called, their conversation was brief, his mood tense. He was angry and she didn't blame him. For the last three months, they'd been sneaking around, and aside from her friends, no one knew they were a couple. The restrictions she'd imposed on them were trying his patience. Kenyon's friends were his family and refusing to meet them was an insult. Makayla suspected he was more frustrated about not having his way than her not attending his party. Kenyon liked running things, liked being in control, liked being "the man," but Makayla wasn't going to put herself out there just to make him happy. If it weren't for Desiree and Sydney pressuring her to get out of the house, she'd be on the couch waiting for the ball to drop in Times Square.

"Of course he wants to see you!" Desiree assured her. "And besides, I didn't spend an hour on my hair and makeup for nothing. I came to get my party on and I'm not leaving here until I do."

Sydney smiled. "We can always go back home. I bet the pizza's still warm."

"No!" Makayla stepped down from the truck. She had arrived at Desiree's expecting a lobster dinner, merlot and a Jackie Brown flick. Instead she'd found pizza, fruit punch and an action movie staring some rapper-turned-actor. If that wasn't bad enough, her girlfriends were plodding around the house in shower caps, zit cream and sweat pants. Five minutes into *Soul Plane*, Makayla suggested they go to Kenyon's party. After shopping in Desiree's closet for the perfect dress, curling her hair and applying some makeup, Makayla was ready to go.

Desiree linked arms with Makayla. "My mantra is simple—eat, drink and be merry. Now let's go party the night away!"

Kenyon's house was alive with music, lights and laughter, and as Desiree rang the doorbell, she glanced at Makayla. "Relax, girl. You look terrified."

Chilled, timorous and fighting the overwhelming urge to spin around and run for cover, she splashed her best Tammy Faye Baker smile on her face. "I'm fine."

Sydney touched her shoulder. "We're right beside you."

Makayla's insides were in knots. Her heart, which seemed to be out of order these days, was thrashing around in her chest. The bone-chilling wind made her hands tingle, but she was sweating like a four-hundred-pound sumo wrestler selling tacos in Mexico City.

Patting her clutch purse, Desiree said, "Don't worry, Makayla, we've got your back. I've got my taser gun in here, just in case Lucas the leech starts acting funny."

Makayla burst out laughing.

The door swung open, illuminating her wind-bitten face. Kenyon stared down at Makayla as if she'd just fallen from the sky. But he quickly recovered from his shock. The last thing he wanted was for her to think he wasn't happy to see her. Kenyon bowed in an exaggerated flourish. "Welcome to my humble abode, ladies."

Desiree and Sydney giggled. "Thanks, Kenyon."

Kenyon ushered them inside and took their jackets. He was surprised to see Makayla in a tight champagne-colored dress and provocative ankle-tie pumps. They had been dating for months and he had never seen her this dolled up. With sultry eye shadow, diamond earrings and flowing curls that tumbled across her shoulders and down her back, her look was screaming "do me." And he was more than ready to oblige. He wished he could blow off his party and take her upstairs.

"I'm glad you guys could make it." Kenyon directed the comment to Makayla. He'd thought of her off and on all day. The urge to call her was overwhelming, but he had pushed it aside. He wanted her to be his date for the party but he wasn't going to beg. Not because Makayla wasn't worth it, but because he didn't want her to think he was less of a man. Real men didn't beg. At least, that's what his stepdad had always told him.

Desiree turned to Kenyon. "Thanks again for inviting us."

"Yeah, thanks," Makayla echoed, her tone flat.

Undaunted by her sedated response, Kenyon took Makayla by the hand and led her down the hall where women in cocktail dresses and men in black tie gathered around the fireplace and the buffet table. Sydney and Desiree headed straight for the bar, leaving Makayla alone with Kenyon.

Kenyon draped an arm around Makayla's waist. It felt good holding her again. Showing a rare measure of restraint, he dropped his mouth to her ear and said, "You're the finest woman in here tonight."

The sound of his "bed-me" voice drew a smile to her lips. "I bet you say that to all the girls."

"No, just you."

Makayla glanced around the room, then strained her eyes down the hall.

"She couldn't make it."

"Who?"

"Alexandria. That's who you're looking for, right?"

"You must be disappointed."

"Hardly. Like I said before, I don't want Alexandria. I want you." His eyes spoke volumes. Kenyon rubbed a hand over his head. He knew what he had to say but it wasn't going to be easy. "When I was a kid, I had to win everything. Every game. Every contest. Every competition. I'd never do anything if I couldn't be the best. Sometimes I take things too far, Makayla. Asking Alexandria to be my date wasn't cool."

"You're right, it wasn't."

"I didn't mean to upset you."

"And?" she prompted.

"And I'm damn glad you're here."

"Actions speak louder than words."

"Then let me show you." He lowered his head and kissed her. Kenyon touched her with a sculptor's finesse. His hands stroked her arms, her back, her hips. Guests passed by but he didn't care. Seeing Makayla was the best part of his day and he wanted the whole world to know how he felt about her.

Seven days without holding her was seven days too long. Makayla hated public displays of affection, but they weren't at some restaurant or some far-away movie theater. They were in the comfort of his home, surrounded by his family and friends. In the hopes of persuading Makayla to be his date, he'd pushed her too far. This was his way of making things right.

Somewhere in the distance someone called his name, but Kenyon didn't budge. He was with his girl and that was all that mattered. Makayla was the most authentic woman he had ever met. She didn't need thousands of dollars of jewelry or designer clothes to feel beautiful. Independent, honest and caring, she had a sweet nature and killer looks. He embraced the idea of them being together. A couple. Two people trying to make a go at this thing called love. Marriage wasn't on the horizon. Kenyon didn't know if it would ever be, but he wanted to continue dating her. Only when he'd had his fill of her, did he release his hold.

"Damn, cuz, give the li'l woman some air!"

Kenyon laughed as his cousin approached. "Quit talkin' smack and say hi to my girlfriend."

The teenager did as he was told. "You look familiar. Are you a model, too?"

Giggling, Makayla swatted Kenyon's arm. "Did you pay him to say that?"

"Not a dollar!"

After a few minutes of conversation, Makayla excused herself to join her girlfriends at the bar. Kenyon watched her cross the room, proud when several men turned to look at her. Beside him, Seth judged every woman who walked by. Kenyon didn't care who his cousin thought had the biggest chest, the longest legs or the sexiest mouth. Makayla was the only woman he wanted, and when the party was over, he'd show her just how much.

This Kahlúa is definitely doing the trick, Makayla decided, emptying her glass. She'd started the evening sipping white wine, switched to a Long Island iced tea with dinner and then had several glasses of Sambucca. Kenyon had been by her side all night, introducing her to his friends, ensuring her glass was full, stealing kisses when she least expected it. Having Kenyon at her side calmed her, but she wouldn't feel comfortable until her reunion with Lucas Shaw was behind her.

"Thailand is one of the most beautiful countries I've ever been to." Kenyon rolled his empty drink glass in his hands. "But there are stray dogs everywhere. That freaked me out! I love animals as much as the next guy, but it was insane. I spent more time running from the dogs than taking pictures!"

Everyone at the table laughed.

Desire put down her wineglass. "Since you're a seasoned traveler, maybe you can help me convince Miss I'm-Scared-of-Flying to go with me to Hawaii for spring break."

"You've never been on an airplane?" Kenyon asked, turning to Makayla.

Makayla shook her head and made a mental note to smack Desiree later.

"Are you afraid of heights? Claustrophobic?"

"All of the above," Makayla replied, growing uncomfortable. She couldn't admit the real reason why she'd never been on a plane. It had nothing to do with her fear of heights and everything to do with her weight. She could never have fitted into a regular-size seat. Her wide bottom and those narrow seats made as much sense as Michael Jackson opening a day-care center.

Desiree thumbed a finger in Makayla's direction. "I told her she has nothing to worry about, but she doesn't believe me. Maybe one of you can talk some sense into her."

"I don't need any convincing. Did it ever occur to you that maybe—" Makayla lost her train of thought. She blinked hard, but that didn't change what she saw. Bounding into the dining room was her arch-nemesis, Lucas Shaw. He was shorter than she remembered. In high school, he had seemed larger than life, but he couldn't be more than an inch or two taller than her. Her palms were damp, her mouth dry, her teeth on edge. Lucas wore a black pinstripe suit and so many gold chains he reminded her of Mr. T. His skin was blotchy and his hairline was receding. *I can't believe I let this shrimp bully me!* Makayla shook her head. *I guess it's true what they say. God don't like ugly.*

"Now I see why you forgot you're hosting a party," Lucas said as he approached the table. "You've landed in an abyss of beauty."

Nothing's changed, she thought. *He's still as corny as ever.*

Kenyon addressed Makayla. "Believe it or not, this clown and I go back almost twenty years."

If Lucas remembered her, his face didn't show it. He directed a smile at her. "You're much prettier than Kenyon described. You've been holdin' out on me, QB. What? Scared I might steal her away?"

Kenyon's laughter blew the roof off the house. "Keep dreamin', playboy."

Makayla didn't know what to do if Lucas took her hand but she had nothing to fear. One look at Desiree, sitting pretty in an indigo-colored dress, and Lucas was smitten. He picked up a beer, bit the cap off with his teeth and fed Desiree a hungry grin. "Save me a dance, sexy."

"What happened to the music?" Kenyon asked, finally noting the silence. "I thought you were my DJ?"

"I was until LaDonna rammed her fat ass into the table. Now the equipment won't play. I came up here to get you because I thought maybe you could fix it."

"I'll take a look at it." Kenyon kissed Makayla on the cheek and promised to return soon. He excused himself from the table and Lucas took his seat.

"I told LaDonna she was going to hit the table but she wouldn't listen. She was too busy cramming shrimp into her mouth to watch where she was going."

The men snickered, the women sneered.

"Leave LaDonna alone," a caramel-skinned woman said. She was dripping in jewelry, makeup and big hair. "That's my girl."

Lucas snorted. His stentorian voice carried across the room. "Well, your girl could stand to lose some weight. A *lot* of weight."

More laughter.

Desiree shot Lucas a look. "And you could stand to gain some weight. You're nothing but flesh and bones. Women like men with muscles. *Lots* of muscles."

"Hold up, baby doll. Don't let the suit fool you. I might not have a six-pack but I'm built like a truck. Just ask my ex-wife. She'll tell you. I aim to please."

All of the women at the table chortled.

Lucas gripped the neck of his beer bottle. "What the hell is so funny?"

Makayla couldn't resist joining in the ribbing. "You guys are being mean. Leave Lucas alone. It's not his fault he's thin."

"Thanks, Makayla."

After being on the receiving end of Lucas's insults and teasing, it felt good giving him a taste of his own medicine. "Lots of women like little men. From what I've read Gary Coleman, Webster and Danny Devito are all lady killers!"

More laughter.

For the next ten minutes, Lucas tried to convince Desiree that he was the right man for her. The more frustrated he got, the more the women at the table teased him.

"Give me a chance, baby doll. I know I could make it worth your while." Lucas wore his most convincing smile. "Judging someone based on their looks is kinda superficial, don't you think?"

Desiree stood. "I couldn't agree more. I hope you remember that the next time you call someone fat ass."

"That's right!" yelled a voluptuous woman at the end of the table.

Lucas sagged back in his chair. "Whatever. You women are all the same, uptight, hard to please, emotional—"

Sydney cut him off. "Hey, the music's back on. Let's dance!"

A dark, heavy-set man smiled at Desiree. "You promised me a dance and I'm going to hold you to it."

She smiled, and then winked at him. "I'll be waiting, Fredrick."

Makayla glanced at Lucas. He was such a pitiful sight, he looked like he was about to cry.

Standing, she tossed him a sympathetic look. Thanks to Desiree and Sydney, Lucas Shaw would never hurt her again. "Let's go!" she told her girlfriends. "I'm ready to party!"

Desiree patted Lucas on the head, which drew even more laughs. "It was nice meeting you, little guy. See ya!"

Laughing hysterically, Desiree, Sydney and Makayla sauntered out of the dining room, their shoulders rocking to the music.

Chapter 20

Kenyon's eyes followed Makayla's every move. They had been to a club once or twice before but he had never seen her dance like she was now in his basement, thanks to his friend Alston, who played a mix of reggae, R & B and hip-hop. Hands out-stretched, hips twirling, she screamed along with the other dancers as Missy Elliott's high-pitched voice filled the room. Makayla moved like she didn't have a care in the world. His eyes gobbled her up. The soft outlines of her breasts were visible under the hushed lights, and her legs looked long and shapely. There was nothing Kenyon liked more than watching a woman dance, especially one who knew how to work her hips. A woman who was confident, not conceited; open-minded but not buck wild. Like Makayla. Kenyon wanted to go to her, but knew if he did, an innocent dance would lead to much more.

The anthem of many love-struck couples, *Caught Up in the Rapture,* came on and a ripple of moans whipped across the packed dance floor. Kenyon glanced at Makayla. Their eyes connected from across the room. He smiled and she waved back. Her sweet, soft cheeks and glossy lips beckoned him but he stayed put. Now that she had spotted him, he was sure she would ditch her partner and come to him. But he had hosting responsibilities to attend to. The bar was running low on champagne, so he grabbed a few of his friends and went into the wine cellar and retrieved a dozen bottles.

When he returned to the basement ten minutes later, Makayla was still on the dance floor. Kenyon didn't like what he saw. Now her partner was a stocky man with dreadlocks. Kenyon covetously looked on as the bushy-haired stranger wrapped an arm around her waist. The dancer's hands settled on her hips as he tried to keep up with her sensual movements. He whispered in Makayla's ear and to Kenyon's surprise, she laughed. Before he could stop himself, he was tapping Mr. Feel-Good on the shoulder. "I hate to bust your bubble, but the woman you're drooling over belongs to me."

"Hey, man, we're just dancing," he replied, reaching for her again. "Chill out."

"My party, my rules." Kenyon thumped the man on the chest. "Go grab a beer. It'll help cool you off."

The stranger disappeared into the crowd.

Kenyon wore a superior smile. He had broken the cardinal rule of hosting, but he didn't care. He didn't want anyone touching or feeling on his girl.

Makayla shook her head, laughter in her eyes. "That wasn't very nice. I think you hurt his feelings."

"Oh well. I'm a jerk. Sue me." Kenyon pulled her into his arms. Their bodies came together like copper and zinc. It didn't matter that a rap song was playing or that they were drawing admiring looks from the other partygoers. His affection for her was obvious to all. He whispered in her ear, enfolded her in his arms and stroked her back. Kenyon liked the feel of her soft body moving against his hard one. The sweet scent of her perspiration was wild and sexy. Makayla was a strange, erotic creature that he would never be able to figure out completely. He loved that about her. Their eyes engaged in a secret conversation. He dropped his mouth to her ear and projected his voice above the music. "You sure know how to party!"

"Should I take that as a compliment?"

"Definitely." Kenyon licked his lips. Makayla was grinding on him, touching him, feeling his chest through his shirt. He was enjoying every second of it. "I like the way you move. How 'bout a private show?"

"Are you serious?"

"Let's go upstairs. I have something to show you."

"What is it?" Makayla asked, linking her arms around his neck.

"I still haven't given you your Christmas gift."

"You could always give it to me after the party."

Kenyon could tell by the sound of her voice that she was aroused. His breathing deepened. He held Makayla closer so she could feel the bulge in his pants. "But I want to give it to you *now*."

Makayla giggled. This was like a scene out of a movie where the hosts sneak off into the bedroom for a quickie. "What if someone needs you?"

"I need you now," he said, his eyes flowing over her body. "Are you coming or not?"

Kicking their flirtation game up a notch, she touched his forearm and allowed her fingers to linger a second too long. She teased him with her best "bad girl" look, her lips puckered into a sexy smirk. "Lead the way."

"Drive safe!" Kenyon called, closing the door on the last of the guests. There was a fierce wind and thick, heavy snowflakes were falling from the sky. The street was surprisingly quiet. Normally, Kenyon allowed guests to sleep over after a long night of partying, but he wanted to be alone with Makayla, free of interruptions. It had taken three quarters of an hour to arrange rides for everyone but now they had the house to themselves.

Kenyon picked up empty soda cans, half-eaten plates of food and dumped them into an orange plastic bag. He found Makayla in the kitchen, piling glasses and dishes into the dishwasher.

He came up behind her. Makayla turned to face him and he kissed her hard on the lips. Their tongues teased and stroked like two lovers salsa dancing.

"Had a good time?"

"Yeah, that was some party."

"Especially the part where you lured me into the laundry room."

Laughing, Makayla pushed him away. "Liar! I didn't lure you anywhere!"

"Oh, yes you did." His jaw had dropped when she pulled him into the laundry room and locked the door behind her. She'd hopped onto the washing machine, hiked up her dress and said in a sultry voice, "I'm waiting—" Kenyon was scared he was going to come right then and there. Makayla had never been that misbehaving before but he liked it—a lot.

Kenyon stared down at Makayla. Her full, pouty lips were screaming out to be kissed and she was wearing a sensuous smile. If he didn't get her upstairs soon, there was no telling what would happen. "Let's go to bed. We'll finish up in the morning."

"I don't know how you can go to sleep knowing your house is a mess."

"That's the difference between men and women. We don't sweat the small stuff."

Makayla followed Kenyon out of the kitchen and down the hall.

"I didn't bring my overnight bag with me. Do you have an extra toothbrush?"

"There should be some in the spare bedroom."

"Okay, I'll meet you upstairs."

Kenyon patted her on the butt. "Hurry up. I'll be waiting."

Makayla returned twenty minutes later. After showering, she had searched the closet for something clean to wear. She had laughed out loud when she saw Kenyon's old high school jersey hanging at the back of the closet. It had taken her fifteen years, but she had finally snagged the captain of the football team.

"What do you think?" Makayla held her hands out and did a small spin. "Cute, huh? I look like a cheerleader."

"Where'd you find that?"

"At the back of the closet."

"It's never looked better." Kenyon sat up. "Seeing you in that jersey brings back memories."

"Yeah, probably of making out with Angela Tucker or the threesome you had with the Cruz sisters." Makayla cupped a hand over her mouth. "Oh my God, I didn't mean—"

Kenyon's eyes narrowed. "What did you just say?"

"Nothing. I—I—" Makayla sputtered like a fish out of water.

"How do you know about Angela Tucker and the Cruz sisters? Did Lucas say something to you?" Kenyon swore. "I'm going to kick his ass."

He reached for the phone.

"Lucas didn't say anything."

"Then how do you know?"

"You don't remember me? Not even a little?"

"Should I?"

"No, I don't expect you to." Makayla stared down at her hands. "I was real ugly back in high school."

His eyes flared. "We went to school together?"

"Same math class for three years."

Now it was Kenyon's turn to stutter. "I—I don't believe it."

"I'll show you. Where's your yearbook?"

"Only God knows. It would take me weeks to find that thing. In case you haven't noticed, I'm not the most organized guy."

Makayla slipped out of bed. She opened her purse, pulled out her wallet and took out an old, wrinkled picture of her and her mom. She stared at the photograph for several minutes before handing it to Kenyon. "This is the last picture we took before she died."

The only thing the girl in the picture and Makayla had in common was their smile. "Is this for real?"

"That picture was taken a few days before graduation."

Kenyon couldn't believe his eyes. Either she had gone to great lengths to play a prank on him or she was telling the truth. He scrutinized the photograph, then held it out in front of him. His eyes darted between Makayla and the picture. "You tutored me senior year!"

"Yup, that was me."

"Damn!"

"I told you I was a mess."

"Man—you said you'd lost some weight, but damn!"

"Are you going to keep saying that?"

Kenyon chuckled, shaking his head in awe. "Sorry, babe, I can't help it. I can't believe it's you! You look like a totally different person."

"Thank God for that!"

They shared a laugh.

"Why didn't you tell me who you were?" he asked, handing her back the picture.

"I don't know. I guess I didn't have the guts to tell you the truth."

Kenyon cupped her chin. He wasn't going to let her off the hook. "There's a lot more to it than that, Makayla. Be honest.

Why'd you keep this from me? We've been kicking it for months and you never said anything."

"I was embarrassed," she began. "I was scared if you knew who I was you wouldn't want to be with me." Makayla thought long and hard before saying, "You're always telling me to keep it real, so here it is. I've lost almost sixty pounds but I'm still not a size five. I'll never be. I have hips and thighs and cellulite and that's not sexy. Men don't want women like me. They want rail-thin, Barbie-doll types with long hair and fake boobs."

"Do you think I'm that shallow?"

Her lips parted into a sad smile. "Kenyon, I don't blame you. I wouldn't have dated me back then, either. I was fat and ugly and you were tall, dark and handsome. You had a flock of beautiful admirers. Why would you take a second look at me?"

The sound of her injured voice stirred his emotions. Kenyon had never felt so low. Makayla was right. It was tough to admit, but before meeting her he thought women were only good for one thing. He hadn't been interested in settling down or having a family. Women were a distraction and he'd had only one thing on his mind: being at the top of his field. But when Makayla stormed out of the Barbecue Kitchen, he had realized there was more to her than just a nice body. No one had *ever* put him in his place and he found himself oddly intrigued. Suddenly, dating a different woman every night of the week wasn't enough. Thoughts of waking up with Makayla in his arms and spending the cold winter nights making love to her dominated his mind.

Kenyon kissed her softly on the lips. "I never thought you were ugly."

"Yeah right. Everyone did."

"Not me."

Makayla stared out the window, her face a blank expression. Kenyon kissed her again, and this time it lasted twice as long.

"If it wasn't for your help I never would've graduated. You helped me back then, just like you're helping me now. I'm not the same man I was when we first met."

"You're just saying that."

"I'm serious. I'm the one who should be worried about you kicking me to the curb. I was a jerk back then."

"You weren't that bad," Makayla said with a small smile. "It was Lucas who made my life miserable."

"Man, I can't wait to see the look on his face when he finds out! Damn! He'll probably pass out, or worse yet—"

"Can we talk about something else?"

"Sure." Kenyon stretched out on the bed and pulled Makayla down beside him. He wrapped her in his arms and gently stroked her hair. His heart brimmed with respect and admiration. Few people could do what she had done. It must have been painful being the butt of everyone's jokes but she had risen above her hurt and transformed herself into a gorgeous, successful woman. That took guts.

Guilt weighed heavy on his heart. He may not have been the one making the jokes, but he'd laughed along with everyone else. Makayla said she didn't blame him, didn't hold him responsible, but Kenyon was angry at himself. His mother had raised him to be respectful of people's differences but he hadn't always followed her teachings. But if there was one thing he had learned in life, it was that it was never too late to change.

It was 3:30 a.m. but he wouldn't be able to sleep until he apologized. "I know you don't want to talk about this anymore, but you don't have to say anything. Just listen." Kenyon took a deep breath and stared outside. If he saw the pain in Makayla's eyes, he'd lose his nerve. "I can't tell you how bad I feel. I know there's nothing I can say or do to erase the past, but I'd like to try. I wasn't one of the kids who bullied you but I'm just as guilty because I didn't stop it. I'm really sorry for the way I treated you. I—" The words stuck in his throat. He rolled his tongue over his mouth and tried again. "I love you, Makayla. Can you ever find it in your heart to forgive me?"

She remained silent.

"Did you hear me?"

Nothing.

"Babe?" Kenyon stared down at Makayla. She was curled up beside him, fast asleep.

Chapter 21

"Terrance, don't track snow through your uncle's house!" Veronika warned as her son preceded her into the foyer. Slamming the door on the blistering wind, she dropped her bags, slumped against the wall and released a deep sigh. *Thank God we made it,* she thought, running a hand through her tangled locks.

After hearing the snowstorm advisory for Philadelphia and surrounding areas, Veronika had called the airlines and booked an earlier flight home from her parents' home in Albany. Theirs was one of the last flights to land before the airport closed.

Catching a cab had taken hours. Then, when traffic stalled, she directed to Kenyon's house, which was closer than her own.

Terrence blew by her, burning off the energy he'd held in check all morning. "Keep it down, son. Your uncle's still sleeping."

Veronika shrugged out of her coat and boots and shuffled down the hall. The living room looked like it had been ransacked. And, she noted as she walked farther, the kitchen was no better. Kenyon and his friends had apparently partied all night and now he was sleeping off the mother of all hangovers.

Veronika turned on the coffeemaker. She'd watch the news, make breakfast and then see about cleaning her brother-in-law's mess.

Makayla rolled onto her back. The bedroom was dark, betraying the fact that the alarm clock read twelve-forty-five. Rubbing the sleep from her eyes, she glanced over at Kenyon and smiled. Last night she'd awoken to the taste of his kiss. Her body had come alive with his skillful touch. The night had been filled with long, languorous lovemaking, and despite being physically spent, they had talked until sunrise. Makayla had dozed off midsentence, but she could have sworn Kenyon had kissed her lightly on her lips, cuddled her in his arms and said, "I love you." But it could be all the alcohol she'd drunk clouding her memory.

Makayla slipped out of bed. She wanted to have breakfast ready for Kenyon when he woke up. But when she passed the mirror, she decided a bath would do her some good. Not only did she have a serious case of bed head, she had dark circles under her eyes and, courtesy of Kenyon, faint bite marks across her neck.

As she soaked in bubbles up to her neck, she closed her eyes and thought of Kenyon. Confession aside, she had never felt more comfortable with him than last night. Their time together had been filled with intimate conversation, passion and more than its fair share of surprises, like Kenyon's Christmas gift. She'd sat dumbfounded when she unwrapped a BlackBerry 8800. A BlackBerry would make it easier for her to keep in touch with everyone, Kenyon had said. To show her gratitude, she had climbed on top of him and kissed him with so much heat he almost rolled off the bed.

Giggling at the memory, Makayla stepped out of the tub and

toweled off. When she emerged from the bathroom wrapped in a towel, she felt like a new woman.

Makayla sniffed the air. She loved the smell of coffee first thing in the morning. Coffee was brewing, bacon was frying and if she wasn't mistaken, strawberries were on the menu, too. That sly! Kenyon had pretended to be asleep, only to go downstairs to make them breakfast. Her heart overflowed with love. No one had ever done anything like this for her. This was definitely something she could get used to. She thought of bypassing the bedroom and heading straight to the kitchen, but changed her mind. If Kenyon saw her in a towel, they'd end up back in bed. It was tempting, but she was starving. Breakfast first, loving later. Smiling, she hurried toward the master bedroom.

"What the hell?"

Makayla froze. She didn't have to turn around to know who the calloused voice belonged to. Her stomach plunged with fear. This couldn't be happening. Not to her…. *Not* today. This was no way to start off the new year. Makayla wanted to die, right then and there. Death would have been a thousand times better than facing the Wicked Witch of the West.

Oh God, Terrance must be here, too! If he saw her at the house he would figure out what was going on. *What if he told his class-mates? What if word got back to administration?*

"What the hell are you doing here?"

The sound of Veronika's voice put the fear of God in her. Shame washed over her like water from a dam. If she hadn't been gripping the door handle, she would have slumped to the floor in shock. Turning, she forced her hands and legs to stop shaking. Veronika looked like a soldier ready for battle. Wrinkled brows, folded arms, face masked in rage.

"K-Kenyon invited me to his New Year's Eve party. I—I was too tired to drive home, so I thought it was best to—"

"Spend the night," Veronika finished, her voice bathed in sarcasm. "If that's the case, then why are you creeping into his bedroom buck naked?"

Makayla tightened her grip on the towel. She had never felt so exposed, so helpless, so vulnerable. This woman had the power to ruin her, but Makayla wasn't going down without a fight. "Like I said before, I came to the party with my girl-friends and—"

"How long has this been going on?"

"It's not like that. I told you—"

"Do I look stupid?"

Makayla gulped. Fear gripped her heart in a choke hold. Words escaped her, but she quickly found her voice. "No, but you don't understand. Kenyon and I are—"

"What do you think Principal Gibson will do when he finds out you're sleeping with my brother-in-law?"

Is she threatening me? Makayla felt as if she were back in Lincoln High. Only this time it wasn't Lucas bullying her, it was Veronika. There was a time when she'd thought she deserved everything Lucas dished out. Insecure and fearful, she didn't have the confidence to stand up for herself. But she wasn't a timid teenage girl anymore. Educated, intelligent and mature, she refused to be insulted or bullied for spending the night with the man she loved. "This is a personal matter between me and Kenyon. I don't have to explain myself to you."

"Oh no?" Veronika's eyes blazed murderously. "This is not over, *Ms. Stevens.* Trust me. I'll see to it that you never teach in this city again!"

"Kenyon and I are dating. That's not a crime."

The bedroom door swung open and Kenyon stood there, shirt-less, yawning, a dreamy look in his eyes. His face brightened when he saw Makayla. "Are you coming back to bed?"

Veronika cleared her throat, drawing his attention away from Makayla.

His smile lost its warmth. "Hey, when did you guys get back? Where's Terrance?"

Makayla brushed past Kenyon and slammed the bedroom door. She had to get out of the house fast! By the time Kenyon returned, she was sitting on the edge of the bed, dressed, a terrified look on her face. Her legs were bouncing restlessly and she was practically twisting the leather off her purse. "I need you to take me home. *Now.*"

"I want you to stay."

"I can't." Then, "Why didn't you tell me they'd be here?"

"This is a surprise to me, too. I wasn't expecting them for another week. Because of the snow Veronika decided to catch an earlier flight home."

Crossing her arms, she asked the one question circling her mind. "Why does she have a key to your place?"

"I gave her one after Felix died. Sometimes when I'm out of town, they'll spend the weekend here. And if my parents want to drive down from Wilmington and see Terrance, at least they have somewhere to stay."

"Where is Terrance now?"

Relief washed over Makayla's face when Kenyon told her Terrance was sleeping. If she was lucky, she'd be out of the house before he woke up.

"Makayla, stay. We have nothing to be ashamed of. We're adults and what we do is between us."

Silence followed. Outside they could hear brakes squeal, the crunch of snow and the blaring roar of snowplows.

Kenyon stretched his hands above his head. "Veronika said it's pretty bad outside. Said the blizzard hit sometime last night and the city's bracing for more snow." He grabbed the remote control and turned on the TV.

According to the news bulletin, two feet of snow had fallen and it wasn't letting up anytime soon. Temperatures were at record lows, and wind gusts had reached a blistering sixty miles per hour. A second wave of snow was predicted for Monday, and as a result all public schools would be closed until further notice.

I can't spend the next twenty-four hours here! Makayla thought, clutching her chest. She couldn't breathe. It felt as if her chest was caving in on her.

"I'm going to grab some breakfast. Want anything?"

Makayla shook her head. Food was the last thing on her mind. She'd eat when she was at home, far away from Veronika and her hurtful accusations.

Kenyon pulled on a pair of sweatpants and a long-sleeved T-shirt. He lifted her chin and held her gaze. "I hope you're in a better mood when I get back. Is spending the day with me that bad?"

Makayla forced a smile. She watched Kenyon leave, her mind racing. When he closed the door, she sprang to her feet. She picked up the phone and dialed Desiree's number. Her friend was probably sleeping, but this was an emergency.

Desiree answered on the second ring. "Hello?" Her voice was surprisingly bright.

"Desiree, I need a favor. Can you pick me up at Kenyon's?"

"Have you looked outside? There's so much snow I can't even see my car!"

Makayla went over to the window and pulled back the curtain. It looked like a winter wonderland outside. Snow covered the trees and ice clung to rooftops. A mountain of snow blocked the driveway and unless Kenyon had a snowplow, he wouldn't be driving anywhere anytime soon.

"Please, Desiree? I'm begging you."

"I would if I could, Makayla, but I can't. Stay with your man, cozy up on the couch and enjoy the extra days off."

"You don't understand. Veronika and Terrance just showed up."

"Oh. So much for a romantic weekend."

"I know. I need to get out of here."

"Good luck. Call me later, okay?"

Makayla dialed another number. Brandi loathed cold weather, but that wouldn't deter her from coming. They had always been there for each other, through thick and thin. But Brandi laughed when Makayla asked for a ride.

There was only one other person she could ask. Though Sydney lived the farthest away, her husband had one of those big monster trucks. But Sydney's answering machine came on and prompted her to leave a message. Frustrated, Makayla banged down the phone.

She spent the next hour calling taxi services. Either the lines were busy or she was left on hold, stuck listening to dreary elevator music. Makayla dialed the last company on her list. It was a limousine service that catered to an exclusive clientele. They charged a flat rate of one hundred and fifty dollars, twice as much as any other company. It was expensive but now was not the time to pinch pennies. A prerecorded voice asked her to leave a message. Makayla stared down at the phone, a doleful expression on her face. *This is ridiculous. Doesn't anybody work anymore?*

Chapter 22

Makayla pounded the car horn. Just her luck to leave an hour early and spend it sitting in traffic. Principal Gibson was a fiend for punctuality and she didn't want to start off the new year on his bad side.

Makayla pulled down the visor against the sun that glowed off the snow blanketing the blizzard-beaten city. For the first time in days, the roads were clear, and she was anxious to get back to work. Desiree said she was crazy, but Makayla needed something to get her mind off her troubles.

When her cell phone rang, she picked it up and checked the number. Kenyon. He had been calling all morning. If she talked to him now, they would likely argue and she needed a clear head this morning. Today was the weekly staff meeting and no doubt Mr. Gibson would have a lot to say. Makayla didn't want to miss anything. Resting her phone on the seat beside her, she turned her eyes back to the road and prayed traffic would clear soon.

A Jaheim song came on the radio. Three months ago, Makayla didn't even know who the young R & B crooner was. But thanks to Kenyon, she knew a whole whack of things. Like how to play pool, different ways to mix tequila and a slew of dirty Spanish words. Turning up the volume, she rested back in her seat and closed her eyes. She thought back to New Year's Eve. Despite her reservations, it had turned out to be the perfect night, a night she would never forget. Dancing with Kenyon, slipping out of the party to make love, cuddling until sunrise. They were all cherished memories that held a special place in her heart. They were supposed to spend New Year's Day together, talking, eating, making love. Instead, they had spent the day arguing. Makayla didn't leave the bedroom all day, not even for dinner, infuriating Kenyon.

Makayla got angry every time she thought about him yelling at her. What did he expect her to do? Sashay downstairs in her crumpled party dress and sit down to steak and potatoes with her enemy? Veronika hated her and the farther Makayla stayed away from the woman the better. Sure, she felt silly holed up in the bedroom while the family ate downstairs, but she had no choice. It was bad enough she'd been caught creeping into Kenyon's bedroom wearing nothing but a towel. If Terrance saw her, he would know she was dating his uncle and there was no telling what the clever first-grader would tell his classmates. And Makayla would do anything to preserve her dignity.

In the middle of the night, Makayla had grabbed her purse, tiptoed downstairs and left. Waiting for a taxi outside in the frigidly cold weather was brutal, but it was better than spending another day under the same roof as Veronika.

Five days had passed since she had walked out on Kenyon and being without him was killing her. It would take a few weeks for things to blow over but once things cooled down, they could pick up where they left off. Until then, they had to lie low.

A horn honked behind her. There was a huge space between her car and the one in front. Traffic was finally moving.

Thirty minutes later, Makayla pulled into the school parking lot. Principal Gibson's vehicle wasn't parked in its usual space. Sighing in relief, Makayla slipped out from behind the wheel. At least she wasn't the only one late.

As she walked down the hall to the faculty lounge, an unexpected smile blossomed on her lips. The memory of how she had met Kenyon, so many months ago, brought a short laugh. One day when she was old and gray, she would tell her grandchildren the story of how she had fallen head over heels—literally—for a handsome photographer from north Philly.

Makayla pushed open the lounge door. Several women were crowded around the coffeemaker, talking quietly, and Wanetta, the school secretary, was digging around in the refrigerator.

Wanetta slammed the fridge door. "I heard she was caught walking around the house naked," she said, turning around. When she spotted Makayla, a look of regret flashed in her eyes.

The music teacher cleared her throat.

"Good morning, Makayla," greeted the librarian.

"Welcome back," another said.

"Yeah, welcome back," Wanetta echoed.

Makayla didn't know if she should run out of the room or pretend she didn't hear what Wanetta said. Her eyes were moist with tears but she wouldn't give her co-workers the satisfaction of seeing her cry. When news broke about her relationship with Jared, most of her colleagues had ignored her. A few of the nicer ones, like Desiree and Wanetta, had remained steadfast friends. But this time, it looked like she was on her own. At least where Wanetta was concerned. This wasn't the first time someone had betrayed her. She had conquered ignorance before, and she would do it again. "Good morning."

Maintaining her too-bright smile, she went over to the cupboard for a mug. Guilt was a tricky emotion. Makayla had done nothing wrong, but she couldn't help feeling bad. Her hands wobbled as she picked up the teapot and filled her cup to the brim. At least now she could escape to the safety of her classroom. She turned toward the door, surprised to find everyone watching her. Though she wanted to defend herself, to set the record straight, she had learned a long time ago the quickest way to kill gossip was to ignore it.

Holding her head high, she exited the room. Before she was completely out the door, she heard snickering and whispering behind her back. Makayla rolled her eyes. They were worse than sixth-graders. It never ceased to amaze her how mean-spirited women could be. Making a mental note to avoid the staff room for the remainder of the week, she blazed down the hall toward her room.

"Ms. Stevens!"

The thunderous roar of her boss's voice startled her. She stopped, almost tripping over her feet. Tea sloshed over the rim of the cup and dribbled down her arm. She glanced over her shoulder, terrified of what she would find.

Principal Gibson was standing in the middle of the hallway. His eyes were tiny, angry beads, his lips tight, his hands fisted at his waist. "Follow me to my office."

So much for escaping to my room, she thought. Makayla trailed Mr. Gibson into his office, dragging her feet as if she had an appointment with the dentist. Once seated, he clasped his hands together and cleared his throat. Makayla knew what was coming next. The rumor mill had reached her boss and now he was going to reprimand her. He would raise his voice, yell, curse, then he'd end his lecture with a summary of her moral obligations as a teacher. Over the years, she'd had the unfortunate pleasure of hearing this talk several times and she dreaded it. He used the same speech on all the faculty and staff, regardless of the offense.

"Thirty years ago when I became a teacher, there were few blacks in the profession. And certainly no principals or super-intendents. My colleagues and I fought to be treated equally and worked hard to rise above racism, prejudice and inequality. We stuck together in those days, supported each other, looked out for each other. We were a strong, unified team of educators who—"

Makayla swallowed a yawn. The speech never changed. He recited it faithfully, word for word. Inside her jacket pocket, her cell phone hummed. It had to be Kenyon. Who else would call her at this time? The hands on the clock mocked her, declaring it was seven-forty-five. Makayla heard the squeal of tires, a horn, and then a multitude of small voices. It wouldn't be long before the halls filled with chatter. As a result of the storm, elementary schools had been closed for days. Makayla was sure the frigid temperatures, fierce winds and blowing snow had kept most, if not all, of her students at home. Being cooped up for days would make them a hyper, rowdy bunch.

"As a teacher, it's your responsibility to model values, morals and integrity. Especially to the kids who lack structure and dis-cipline at home. Don't you agree?"

"Absolutely."

"You shape who they are and ultimately who they will become. It is a serious job that should not be taken lightly. Educators have the power to—"

Makayla sighed. This was taking longer than she had expected. To keep from keeling over in boredom, she made a mental list of all the things she needed to do if she ever got to her classroom.

The bell rang, cuing staff and students that the day had offi-cially begun. Makayla should be standing in front of her door greeting students, not sitting in Principal Gibson's office plotting her escape.

Wearing a smile, she uncrossed her legs and leaned forward in her chair. "I'm sorry to interrupt, Principal Gibson, but can we continue this discussion at the end of the day? I'm more than happy to stay late."

Principal Gibson's brows bridged together, forming a long, straight line. His glasses magnified the anger in his eyes. "I don't think you understand the seriousness of this situation, Ms. Stevens." His voice was harsh, mean. "I have been fielding complaints from teachers and parents all morning."

"What happens in my personal life is private," she said, projecting calm. Makayla couldn't imagine anyone on staff criticizing her, but after hearing what Wanetta had said, it was possible. "Which of the teachers complained?"

"I'm not at liberty to divulge that information. It's confidential. But know that your actions have affected us all." His eyes bore down on her. "Not only have you embarrassed yourself, you've tarnished the reputation of the school."

Makayla couldn't believe what she was hearing. There were two teachers on staff who gambled heavily, a single mom who moonlighted as a waitress at a gentleman's club and last year the superintendent had been arrested for driving under the influence. So what if she had a relationship with a relative of one of her students? She wasn't hurting anybody; she wasn't breaking the law.

"This is not the first time you have done something of this nature. Not too long ago we had a similar situation, didn't we, Ms. Stevens? I remember warning you then, but you obviously did not take me seriously. You think because you're pretty the rules don't apply to you. Well, I'm here to tell you they do!" He slammed his hand against the desk, rattling the items on top.

Makayla was on the verge of losing it. She wasn't going to

sit there and be insulted. Her students needed her and she needed to get out of the room before she reached across the desk and strangled her boss with his tacky red bow tie. She collected her purse and tote bag. "If you'll excuse me, I have a class to teach."

"No, you don't. You have been relieved of your duties until further notice."

"What?" Her voice was a mangled scream. "You can't be serious. I've been teaching here for years!"

"You have been replaced."

Gripping the side of her chair, she dug her fingernails into the cushion. Makayla couldn't breathe. The walls were closing in, suffocating her. She felt as if her world was collapsing around her. Her head throbbed in pain and her eyes burned.

"Administration will discuss this matter on Thursday and decide what course of action to take. You are more than welcome to attend the meeting, but be aware if you choose to attend you will be questioned."

Makayla had given her heart and soul to the school for the last ten years. It hadn't mattered what she was called to do, she did it and she did it well. Most of the longtime teachers weren't involved in extracurricular activities, but Makayla volunteered for committees, provided free tutoring and served as a mentor to troubled girls. And what did she get in return? Nothing.

"I do hope you will use this time off to consider your future at Springs Park Elementary. I won't have my faculty or staff fraternizing with parents—" his eyes were thin, sharp blades and a sneer was on his lips "—or relatives. Do you hear me, Ms. Stevens?"

This wasn't about Principal Gibson or the teachers or the parents. The only thing that mattered to Makayla were the twenty-two students waiting for her in room 1C. They were depending on her. She would go to class, tell the students she was sick and while she was there retrieve her day planner. In her haste to leave the last day of school, she had forgotten it in her bottom drawer. Thank God she kept her desk locked at all times. Sure, it didn't hold any incriminating evidence, but Makayla would feel better if she had it in her possession.

"I'll clean my desk and be on my way."

"I don't think that would be best. Classes are under way and students are hard at work. We don't want to upset the kids, do we? Call me later this week and we will arrange a more suitable time."

Anger propelled Makayla out of her chair. She wasn't going down without a fight. She was a good teacher, a damn good teacher, and she refused to be punished for having a private life. Veronika Blake had been gunning for her since the first day of school and Principal Gibson had always been on the woman's side. "Show me somebody else on staff who works as hard as I do. Show me! I give a hundred and ten percent every day." Makayla continued, gathering steam. "I've worked tirelessly for this school for years. I rarely call in sick, I stay late and there's nothing I wouldn't do for those kids."

"Like push them off the play structure or send them to the janitor's office to work!" Principal Gibson stood, his arms doubled across his meaty stomach. "I know everything that goes on in your class, Ms. Stevens. Nothing escapes me."

"I quit! I'd rather be unemployed than work for an egotistical dictator like you!" Makayla turned toward the door, her vision blurred by tears and fury. With great difficulty, she jerked open the door and slammed it with such force, the windows vibrated. The first tear hit her cheek as she stepped outside the school and, like rain, they didn't stop coming.

Chapter 23

Kenyon peeked inside the house. The living room was dark, but the lights in the kitchen were on. He rang the bell again. Nothing. Banging on the door didn't produce any results, either.

He'd been calling Makayla nonstop for days with no luck. The last time they spoke was a week ago and talking on the phone for ten minutes wasn't enough. Makayla had been dealt a tough blow and Kenyon wanted to be there for her. He had to see her for himself, had to know that she was okay. Oh, she tried to play it off, claiming she was ready for a career change, but he knew differently. Makayla loved her job and adored those kids; losing it had to be devastating.

The news had shocked him, too. He had picked up Terrance from school and was troubled when he saw his nephew's tear-stained face. Kenyon had questioned him, but his inquiry had gotten him nowhere. Fearing the worst, he had returned inside in search of Makayla. On his way to the office, he had run into Desiree, who had told him what happened.

Kenyon tried Makayla's cell phone again, but the call went straight to voice mail. He had a sneaking suspicion she was home, but didn't want to be bothered with visitors. Well, that was too bad. He wasn't leaving. He couldn't go another day without hearing her voice. Accustomed to their daily phone calls and weekly dates, his life suddenly felt empty without her in it.

His feet crunched through the snow. As he walked around the side of the house, he remembered something Makayla once said. After losing her house keys a third time, she had decided to keep a set in the backyard. He spotted the silver ornament by the patio and retrieved the hidden key.

He let himself in through the side door. The air was heavy with perfume and he could hear music playing. Could she have company? Male company perhaps? Closing the door behind him, he shook off the thought. If Makayla was seeing someone else he would know.

Kenyon unzipped his jacket and chucked it on the couch. The light on the answering machine was blinking; the message box displayed fifteen new calls. *I guess I'm not the only one worried about her,* he thought. Strolling through the main floor, Kenyon was struck by how clean the house was. Makayla was experiencing a major life crisis but still found time to clean.

The kitchen resembled a florist shop. Gigantic bouquets sat on the counter, among cards, boxes of chocolates and teddy bears. Curious, he picked up one of the cards and looked inside. It was from Chelsea O'Neal, a parent volunteer Kenyon remembered from the zoo field trip. Her words were kind, sympathetic, sincere. She labeled Makayla "an amazing and thoughtful teacher" and wished her success in her future endeavors. The card must have brought a smile to Makayla's face. Kenyon sure hoped so, because after the week his girlfriend had had, she needed some cheering up.

As he made his way down the hall, he heard the sound of running water. No wonder she hadn't answered the door. Makayla was in the shower. But that didn't explain why she hadn't returned any of his calls. Kenyon entered the bedroom. From the mess inside, it was evident this was where Makayla had been spending her time. Bags of cookies, potato chips, soda cans and plates plagued the floor, and clothes and magazines were scattered about.

Kenyon stopped outside the bathroom door, unsure of what to do. Should he wait for her to come out or go in? The image of Makayla, naked, lathered in soap, was more than he could take. He lifted his hand, but stopped midknock. He had never given so much thought about what to do concerning a woman. But Makayla wasn't just anyone. She was his girl, his love, the only woman to ever capture his heart.

Specks of sweat dribbled down his face as he turned the handle and entered the room. He felt like an intruder. But what choice did he have? She had shut him out, albeit deservingly, and every attempt he'd made to reach out to her had failed. Makayla would either welcome him with open arms or throw him out. Regardless of the outcome, he would finally see for himself how she was holding up.

Through the steam he saw Makayla standing beneath the showerhead, her back toward the glass door. Kenyon couldn't put into words how happy he was to see her. Overcome with relief, he stood there for several moments, watching her. When she turned sideways, he caught sight of her profile and his pulse soared. His throat felt tight, thick, constricted. Desire and lust flowed through him. Her body, glistening and wet, was a sight to behold. Full, perky breasts that fit into the palms of his hands. Smooth brown legs that wrapped perfectly around his torso. And a butt so tight it could give J-Lo a run for her money.

He released a long, deep groan. The room was getting hotter by the second. Kenyon had never been more aroused. His heart was racing, his breathing labored and he felt faint. He closed his eyes, imagining her hands were his hands, but quickly squelched the fantasy. If he was going to help Makayla, he had to remain focused. Their once smoldering-hot relationship had cooled and this scandal didn't help matters. All he could do was be there for her and hope for the best.

Kenyon thought of calling her name, but with the water running and the music playing, she wouldn't hear him. There was only one thing left to do. He undressed and opened the door.

Makayla stared at him, unshed tears lining her eyes. He waited for her to ask him what he was doing, but she didn't. He stepped inside, his eyes fixed on her pretty face. Lifting her chin, he placed soft kisses on her neck, cheek, lips.

Kenyon didn't know how much time passed, but it seemed like an eternity. They touched, kissed and caressed each other's bodies as if this was their first time. Makayla ran her fingers over his hair, then across his neck, chest and abs. She slid her hand down his stomach, gripped his penis and steered it between her legs. Floored by her boldness, he examined her face. Her eyes were closed, but there was no mistaking the sensual smile on her lips. Kenyon would never dream of turning down sex, especially after a two-week lapse, but he didn't want Makayla to think that's why he was here. Tonight wasn't about sex; it was about being the support she needed.

"Are you sure you want to do this?" he asked, cupping her chin.

Nodding, she shifted her hips forward.

"Makayla, look at me."

She opened her eyes, and that's when he saw the tears.

Kenyon saw her pain, the hurt, the confusion. There would be plenty of time for lovemaking. Right now, he had to take care of her. Shutting off the water, he pushed open the door and helped her out. Once she was swathed in a plush, oversize towel and Kenyon was dressed, they returned to the bedroom.

The curtains were drawn, flaunting the sky's matchless beauty. It was a clear night, calm, quiet. Stars twinkled, just inches from the moon.

Kenyon wondered what was going through Makayla's mind. She stood beside the dresser, her arms crossed tightly above the towel.

"I really appreciate you coming to check on me, but you don't have to stay. I'm okay now. I feel much better."

The tears in her eyes told him otherwise. It had taken him a week to track her down and he wasn't going anywhere until they talked. "Why don't I order in some food from the Barbecue Kitchen? I know how much you love their mashed potatoes and baked chicken." Kenyon pulled his cell phone out of his pocket. "Hold on a sec, I think I have the number in here somewhere."

"No thanks. I'm not—"

"Get dressed and I'll meet you downstairs."

"But I'm not hungry. If you don't mind, I'd really like to be alone."

He put the phone to his ear and exited the room. "Hello, Hubert? What's up? It's Kenyon. I need some food delivered to—"

Containers of chicken, potatoes, fries, mixed vegetables and gumbo covered the kitchen table. Balancing his plate in his left hand, Kenyon opened the fridge in search of something cold to drink. Milk, eggs and a half-eaten loaf of bread sat on the top shelf. A case of beer and a box of baking soda were at the back of the fridge. First thing tomorrow, he would go to the store and stock up on groceries. Now that he had a set of keys, he could come and go as he pleased. He grabbed a beer, slammed the door and went into the living room.

Makayla sank into the couch and tucked her legs beneath her. Her look was simple. A black V-neck sweater, leggings and fluffy pink slippers. Her hair was concealed with a silk, multicolored scarf. Without makeup, she looked incredibly young and pretty.

"You sure you don't want more? A scoop of vegetables isn't going to fill you. Let me get you some chicken."

"I'm fine, Kenyon. Quit worrying."

"I can't help it. You're not acting like yourself."

"How would you act if you lost your job?" she snapped.

"There, you said it. Let's talk about it."

"There's nothing to talk about." Makayla pushed a carrot around her plate with her fork. "I resigned. People resign from their jobs every day. It's no big deal."

"If it's no big deal, then why are you miserable? And why haven't you answered the phone or left the house all week?"

"Because I have plenty of things to do here."

"Like what?"

Makayla studied him through her lashes, her brown eyes at half-mast. "Kenyon, why are you here? I thought I told you we couldn't see each other until things cooled down."

"Cooled down? Everything's out in the open. We don't have to sneak around anymore. You're trippin' if you think I'm going away. You need me."

"My lawyer said we should take a break until the case goes to court."

"You're going to sue?" Shock registered on his face. "For how much?"

"It's not about the money. To be honest, I don't care if I ever see a dime. I have enough saved to cover my bills, and my dad and Desiree said they'd help me if I need it."

"Add me to the list. If you need anything just let me know." His voice was textured with concern. "I mean it, Makayla. Just ask."

Kenyon gulped down some beer. "If this isn't about money, then what's it about?"

"Administration had no right to treat me the way they did. My personal life wasn't interfering with my job. I rarely missed work, stayed late most days and was a good teacher. I was forced out of my job and my final paycheck was withheld. All I want is a letter of reference, my pay and a chance to say goodbye to my kids."

"That sounds fair."

"I think so. My lawyer does, too."

A fog of silence seeped into the room. Kenyon watched Makayla. It was hard not to. She looked so vulnerable, so sad, so scared. He racked his mind for something to say. Kenyon thought of telling her about his new assignment, but decided against it. Now was not the time to tell Makayla he would be doing another photo shoot with Alexandria.

"How is Terrance doing? Does he like his new teacher?"

"No. He's been acting up again."

"I heard." Makayla wore a soft smile. "Desiree told me about the 911 call."

Kenyon shook his head, chuckling. "Can you believe the little bugger called the fire department? Principal Gibson called Veronika at work to come pick him up. She grounded him for the rest of the month."

"Poor thing."

"He misses you."

"I miss him, too. I miss all of the kids."

Kenyon slumped back in his chair, a look of contentment on his face. "Now, that's what I call dinner."

"I'm glad you enjoyed it."

"I'm sorry you didn't."

"I might eat some later."

Makayla stood, picked up their plates and went into the

kitchen. She returned seconds later, carrying a glass of water. "Can I get you anything else before you go?"

"No, 'cause I'm not leaving."

"Kenyon, I told you, my lawyer said—"

"I don't care what he said. I'll sleep on the couch if you want, but I'm not leaving you alone." Kenyon finished his beer, placed the empty bottle on the table and stood. "Don't argue with me about this, Makayla. I'm going to Belize on Saturday, then I'll be in Costa Rica. I was hoping we could spend some time together before I leave. Not seeing you for two weeks is gonna be a bitch."

Despite her mood, she smiled. "Ah, the glamorous life of a photographer. Poor thing. You have to spend the whole day on the beach taking pictures of Alexandria."

He raised a brow. "How did you know she was going?"

"I didn't. I was joking."

"Oh."

Makayla cleared her throat. "So, she's going to be there, too?"

"If you don't want me to go…"

"Oh, please, Kenyon. I'm hardly in a position to tell you what to do. You have your life, I have mine, right?"

Baffled by her response, he said, "Is that how it is?"

"What do you expect me to say? Don't go? We never made any promises to each other. We both knew what this was from day one."

Kenyon didn't like Makayla's tone. She was implying that their relationship didn't have merit, that it was just a fling. He had told her he loved her. Didn't that mean anything? "Black women are always complaining there are no good men left. We're all cheaters, players, dogs and deadbeat dads. But here I am, trying to do right by you and you're shutting me out. Why?"

"Why? Why?" she roared, her voice in a dangerous crescendo. "None of this would have happened if it wasn't for you! I told you what happened in the past. I told you we had to be discreet, but you wouldn't listen. You know how much teaching means to me, how much I love those kids!"

"I didn't know Veronika and Terrance were coming! It was as much a surprise to me as it was to you."

"If you hadn't pressured me to come to your stupid party, I'd still have my job and I'd still be teaching my kids."

"No one twisted your arm, Makayla. You didn't have to come." Feeling remorseful, but angry that she was blaming him for what had happened, he said, "I'm sorry you lost your job, Makayla, really I am. But it's not my fault Veronika and Terrance showed up."

"No. No, it's not. But I was the one who was humiliated." Her face twisted in anger. "I'm the one who took the fall, so excuse me for not running into your arms. If I had followed my instincts and stayed the hell away from you in the first place, I wouldn't be in this predicament now."

Kenyon rubbed a hand over his head. He wasn't surprised that Makayla blamed him for what had happened; she was right—it was his fault. But he would never do anything to intentionally hurt her—didn't she know that? In the beginning he had been selfish, arrogant, insensitive, but that was before he got to know her. Now he couldn't imagine being without her. "Maybe this is for the best." When her eyes narrowed, piercing him with their fury, he hurried to explain. "You've been wanting to be a travel writer for years. Touching the Taj Mahal, gazing at the pyramids of Giza and climbing the Great Wall of China is all you ever talk about. Now you finally have the freedom you've been craving."

"But I didn't want to lose my job! I wanted to do both." Lowering her eyes, she stared down at her hands. "Do you know how humiliated I was when Mr. Gibson told me I had been replaced?"

He reached out and pulled her into his arms. "I know. It must have been horrible. You didn't deserve that, baby. You're a great teacher and the staff and parents know it." He turned Makayla around, so she was facing the kitchen. "Look at all the cards and flowers you got."

Her smile was brief. "But what now? I've been teaching for a decade. It's all I know. I can't give that up."

"You can and you will. It's time to start another chapter of your life." Kenyon wanted to say more, wanted to tell her he would be there every step of the way, but didn't. His hopes and dreams for their future could wait.

"There's no guarantee that I'll be a successful travel writer. Even Brenda said she didn't think I had what it takes."

Realizing she needed the space to express her feelings, Kenyon tightened his hold and listened as she gave voice to her fears.

"What if my dad and Brenda are right? What if I'm not cut out to—"

Kenyon had heard enough. "Makayla, not only are you an incredibly talented writer, you're smart and savvy and self-reliant. You've been hiding behind your teaching career long enough. It's time you followed your dreams."

"But—"

"But nothing. Take it slow, Makayla. It doesn't have to be all or nothing. Travel for three months, then decide if you want to return to teaching."

Moving out of his arms, she smoothed her fingertips under her eyes. "You should go. I'm exhausted and—"

"I'm not leaving."

"Kenyon, I don't need you hovering over me like a fretful parent. You shouldn't have come over in the first place. It's even riskier now."

"What are you saying? Are you telling me it's over?"

"I need some time."

"How much?"

Her silence stretched into minutes. "I don't know."

"You know what—you're right. I should go." His voice was squeaky, like an adolescent boy on the verge of puberty.

Kenyon looked straight into her eyes, hoping she would reconsider and ask him to stay. Surely she didn't mean what she said. She was upset, and his untimely appearance had only confused her more. He would give her the space she needed, and by the time he returned from Costa Rica, Makayla would be her old self, the woman he loved and adored.

They shared many similarities—their upbringing, their background, their love of Black exploitation films—but it was their differences that kept them together. They were an ideal match and with Makayla in his corner, there was nothing he couldn't do.

Kenyon wanted to kiss her, but didn't want to upset her any more than he had. However, if he left now, the way things stood, their relationship might be permanently damaged. No, he had to show Makayla what she meant to him, had to show her how much he cared. Yielding to his need, he lowered his head and kissed her softly on the lips. Then he turned, grabbed his jacket and walked out the back door.

Chapter 24

Makayla reviewed the two-page itinerary Roman Douval sent her. Next month she would be in St. Croix, one of the most beautiful islands in the United States, Virgin Islands. Beaming from ear to ear, Makayla shook her head in disbelief. Three weeks ago she was curled up on the couch, sobbing. Now her schedule was overflowing. Makayla couldn't believe how her luck had changed.

She had wasted the first few days after quitting, lying in bed staring at the ceiling. The second week she moped around the house, contemplating her future. Should she pursue a full-time writing career? Get a part-time teaching job? Writing a monthly article for *Travel and Entertainment* magazine wasn't going to pay the mortgage. Makayla had enough saved to cover her bills for the next three months but then what? Her friends and family loved her, but she couldn't depend on them to support her.

In a moment of desperation, she had contacted Brenda Van Buren. Her article "Thrill Every Inch" had run weeks ago but

Makayla knew from reading the "Letters to the Editor" section her fans wanted more. It wouldn't kill her to resume writing the Sexpot Files. It paid well and if she truly did have complete creative control, she could delve into meatier subjects such as sexual addiction, date violence and sexually transmitted diseases.

Five minutes into the conversation, Brenda had offered her a more lucrative contract. A daily column, a generous salary and an office on the twentieth floor with a view of downtown Philly. It was more than Makayla could have hoped for. She'd have the best of both worlds. She'd work from the offices of *The Philadelphia Blaze* when she was in town and send in articles when she was away. Makayla had had every intention of taking the job, but hadn't wanted to seem too eager. After promising to call Brenda back within twenty-four hours, she'd hung up the phone, flopped onto her bed and screamed into the pillows.

She was still excited. Now craving something sweet, she went into the kitchen. Makayla pulled out a half-eaten container of ice cream from the freezer and retrieved a bowl and spoon from the dish rack.

Her eyes strayed to one of the many pictures on the fridge. Kenyon had taken it at the Philadelphia Zoo. Terrance had a wild-eyed look and his peers wore equally funny faces. She missed the kids. Makayla smiled when she thought about the plans she had made for next Saturday afternoon. Every year she threw a Cupcake Party for her class. It was a ten-year tradition and her students had been looking forward to it since the start of the school year. Even though she was no longer their teacher, she wouldn't disappoint them. With Desiree's help, she had designed heart-shaped invitations, mailed them and compiled a kid-friendly menu for the day's festivities. Since it was probably the last Cupcake Party she would ever throw, she had gone all out. A magician was booked, Desiree was dressing up as Strawberry

Shortcake and if the weather permitted, there would be a scavenger hunt in her backyard.

With her ice cream Makayla returned to her office. She nibbled on her spoon, relishing the thick, creamy texture of her snack. There was nothing better than a rich, gooey treat at the end of a long, taxing day. *Nothing could top making love to Kenyon.* Ignoring the thought, Makayla stuck her spoon into the mound of ice cream. She didn't have time to fantasize. Daydreaming about sex would ultimately lead to thoughts of Kenyon and she had thought about him so much today she had a headache. He had loomed in her thoughts like a welcome intruder. Makayla had too much to do to get sidetracked. If she worked hard for the next hour, the article would be finished and off to Brenda by four o'clock. It was a fun piece in honor of Valentine's Day, entitled "Sexy Romantic Treats." After a rousing discussion about multiple orgasms at the last book club meeting, Makayla had compiled a list of unique "gift ideas" that couples could do in bed.

Her fingers pounded the keys. Three more paragraphs to go. When she typed the word *arousal* an image of Kenyon, dressed in his leather jacket and boots, popped into her head. Her mind wandered back to the day he'd cornered her in the classroom. They had shared their first kiss. It was sensually erotic and just thinking about it made her moan. If Makayla was being honest with herself, all of their sexual encounters were steamy. In the back seat of his car, in the laundry room, the shower.

Concern clouded her face. Unlike all the other times Kenyon went away, this time he didn't call or check in.

She stopped typing, her thoughts on their relationship and what his uncharacteristic silence meant. Could he be back with Alexandria? Or had an equally stunning supermodel caught his eye? If that was the case, Makayla had no one to blame but herself. She had pushed him away. Kenyon had showed himself to be spontaneous and daring, but was sensitive and considerate when the situation called for it. Like most men, he had a lot of pride and would never admit that she'd hurt him. But she had. There'd been no mistaking the pained expression in his eyes when she'd asked him to leave.

Emotions were running high that night. A part of her wanted Kenyon to stay, wanted his to be the shoulder she cried on. But an even bigger part of her felt the need to shut him out. If it wasn't for his relentless pursuit and constant advances, she would still have her job. Makayla winced. Okay, that was a lie. She had been ready for a job change for months, but was scared to follow her heart. Fear of failure had kept her at Springs Park Elementary. Teaching was safe and she was good at it. But her interests had changed and those closest to her knew it.

Makayla ignored her thoughts, and worked attentively to finish the article. When she felt a musing coming on, she pushed past it and typed faster. *I wouldn't have had such a hard time concentrating if this article wasn't about sex,* she decided, hitting the Save button and pushing herself away from the table.

Bowl in hand, she exited her office and went down the hall to the bedroom. Her room needed a thorough cleaning, but after spending most of the day in her office, the last thing she wanted to do was housework. Outside, the sun was shining, there wasn't a cloud in the sky and the delightful squeals of small children could be heard. A walk to the park would boost her energy and then she would think about tidying up. Or maybe, she would think about calling Kenyon.

The phone rang, providing just the distraction she needed. It was Brandi, and Makayla could tell by the sound of her friend's voice that she was in a good mood. "Hey, girl, what are you up to?" Makayla asked.

"Guess what? I landed that multimillion-dollar shoe contract!"

"Congratulations, Brandi! I know how hard you've been working on that account."

"There's more. This morning my boss handed me three tickets to see Mary J. Blige at the Martini Lounge! She's doing a special Valentine's Day show."

"But Valentine's Day isn't for another week."

"So she's celebrating early. Who cares? We're going to see the Queen of Hip-Hop Soul!"

"I've never really been a fan but it sounds like fun."

"And here I thought Kenyon would hip you to what's hot. Boy, was *I* wrong."

"Ha, ha, very funny. It'll be nice to hang out with you and Jamaal, even though I'll be a third wheel."

"Jamaal has to work the midnight shift. It's just us girls. Hey, why don't you call Desiree and Sydney to see if they're interested in going? Mr. Lowenthal said he could get me more tickets if I need them."

"Okay, I'll ask them and get back to you tomorrow."

"Sounds good. I'm going to get some dinner on the table before this man eats me alive!"

"Bye, girl." Laughing, Makayla hung up the phone.

Kids raced around the room, bouncing off furniture, plucking each other's party hats, stuffing their mouths with popcorn. Plastic heart-shaped bowls overflowed with chips, jellybeans and tasty treats.

Careful not to knock over the trio of girls stretched out on the floor playing Go Fish, Makayla carried the pizza boxes over to table and blew her whistle. Everyone in the room stopped, looked and listened. "The pizza's here!"

Loud, jubilant screams filled the room.

Makayla opened the boxes and started filling plates. "Who can tell me what we do when we're eating?" she asked, facing the group.

Everyone spoke at once.

"Yes, Francis?"

"We sit down on the floor." She paused. "Oh yeah, and we don't talk with our mouths full. That's gross."

The kids giggled.

"Now, everyone form a line behind Olga and don't forget to take a napkin. After you've finished eating you can have juice."

Makayla was picking a piece of pepperoni out of the carpet when the doorbell rang. Smiling, she wiped her hands clean on a napkin. "Keep an eye on them. I'll be right back."

Desiree nodded. Every time Makayla looked at her co-worker, she had to swallow a laugh. Her friend could pull off any style, from skinny jeans to cargo pants and heels, but she looked like an overgrown kid in the costume. The pouffy floor-length dress was embellished with sequined strawberries, lace ruffles and an emerald-green trim. But it was the cheap, silk shower cap and curly reddish-brown wig that made Makayla crack up each time Desiree smiled.

Makayla walked carefully through the room. Since she was the hostess, her outfit had to be practical. She couldn't chase kids in a long, frilly dress, so she had decided on a Hello Kitty costume. The character didn't fit in with the theme, but the kids had gotten a kick out of seeing her dressed up and seeing them smile was all that mattered. Her costume consisted of a hat, complete with ears and whiskers, a tail and a pink vest. Makayla felt silly in the hat, but if Desiree could walk around in that ridiculous getup, surely she could play along for the kids' sake.

As Makayla made her way down the hall, she heard Terrance's

voice through the door. Her mouth grew dry and her feet slowed. If Terrance was here, that meant… She took a deep breath. Seeing Kenyon was nothing to panic about. Smiling brightly, she opened the door, prepared to face the man she loved. Only, it wasn't Kenyon standing beside Terrance, it was Veronika. Makayla maintained her smile. "Hi, Terrance."

His face shone with happiness. "Ms. Stevens!"

Laughing, she hugged him tight. "You're just in time. The kids are in the living room eating pizza."

"Yay! I love pizza."

Makayla held him at arm's length. "I heard you've been giving your new teacher a hard time. Is that true?"

Terrance shook his head emphatically. "No way, Ms. Stevens. I've been a good boy. Just ask my mom and Uncle Kenyon. They'll tell you."

Draping an arm around his shoulders, she stood and addressed his mother. "The party will be finished at four-thirty."

"I was hoping we could talk."

"I'm sorry, now is not a good time."

"What I have to say will only take a few minutes."

Makayla didn't wish Veronika ill will, but that didn't mean she wanted the woman in her house. She didn't. "Like I said, now is not a good time. I have a house full of kids waiting for me."

Veronika patted her son's cheek. "Why don't you go inside and show the other kids your new Superman watch?"

Terrance turned and sprinted down the hall. "Bye, Mom!" he called over his shoulder. "See you later!"

"Can I come in?"

Makayla crossed her arms across her chest. "I'd rather you didn't."

"Okay, fair enough." Veronika took a deep breath, the expression on her face one of regret. "I told Mr. Gibson about you and

Kenyon but I didn't mean for you to lose your job. I didn't think things would go that far."

"What did you expect, spreading vicious rumors about me?"

"I wasn't thinking about the repercussions. Sometimes when people are angry they do stupid things."

"What's it to you if Kenyon and I are dating?"

Veronika took a moment before answering. "After my husband died, Kenyon stepped in and filled that void. I've gotten so used to him being around that when I saw you guys together, I felt threatened."

"Are you in love with him?"

"No, of course not. Why would you ask something like that?"

It was a lie if Makayla had ever heard one. Veronika's feelings for Kenyon had fueled her rage. In a way, Makayla felt sorry for her. It couldn't be easy being a widow and a single mom. Personal issues aside, there was no excuse for what she did. It was mean and vindictive and her actions had affected a lot of people. Just thinking about what Veronika did made Makayla's temperature spike. As hard as it was, she was going to rise above her feelings and be the bigger person. She took a deep breath and exhaled slowly, expelling all the bitterness she had inside. In a good place now, spiritually and emotionally, Makayla didn't want to waste any more time rehashing the past. "Resigning was my choice. No one forced me to. I could have made the choice to stay, but I didn't."

"I feel responsible."

You should. Makayla dropped her hands at her sides. "Don't. I'm happy. I'm living out my dreams and I honestly can't ask for more than that."

"And Kenyon?"

Makayla paused. This was the second time in months Kenyon had been MIA. No calls, no e-mails, no postcards. Hell, for all she knew he could be in a remote village in Ghana guzzling homemade beer and chanting with the locals. Their relationship hadn't played out the way Makayla thought it would, but she had been a fool thinking things would lead to marriage. "Kenyon's a good man and I hope we can remain friends."

"He loves you, you know."

Her stomach flipped. He did? Speechless, she took a moment to gather her thoughts. Was this another ruse? Or could she be telling the truth? Makayla was dying to know what Veronika knew but couldn't bring herself to ask. This was the same woman who had mistreated her for months, lied about her and soiled her name, which had ultimately led to her resignation. "Well, thanks for stopping by, but I really have to get back to the party."

"Okay, well, I just wanted to clear the air."

"I appreciate that. Goodbye." Closing the door, Makayla released a deep sigh. If someone had told her Veronika would show up at her door to apologize, she never would have believed it. As she walked down the hall, Veronika's words replayed in her head. *He loves you, you know.* Makayla shook her head, a frown on her lips. *If that's true, then where the hell is he and why hasn't he called?*

Chapter 25

"To sisterhood, good lovin' and great shoes!" Desiree screamed, hoisting her glass of champagne in the air.

"Cheers!" Sydney, Makayla and Brandi clinked glasses. Some of the liquid sloshed onto the table, leaving a large wet stain on the tablecloth.

The bubbles from the champagne tickled Makayla's upper lip. Resting her glass on the table, she said, "I'm glad I decided to come. It's been a while since we all hung out."

Sydney agreed. "It's too bad Jo couldn't come. Pneumonia's no joke though and I am too cute to be sick!" Addressing Makayla, she said, "From what Desiree told me on the drive over it looks like things are on the up-and-up for you."

"Well, not exactly. My case against the school still hasn't been resolved. The court date won't be set for another month, but my lawyer doesn't think things will get that far. He's confident we'll reach an agreement with administration in the next few weeks. I sure hope so, because I'm ready to move on."

"I hear you," Desiree said, propping her elbows on the table. "Lately, I've been thinking about a career change."

Brandi pitched an eyebrow. "Really? You never mentioned it before. What do you have in mind?"

"Promise you guys won't laugh?"

The trio nodded.

"Well," she began, her voice losing its usual flair, "I've never told anyone this, but I've always dreamed of being a dancer."

"Like at a strip club?" Sydney asked.

Brandi and Makayla snickered.

"No, silly, like one of those girls in the music videos."

"Oh, hell no!" Brandi shook her head, her side-sweeping bangs whipping her face. "You've got to be kidding. Are you out of your damn mind? You want to quit your job and become a video girl?"

Sydney reached over, picked up Desiree's glass and took a whiff. "What's in here? Liquid crack? That's it, no more drinks for you."

Makayla and her friends screamed in laughter.

"You're a pretty girl and all, but it's not going to happen." Brandi put a hand on her shoulder. "Desiree, you're going to be thirty-two this year. That ship has sailed and sunk, my friend. I'm a marketing exec. I know what I'm talking about."

Desiree's smile withered. She turned to Makayla, her eyes begging for support. "What do you think?"

The timely arrival of their waiter saved Makayla from dashing her co-worker's hopes and dreams. Appetizers arrived, and once food orders were placed, the conversation turned to Makayla's stalled love life. Her attempts to change the subject failed and when she realized her girlfriends weren't going to leave her alone until she told them something, she stopped sipping her drink and answered their questions.

"No, I haven't spoken to Kenyon and no, it doesn't bother me, and no, I'm not about to have an emotional breakdown."

Sydney plucked a stuffed mushroom off the plate. "Why don't you call him? He's into you, you're feeling him and the sex is outta this world."

Makayla held back a smile. "And how do you know that?"

"Because you haven't walked straight since the two of you hooked up!"

Desiree and Brandi chuckled.

"Keep it down," Makayla whispered, taking a fleeting look around the room, "or they'll ask us to leave." The Martini Lounge was first-class all the way. Warm terra-cotta tones, opulent stained-glass windows and soft, intimate lights created the feel of a Spanish villa. Half of the room held a handful of booths and an elongated bar, while the other half was a sea of tables surrounding a large dance floor and a sizeable raised stage. Mary J. Blige wasn't expected to perform for hours, but the lounge and adjoining dining room were already full to capacity.

"Please," Brandi said, rolling her eyes. "They're not going to kick out the finest women in here. Am I right or am I right?"

Sydney, Brandi and Desiree smacked hands.

"Now, back to that fine-ass Kenyon." Sydney slung an arm around Makayla's shoulder. "It's just us girls. You can be honest. You miss him, don't you?"

Makayla shrugged a shoulder. "A little."

Brandi humphed. "A little my ass. You've been singing the blues since he left. I don't understand what the problem is. Kenyon's a great catch. Financially stable, too handsome for words and he's crazy about you. What more could you want?"

"What do you guys expect me to do? Track him down and force him to commit to me?"

Sydney giggled. "That's what I'd do!"

"You guys make a cute couple," Desiree affirmed. "And you've changed a lot since you started dating Kenyon. It's like he brought you out of your shell or something. I've never seen you more confident and outgoing, and you positively glow whenever you mention his name."

Makayla sighed. It was true. She was different. Her heart was open to new experiences and now she lived every day to the fullest. Whenever she went out with Kenyon, he was like a bee buzzing in her ear, encouraging her to try something different. *Come on, babe, it won't kill you to eat sushi... Do you really need another black dress? What about this sexy red one?... Roller coasters aren't death traps! One day I'm going to take you to Magic Mountain. You'll love it.*

"Tell him how you feel," Brandi was advising when Makayla returned to the conversation. "If you don't, you could lose him forever."

Makayla felt cornered. Gulping down some of her Long Island iced tea, she considered her friends' advice. There was no end of opinions about her relationship with Kenyon, but they were missing a piece of the puzzle. "There's a reason he hasn't called and I bet it has to do with another woman. Guys like Kenyon might commit for a while, but they're always looking for someone better." Makayla didn't want to talk about Kenyon anymore. Things were too confusing and nothing seemed to make sense anymore. She loved him, maybe he loved her, but either way they were over. He had moved on and she would do the same. No matter how painful it was.

Makayla was thankful when the waiter arrived with their entrées and the discussion turned to the men in her friends' lives. Relieved to know she wasn't the only one having man trouble, she sat back and enjoyed the discussion. Makayla was having such a good time, she temporarily forgot about her problems with Kenyon.

"Can I interest you lovely ladies in something from the dessert menu?" a deep, somber voice asked.

Wiping her mouth with a napkin, Makayla glanced up at the new waiter. It was him. The guy from Alfredo's. The one who had asked for her phone number. What was he doing here? He had called a few times, but once Makayla started dating Kenyon, she hadn't given him another thought. Surely he wouldn't remember her after all these months. Makayla didn't realize it was her turn to order until Desiree waved a hand in her face. "Snap out of it, girl!"

"And for you, miss?" His smile tarnished and his eyes flickered with recognition. Then, "You never returned any of my calls. How come?"

Desiree, Brandi and Sydney stared openmouthed at Makayla.

"I'm sorry, I meant to call back, but—well, you know how it is."

Sydney grinned. "No, we don't. How is it?"

Embarrassed, Makayla ducked behind the two-page dessert menu. Slowly perusing the list, she ignored the envious looks her girlfriends were sending her. After a minute, she said, "I'll have the apple crisp with a scoop of ice cream on the side. Thank you."

He jotted down her order. "I'd still like to take you out sometime. Are you free Friday night?"

When Makayla didn't answer, Desiree ripped the dessert menu out of her hands. "Did you hear him? He just asked you out."

Sydney leaned forward in her seat. "What did you say your name was?"

"Cordell, but my friends call me Cash."

"Okay, Cordell, what do you have in mind?" Sydney asked, eying him warily.

He fed the group a disarming smile. "I have two tickets to see an advance screening of Tyler Perry's new movie."

"She'd love to," Brandi said, fishing in her snakeskin purse for a pen. She grabbed a napkin, jotted down Makayla's address and handed it to him, oblivious to the expression on her best friend's face. "And don't be late."

"I'll be there at six. We'll have dinner first."

Stunned, Makayla stared incredulously at Brandi. She didn't want to embarrass Cordell, or herself, so she waited until he left to give her girlfriends a piece of her mind. "Did it ever occur to you Meddling Marthas that maybe I had other plans?"

The trio broke into laughter. When Sydney composed herself, she said, "No, because we know you don't. Makayla, Friday's Valentine's Day. You don't want to be stuck at home thinking about Kenyon, do you? Go out with the young stud and have a good time."

Brandi agreed. "Twinkie, quit taking life so seriously. It's just a movie."

Spending time with someone else might make her feel better for a couple hours, but it was only a temporary fix. Makayla took a sip of her drink. "It just doesn't seem right, that's all."

"Damn, girl, sometimes you can be so uptight."

Sydney spoke next. "In life you have to just go with the flow. Besides, going out with Cordell will keep your mind off Kenyon."

"Hardly," she murmured, stabbing an ice cube with her straw.

When Mary J. Blige graced the stage an hour later, her shiver-up-your-spine vocals set the mood for romance and the promise of things to come. And when she belted out the soul-wrenching lyrics to "Not Gonna Cry," Makayla did.

Chapter 26

Cordell was twenty minutes late when the doorbell finally rang. Makayla forced herself to relax. She could do this. Cordell was a nice guy and though she wasn't interested in anything more than friendship, it felt good having somewhere to go on Valentine's Day.

Smile in place, she opened the door and greeted him affably. "Hi, Cordell."

"You look good enough to eat, li'l mama. Word is bond."

What happened to the well-spoken waiter I met at Alfredo's? Makayla wasn't familiar with street lingo, but she could tell by the glimmer in his eyes and the way he was licking his lips that he was pleased. Overwhelmed by the strength of his cologne, she stepped back. Makayla recognized the scent. It was Nautica, one of Kenyon's favorites. The very cologne she had bought him for Christmas. Stepping aside, she said, "I just have to get my purse and coat."

"No problem. Take your time." Cordell swaggered into the

living room as if he were the *GQ* man of the year. His multicolored sweatshirt was three sizes too big, his faded blue jeans hung off his hips and he was wearing a gang of chains. They made an unlikely pair, and Makayla could only image the attention they would garner at the restaurant.

"Nice place. You live alone?"

"Yeah, why?"

"Just curious." He flopped down on the couch and propped his feet on the coffee table. "Yo, check this out. The craziest thing happened today. I swung by the bank to get some money for our date and my bank card wouldn't work." Cordell examined the items in the room, as if committing them to memory. "Can I hold a fifty till Wednesday? I'm good for it, yo, I swear."

Do I look like a bank? Makayla couldn't count how many times men had asked her to borrow money. If Cordell could ask her, a virtual stranger, for cash, there was no telling what else he would do. It was Valentine's Day, the most romantic time of year, and she was spending it with a slang-talking-jean-wearing-money-begging pretty boy. *Lord, why me?*

Cordell grinned like a used-car salesman on the verge of making a huge commission. "If you can't spot me fifty, I guess I can make do with forty."

Makayla forced a smile. "I'll just pay for myself, how's that?"

"Cool."

"I'm ready."

"Yo, what's the rush? Let's kick it here for a while. Your place is tight."

"I thought we were going to eat before the movie."

"Naw, we'll just grab some cheeseburgers on our way. We'll eat in the car." Cordell laced his fingers behind his head and crossed his legs. "Yo, where's the TV? I want to check out the score of the Lakers-Miami game before we bounce."

"Sorry, I don't have one."

His eyes opened wide. "Were you robbed?"

"No," she shot back defensively. "I don't watch TV."

"Yo, that's strange."

If he used the word *yo* one more time, Makayla was going to scream. Crossing her arms on her chest, she silently cursed her girlfriends for agreeing to this date. If she wasn't such a big Tyler Perry fan, she'd ask Cordell to leave, order a pizza and curl up in bed with the latest book club selection.

Cordell jumped to his feet. "Yo, can you drive? My Jeep's low on gas and I don't get paid till next week."

"Fine. Let's go. I don't want to miss the movie."

Cordell ambled into the foyer, opened the front door and waited while she activated the alarm. "Yo, who's the dude getting out of the souped-up Escalade?"

Makayla glanced over her shoulder. She blinked her eyes rapidly. It was dark, but the streetlights illuminated the sidewalk. Strolling up the pathway, carrying roses in one hand and a wine bottle and heart-shaped box in the other, was Kenyon. He looked neat, trim and stylish in a black crewneck sweater and slacks. Very sexy and very hot. It staggered Makayla to see him there. Beside her, Cordell plagued her with questions, but she didn't have the presence of mind to respond.

Kenyon approached the steps, wearing his trademark smile. His gaze was so strong, so intense, it took all her effort to speak.

"Hi" was all she could manage.

"Hi, yourself."

It felt good hearing his familiar greeting. So good, her heart skipped a beat.

"These are for you." Kenyon handed her the bouquet, then bent down and kissed her. The kiss was more sweet than passionate, but it excited her all the same.

"Thanks." Makayla clutched the flowers to her chest as if they were a shield.

"You're wearing the dress I bought you."

Glancing down at her outfit, she smoothed a hand over her stomach. "It's tighter than when I first tried it on."

"If you've gained weight, it's in all the right places." Grinning, he touched her gently on the shoulder. "Can we talk?"

"I'm on my way out."

Cordell cleared his throat.

Kenyon turned to his left, as if noticing him for the first time. All the muscles in his face grew tight. He glared at the stranger, the tension in his jaw working its way down his neck. Anger bubbled in his chest like a steaming volcano. "Who the hell are you?"

"Cordell, but my friends call me Cash."

It burned Kenyon inside to see Makayla with another man. He stepped forward, in the hopes of intimidating the stranger with his size. He clapped him hard on the back and steered him toward the walkway. "You should leave."

"Hey, yo, she's going with me to the movies."

Makayla suppressed a smile. Last year she'd spent Valentine's Day at home, marking papers, and this year she had two men fighting over her. Okay, so one of them didn't have a university degree but it was still an adrenaline rush.

"Sorry, kid. Here's something for your troubles." Kenyon pulled out his wallet and handed Cordell a hundred-dollar bill.

His face broke out into a smile. Pocketing the money, he said, "No problem, yo. My baby's mama's home with the kids and I promised I'd bring them dinner. Thanks, yo!" With that, he strode over to his Jeep, hopped in and took off down the block.

Baby's mama? When was he going to tell me about his ready-made family? Shaking her head in disgust, Makayla pushed open the door, kicked off her shoes and stormed down the hall. "You shouldn't have done that. You don't own me."

"You should be thanking me, yo." Kenyon chuckled at his own joke. "I saved you from possibly the worst date of your life."

"Who I date is none of your business."

"What's with the attitude?"

Makayla whipped around. "Excuse me?"

"We haven't seen each other in weeks and this is the welcome I get?"

"You're joking, right?"

"No." Kenyon knew he'd said the wrong thing when he saw her eyes darken. He put the champagne and the box of chocolates on the coffee table. "You're acting like you don't want me here when we both know you do."

He can't be serious. Cocking her head to the right, she studied his face. Steady gaze, tight lips, rigid posture. He sure looked serious. Anger crept up on her, seeped into her heart and took control of her mouth. "I haven't heard from you in weeks! Weeks! What do you expect me to do? Hop into your lap and give you a big, fat, juicy kiss? You stroll in here like Tom Cruise in *Jerry Maguire* and think you'll charm your way back into my life, but it's not going to happen."

"I don't get you. You asked for space, I gave it to you and now you're mad."

"I asked for space. I didn't tell you to disappear."

"What do you want from me, Makayla?"

"I want you to leave!"

Several seconds passed. Then Kenyon parted his lips and very slowly curled the sides into a smile. "You're lying." He stepped into her space and lowered his eyes with calculated slowness. "Your legs look amazing in this dress. And the color's hot, too."

Makayla wished Kenyon would wipe that stupid grin off his

face. He was making her uneasy and if he kept this up, she just might forget she was mad at him. "You still haven't told me why you came back from Belize and didn't call me."

"I didn't want you to think I was sweating you. I'd be a punk if I kept calling and coming around after you told me not to."

"Then why are you here now?"

"Because it's Valentine's Day and you're supposed to spend it with the one you love." Kenyon touched her cheek. He'd been a fool to think he could obliterate her from his mind. He thought he would use their time apart to get hold of his feelings. But Makayla was all he could think of. He was more patient, more considerate, more understanding. His love for her hadn't happened overnight. Makayla had captured his heart by being sincere, caring and incredibly sweet. She was the kindest, most generous spirit he knew and he couldn't live without her.

Gratifying his desire for more of her, he leaned over and kissed the spot where his finger had been. "I care about you, Makayla, but I'm not going to chase you. That's not my style. And I'm not going to stay where I'm not wanted. Do you really want me to leave?"

His smile penetrated her anger. His gentle words were just what Makayla needed to hear. She had been doubting his true feelings for her and it felt good knowing he cared about her. "No, I guess you can stay."

"That's my girl." The amorous sound of his voice and his raw, magnetic energy were overpowering. His explanation about his recent absence made sense, but Makayla needed to know where things stood between them. She put a lot of thought into what she said next. "Kenyon, I'm looking for something long-term."

"Me, too."

"Really? You're not just saying that?"

"No."

"Do you want to get married?"

"Are you proposing?"

Makayla laughed. "No, silly. I just want to know how you feel about marriage."

"To be honest, I never pictured myself getting married. I thought I'd be a lifelong bachelor. Then I met you." His face was the definition of neutral, but his voice was thick and his shoulders were slightly hunched.

If Makayla didn't know better, she'd think he was nervous. But what could he be scared of? Kenyon was the epitome of cool. Confident, secure, focused. He believed in his strengths and abilities and never wavered. That was what she loved most about him. He stretched her imagination, stimulated her desires and taught her how to dream big.

Her heart beat with a mixture of thrill and fear. Kenyon was saying all the right things, but that didn't mean they could ride off into the sunset. "What about Veronika? I talked to her a few days ago and I got the impression—"

"Leave her to me."

"But—"

Kenyon quelled her fears with a kiss. The kiss was long, passionate and deeply intense. They parted and he held her tightly around the waist. "I'll take care of it."

"Are you sure?"

"Positive." He cleared his throat and rubbed a hand over his right cheek. "I'm not good with all this feeling stuff but I have something to say."

Makayla stared at him expectantly. Her heart throbbed in her chest. This was it. He was going to tell her why he loved her but why they couldn't be together. "Go on, I'm listening."

Kenyon took her by the hand and led her over to the couch. They sat together in silence for several minutes. He had broken through her crust of anxiety by listening to her, romancing her and making her laugh. But he had never imagined he would fall in love. He'd lost his heart to Makayla the day she showed up at his house with dinner and since then, he'd only fallen deeper in love. Monogamy was a big step but there was no doubt in his mind that she was the right woman for him. Now, all he had to do was convince her. "There was a time when I was a selfish, egotistical bastard. I used to be a player but those days are far behind me. I'm not that guy anymore, Makayla. I swear." Kenyon pulled at his shirt collar, then shifted around in his seat. "Our relationship has been the most significant thing in my life. We're going to argue and fight like every other couple but I want you to know I'm in this for the long haul. You grabbed my heart from the first time we met and I can't live without you. I love you, yo!"

Makayla burst out laughing. No one had ever made such an amusing declaration. Her heart was full of unutterable joy and her thoughts too deep to put into words. She had always had a special place for Kenyon in her heart and even after all these years the flame had not died. "I love you, too," she confessed, tilting her chin to receive his kiss. Their lips came together in a sweet reunion. Kenyon loved her with his lips, his mouth, his hands. Ignited by his touch, she linked her arms around his neck.

"I have one more confession to make," Kenyon said, stretching out on the couch and pulling her down on top of him. "I hate country music. It's the most depressing music on the face of the earth."

"You do?"

"Yup."

"Then why did you come with me to the Gretchen Wilson concert? And why have you been playing her music all these months?"

Kenyon placed kisses along her neck. "I was softening you up. I figured you'd think I was a sensitive guy. Did it work?"

"No!"

They shared a laugh. It felt good teasing and joking with Kenyon again. He had a wicked sense of humor to go along with his gregarious personality and wit. Their future would definitely be filled with love, joy and laughter. "Is there anything else I should know?"

"Yeah, I can't live without TV! First thing tomorrow we're going to the store. We'll get a plasma screen for the bedroom and a fifty-inch with high definition for the living room. I love you, Makayla, but I can't go to bed without my nightly dose of Stuart Scott on ESPN!"

"I don't care what you get, as long as you don't disturb my sleep." Laughing, she rested her head on his chest. In his arms she felt safe, loved, secure. Kenyon loved her and they were going to be together. Nothing had ever felt so right.

Starving for another one of her kisses, Kenyon cupped her face in the palm of his hand. He'd never understood the expression "appetite comes with eating" until he met Makayla. The more time they spent together, the more he wanted her. His desire knew no bounds where she was concerned and he wasn't afraid to admit it.

He kissed her slowly and tenderly, sending a shiver of pleasure from her fingers to her toes. Tilting her head to the right, she pressed herself against his chest and deepened the kiss. It had taken a lifetime but she had finally found her dream man. Her one and only. Her soul mate. Outspoken and confident, Kenyon made sure to make his opinions known and never shied away from the truth. Makayla was set in her ways but he knew just what to say to change her mind. They couldn't be more wrong for each other, but she appreciated their differences. Kenyon was the protective type who took the reins whenever they were out in public and whenever they were in the bedroom. Definitely, her kind of man.

Book #1 in

THE THREE MRS. FOSTERS

THIS
TIME FOR
GOOD

FAVORITE AUTHOR

CARMEN
GREEN

About to lose her family business because of her late
husband's polygamy, Alexandria accepts Hunter's help.
But she's not letting any man run her life—
not even one who sets her senses aflame.

"Ms. Green sweeps the reader away on the lush carpet
of reality-grounded romantic fantasy."
—*Romantic Times BOOKreviews* on *Commitments*

***Coming the first week of May
wherever books are sold.***

KIMANI™
ROMANCE

www.kimanipress.com

KPCG0650508

Down and out...but not really

Indiscriminate
Attraction

ESSENCE BESTSELLING AUTHOR
Linda Hudson-Smith

Searching the streets and homeless shelters for his missing
twin, shabbily disguised Chad Kingston accepts volunteer
Laylah Versailles's help. Luscious Laylah's determination
to turn "down-and-out" Chad's life around has a heated
effect on him. But Chad's never trusted women—
and Laylah has secrets.

"Hudson-Smith does an outstanding job…
A truly inspiring novel!"
—*Romantic Times BOOKreviews* on *Secrets & Silence*

**Coming the first week of May
wherever books are sold.**

KIMANI™
ROMANCE

www.kimanipress.com   KPLHS0660508

"Byrd proves once again that she's
a wonderful storyteller."
—*Romantic Times BOOKreviews*
on *The Beautiful Ones*

ACCLAIMED AUTHOR

ADRIANNE
byrd

controversy

Michael Adams is no murderer—even if she did
joke about killing her ex-husband after their nasty
divorce. Now she has to prove to investigating
detective Kyson Dekker that she's innocent.
Of course, it doesn't help that he's so distractingly
gorgeous that Michael can't think straight....

**Coming the first week of May
wherever books are sold.**

ARABESQUE®

www.kimanipress.com

KPAB I 000508

Her dreams of love came true...twice.

ESSENCE BESTSELLING AUTHOR

DONNA
HILL

Charade

Betrayed by Miles Bennett, the first man she'd let into her heart, Tyler Ellington flees to Savannah where she falls for photographer Sterling Grey. Sterling is everything Miles is not...humorous, compassionate, honest. But when she returns to New York, Tyler is yet again swayed by Miles's apologies and passion. Now torn between two men, she must decide which love is the real thing.

"A lighthearted comedy, rich in flavor and unpredictable in story, *Divas, Inc.* proves how limitless this author's talent is."
—*Romantic Times BOOKreviews*

*Coming the first week of May
wherever books are sold.*

ARABESQUE®

www.kimanipress.com   KPDH1010508

*Overcoming the past to enjoy
the present can be difficult...*

YOLONDA TONETTE SANDERS

Secrets of a
Sinner

After years of doing whatever was necessary to survive,
Natalie Coleman finally feels her life is getting back on
track. Returning to the home she ran from years ago, she
confronts the painful events of her past. As old wounds
heal, Natalie realizes God has led her home to show her
that every sinner can be saved, every life redeemed.

"Need a little good news in your novels? Look no further."
—*Essence* on *Soul Matters*

Coming the first week of May wherever books are sold.

www.kimanipress.com   KPYTS1320508